OPERATION EMERALD

OPERATION EMERALD

DOMINIC McCARTAN

Dembner Books • New York

Dembner Books
Published by Red Dembner Enterprises Corp., 80 Eighth Avenue, New York, N.Y. 10011
Distributed by W. W. Norton & Company, Inc., 500 Fifth Avenue, New York, N.Y. 10110

Published by arrangement with Pluto Press.

Library of Congress Cataloging-in-Publication Data

McCartan, Dominic.
Operation Emerald.

I. Title.
PR6063.C3406 1985 823′.914 86-6243
ISBN 0-934878-77-3

For Dorrian, Rebecca, Finbarr, Conrad and Benedict

OPERATION EMERALD

Chapter 1

The Maze is situated on the outskirts of Belfast, the largest prison of its kind in Europe. For many years it has contained a high number of Irish Republican activists demanding to be classified as political prisoners and protesting against their treatment. On a bleak April morning, during a period of unrest, a letter from British Government Headquarters was delivered to the Senior Governor by special courier. Above the impressive crest on the crisp, heavy paper was stamped in red the single word: SECRET. The latter paragraphs of the letter read:

> Therefore you are instructed by Her Majesty's Government to ensure that prisoner O'Mara (11176/—), currently in one of the H Blocks, is to be discouraged from continuing his political protest and removed to the appropriate unit where he should be incarcerated with prisoner Wilson (10914/—). After a period of two months prisoner O'Mara and prisoner Wilson are both to be released.
>
> It is of the utmost importance that this directive be carried out efficiently.

The letter was signed by the Secretary of State.

When the Governor had finished reading, he turned in his swivel chair and placed the document in a Chubb wall-safe. Then he rang through to his most trusted officer in the relevant block, requesting his presence in the administrative wing as soon as possible. While he waited, he stood gazing out of his window over the dismal compound, wondering what high-level machinations were at work.

Principal Officer Black was a balding old bull of a soldier who had been in the prison service for 20 years. With the customary pride he took in his uniformed appearance, he was soon marching across the jailyard. When he entered the Governor's quarters, he saluted and came briskly to attention, his cap under his arm.

'Sir, you wished to see me,' he said, gazing at the window a few inches above the head of his English superior.

'Yes, yes, Charlie, relax.' He waved Black towards an easy chair opposite the oak desk which dominated the office. The Governor's orderly served real coffee. Black swelled at the privilege.

'Charlie, I want to talk to you about one of the protesters – Patrick O'Mara. What sort of chap is he?'

The officer perched on the edge of the chair and began eagerly. 'Well, sir, by all accounts he used to be one of the Provos' top hit men. Only, when he first came in here he'd been kneecapped. He'd been stealing IRA funds, from what I could gather.'

The Governor nodded slowly. 'And how's he shaping up now?'

Black played with the badge on his cap, trying to appear thoughtful. 'O'Mara's different, sir. He's not like the others. They seem to believe in what they're doing. He's looking out for himself.'

'It suits him to be on the protest?'

'While he's in here, sir, yes. But he'd turn if it looked like it'd get him out. It wouldn't take much.'

'I see.'

Black was keen to impress his superior. 'Every chain has a weak link, sir,' he said philosophically. 'To tell you the truth, I'm not surprised you're interested in him.'

The Governor sipped his coffee. He smiled ruefully. He had expected something like this. British Intelligence was always thorough in its research: the few Republican 'supergrasses' had always been carefully assessed before they were approached.

'Right, Charlie.' The Governor assumed an authoritative posture. 'I want that man off the political protest and back in prison uniform. Do whatever you have to.'

Black again responded eagerly. 'No sweat, sir, no sweat at all. The fact is . . .'

The Governor stood up brusquely. 'I don't want to know anything about it. Just do it.'

The officer immediately remembered his rank. He stood up too, and looked once more at the space above the Governor's head. 'Yes, sir, is that all?'

The Governor answered with a discreet nod. Black replaced and straightened his cap, saluted and left the room.

Charlie Black marched back to the block with an air of smug assurance. To lean on O'Mara would not be difficult. A well-circulated rumour had reached him only a few days before that the prisoner's girlfriend, a regular visitor suspected as a messenger for the Provisional IRA, had been seen in the unlikely company of a Unionist councillor. The strategic value of such information was never underestimated in the war of attrition against the political internees. Black sensed that he was about to enjoy himself. The thought of promotion was an added incentive.

In the far wing, O'Mara lay on a mattress in the filth of his cell. He shared it with another protester and a single bible. His hair was long and greasy, his beard unkempt. He shivered in the rags of a blanket tied around his waist. His naked body was covered in a weeping rash. The cell walls, like the others in the block, were smeared with excreta. The stench was disgusting, and no less so to those who had caused it, in revolt against the withdrawal of military type status, which had turned the Maze into a prisoner-of-war camp.

As he waited for his midday meal, staring vacantly at O'Hanlon, his fellow-prisoner dozing fitfully across the cell, he heard the sound of the warden's boots in the corridor outside. He expected the food to be shoved as usual into the cell, and the door to be shut behind it. It did not happen this time.

'On your feet, O'Mara.' The prisoner neither moved nor answered.

'The boss wants to see you. Either you walk or I drag you by the hair. It's your choice now.'

O'Mara got slowly to his feet. He looked across at O'Hanlon, who had awoken and now gave him a clenched fist sign of solidarity; then he knotted his blanket and followed the guard out. Numerous grilles and doors were opened before the two men reached the office in the centre of the block.

O'Mara stood defiantly in front of his jailors. Principal

Officer Black stared back at him with the glint in his eyes which always betrayed the pleasure he took in taunting the 'blanket men'.

The old soldier curled his lip. 'Enjoying yourself in here, are you, Mr O'Mara?'

There was silence. The warder standing behind him jabbed O'Mara in the ribs. 'Speak when you're spoken to, boy.'

O'Mara continued to stare at the officer, who shook his head in disgust.

'You dirty bastard.'

Black stood up and turned his back. His tone changed suddenly. 'Well now, how's your girl? Still visiting, is she?'

The prisoner raised his eyes to the ceiling.

'Mary McKee from Ballymacford. Fine-looking woman she is. Known her a long time, eh? Kind of cousin of yours, I believe.' Black went on talking to O'Mara over his shoulder. 'Working at Kelly's near the airport. Aye, well, there'd be plenty of guys passing through there.'

Still O'Mara refused the bait. 'She's far too good for the likes of you, anyway. Take a look at yourself, boy. What woman'd fancy you now?' Black waited, then turned and leant his heavy frame on his desk, bringing his face close to O'Mara's. His eyes were laughing. 'She's getting bucked by an Orangeman, sure as I'm standing here.'

O'Mara could no longer restrain himself. 'Go screw yourself, Black. You're talkin' shite.'

A heavy blow to the kidney sent him forward on the desk. Black bent further down and whispered in his ear. 'I may be talking shite, boy, but you'll eat it before we're through with you.' He stood away again. 'Take the pig back to his sty,' he said, glancing at O'Mara who was straightening up slowly. 'He can start in there.'

As the prisoner was led off, he shouted after him for good measure: 'You can bet that's not all she's doing either. You Fenian bastards all have a price.' His laughter echoed down the corridor.

When he was back in his cell, O'Mara clutched his back where he had been struck and breathed deeply. Then he turned and fired a torrent of obscenities through the locked door.

'Hold on there, man.' O'Hanlon spoke with a familiarity bred of long hours spent in shared squalor. 'Don't lose your rag.'

'Christ!' O'Mara slammed his fist against the door, then turned again. 'Them fuckers are gettin' to me. It's only a bloody rouse but . . .'

O'Hanlon interrupted. 'What they tryin' now?'

'Mary McKee. Black says she's seein' some Or'ngeman.'

'Sure, you're not fallin' for that one? It's the oldest trick in the book.'

O'Mara shook his head. The other prisoner sat up and said simply, 'When's your next visit?'

'Thursday.'

'Is she still runnin' errands for Kelly?'

'Not this time,' O'Mara said quietly.

'Right. So you ask her, straight out, no bullshit. Then you'll know.' O'Hanlon grinned. 'Anyhow, she wouldn't get away with nothin' like that for long, would she? We're fightin' a war here, man.'

O'Mara turned his face away. It was not the political implications which disturbed him.

'So don't let it rile you, man. The only way we're goin' to win this thing is to stick it out. There's no place for toe-rags. Thought you'd know that by now.'

O'Mara merely nodded and threw himself down on his bed.

Thursday 27 April. After several days under further pressure from the warders, O'Mara was taken across the rainy yard to the visitors' block, dressed for once in prison clothing. He sat at a desk and waited. A slim, black-haired girl in her mid-twenties, with a dark complexion and a warm, impulsive air, was ushered in. She smiled at him. He tried to detect some hint of deceit in her eyes as she sat down, but he could think only how clean and feminine she looked. He could smell his own decay. He lowered his eyes with a bitterness which quickly stopped her smiling.

They spent some time exchanging the usual empty phrases under the gaze of the warder. Eventually their small talk trailed into silence. The prisoner gazed at his filthy fingernails, while his bright-eyed visitor became ill at ease. The minutes passed. O'Mara seemed to think carefully before he came to a decision. When he next spoke, it was exactly as his cellmate had advised. He stared at the girl while he waited for an answer; but she in turn looked down at her hands, clutching the strap of her bag. O'Mara said nothing more; then he lifted one finger and pointed at her threateningly. He signalled to the warder, who had continued to watch them with unusual interest, that he wished to be taken away. She watched the door close behind him, sighed heavily with anger and trepidation and left the long bleak room.

Early the next morning, news reached the Maze that Kelly's Motor Inn, the large touring hotel on the main Aldergrove road, had been bombed. Six Catholic employees and an undisclosed number of guests were dead. O'Mara's first reaction was that Mary McKee was among the victims. But intuition, and the suspicions carefully put into his mind, caused him to doubt it. The thought of remaining in the H Block was now unbearable. Not only would he find it impossible to contain the jealousy which had preoccupied him over the last days, but his life could well be at risk if his name was linked with what had happened.

At midday he asked to see the Governor, telling O'Hanlon that he was going to protest at his treatment. Within two hours, he was being marched from the cell again, this time in a different direction. Dressed in his damp, dirty blanket, he walked onto the first carpet he had seen since his arrest. He looked around him at the bright, sweet-smelling office of the Senior Governor and felt a surge of relief.

'Good afternoon.' The Governor rose from his seat. 'Do sit down.'

O'Mara found it hard to believe what he heard, but he sat down in the chair Black had occupied the week before, while the officer himself stood close behind.

The Governor wasted no time. 'Am I to take it that you have at last come to your senses?'

'How do you mean?' said O'Mara.

'How do you mean, *sir!*' Black bellowed in his ear.

'Steady on, steady on now.' The Governor stretched his legs under his desk. 'This man is fragile. He must be treated carefully.' He pushed a silver cigarette case and a gas lighter across the neatly-arranged surface of the desk.

'Would you like a cigarette?'

O'Mara realized that his surrender was already being taken for granted. He did not object. His hand shook as he took a cigarette, lit it, and sucked the smoke deep into his lungs.

'Could I ask you a few questions – sir?' he said, at length.

'By all means.' The Governor leant forward.

'If I come off the blanket now, what happens to my sentence an' what do you do for me when I get out?'

'Well.' A file on the desk was cursorily consulted. 'We'll release you in two or three months' time, provided you stay in line . . . and, of course, co-operate with us if we should ask you to.'

The prisoner raised his eyebrows but wisely said nothing. He was quick to appreciate how much his defection might mean to the authorities.

'And after your release you'll receive the usual welfare and social services to help you find accommodation and work.'

'Och, but that's not good enough, sir!' exclaimed O'Mara. 'There's people who're goin' to be after my blood. I need protection.'

The Governor betrayed the slightest irritation. 'Couldn't you go abroad?'

'With my record? Sure, I'd be sent home on the first plane.'

'How about the Republic, then?' The authoritative facial muscles twitched; the interview could become extremely tedious if it went too far.

The message was not lost on O'Mara. He drew on the cigarette and resigned himself. 'So you're tellin' me I look after meself.'

The Governor appreciated his attitude. 'You never know what may come up,' he said carelessly. 'I wouldn't worry too much if I were you.'

O'Mara nodded sullenly, stubbed out the cigarette and stood up. Principal Officer Black took over. 'Alright, boy, let's go.'

The Governor watched with pleasure as prisoner and escort left the office. He closed the folder and said quietly to himself, 'That's that.' He took a bottle of Bushmills whiskey from his desk drawer. It was, in his opinion, one of the few good things to come out of Northern Ireland. He poured himself a stiff drink.

O'Mara was taken directly to prison reception. This was a squat, grey block surrounded by high wire. On this day as on many others, a bevy of black vans was returning from the High Court in Belfast. While Black waited for the guard to check their passes, O'Mara stood trembling in the wind as it gusted across the empty yard, tugging at the blanket he had pulled tightly round his shoulders. The guard dogs howled.

Eventually the prisoners were marched in single file in to the block, where a small warder, dressed in a brown overall, ambled from one of the side offices to meet them. 'OK boy,' he said to O'Mara. 'Let's have a look at you. Strip.'

O'Mara took off the blanket and stood in the middle of the cold tiled room, his hands over his groin, as the warder walked round behind him and lifted a few strands of tangled red hair.

'Crawling with bloody lice. You filthy Mick.'

Black stepped forward in a direct imitation of the Governor's manner. 'Hold on, there.' They turned their backs and whispered. Then the small man disappeared into his office and returned with a bottle in his hand. He told O'Mara to take a shower and handed him the bottle. 'Use this on your head.'

O'Mara, ignoring Black's watchful eyes, relished the hot water flowing through his hair and coursing through the lather he mulched vigorously on his flesh. After he had washed himself clean, he stepped out, dripping, to be handed a towel.

The warder trimmed his hair and shaved his beard. O'Mara listened to the clipping of the scissors and watched the wet red commas falling round him on the floor. This was, he knew, the point of no return. He had become one of the walking dead for the Provisional IRA.

Chapter 2

While O'Mara was receiving what was to be his last visit from Mary McKee, his prospective cellmate in H9 was released into RUC custody, ostensibly for special interrogation. Sam Wilson was driven along a brief stretch of motorway, across the city to the chief interrogation centre in East Belfast, notorious for its indictment in the European Court of Human Rights. The burly Ulsterman arrived handcuffed to a plain clothes officer. He was handed over to a man in uniform and thoroughly searched, before being led down a series of stairways to the basement. There, he was ordered to stand to attention outside an unmarked door. The door was opened by a civilian official who dismissed the escort and ushered the prisoner, not in to the confines of a cell, but the vestibule of a converted office.

As soon as Wilson entered the office he was greeted warmly by the Commander of British Intelligence in Ulster. He was one man currently in Northern Ireland who would have been fully qualified to answer the Prison Governor's speculations about the nature of clandestine operations in the province. Wilson took his hand in a firm grasp, looking respectfully into the man's sharp features. Unlike his fellow countryman the Commander possessed an air of genuine authority and assurance. In his neutral grey suit, spectacles and old college tie, his appearance would have been appropriate in an academic.

'Good to see you, Sam,' he said amicably. 'Take the weight off your feet.'

Wilson made no attempt to conceal his pleasure. 'Thank you, sir. It's good to be back in civilized company.'

He sat down in a black office chair. Only now did he acknowledge the presence of two other men. Their sour expressions and athletic bodies left him in little doubt as to their occupation. He turned again to the Commander.

'Sam, I want you to meet two chaps who are ready to play an essential part in our scheme.' Wilson nodded to each man in turn as he introduced himself. Both were Americans, of impressive military rank – hard, taciturn characters willing to

He was roused from his reflections by Black's peremptory instruction. 'OK, boy, on your feet. And put these on.'

He took the regulation prison clothing and dressed himself slowly. The he posed in front of the prison camera. Later, in the photographs, with his crew-cut and his gaunt face again exposed, he was immediately recognizable as the sullen-eyed murderer of his former days.

'That's that,' said Black, this time unknowingly echoing the Governor. 'So let's get your stuff.'

They crossed the yard and returned to the H Block. This was part of Black's personal strategy. As O'Mara walked down the corridor, his new boots squeaked on the highly-polished floor. It was a signal the inmates recognized. A barrage of abuse followed him to the office, and again on his way out. His face remained set under Black's faintly mocking gaze.

'Where now?' he asked. There was a new edge in his voice which confirmed the self-reliance he had no choice but to adopt.

'H9', the guard replied curtly.

O'Mara had heard of the block, used specifically for prisoners in danger from their own kind. He was marched a considerable distance before it came into view, past the countless grilles, gates and wire fences. His right leg began to throb painfully at the knee.

express themselves in action. Their attitude contrasted sharply with the scholarly mien of the Englishman who sat facing them across a narrow desk.

'Our friends flew in to Aldergrove a few days ago. Since when they've been getting into the swing of things here. Their credentials are impeccable.' Both men remained impassive. 'Green Berets. Phoenix Operation in Vietnam. Secret activities in Central America and Southern Africa. They have been chosen expressly for the job by our senior partners, so to speak. We should look on them as personal representatives of the commitment being undertaken at the highest level.'

Wilson smiled wrily. 'I have no doubts about the efficiency of the CIA, sir.'

The Commander did not respond to his ironic glance. He turned quickly to the Americans. 'Wilson is one of our top men here. His role is vital to the success of our operation.'

There was a brief silence while the Commander watched for their reaction. He then drew in a sharp breath and pressed the intercom on his desk. 'The Emerald file please. And tea in ten minutes.'

His private secretary entered from the outer room with an official wallet, put it down in front of him, and retired. His slim white fingers delved through a mass of papers while the others sat waiting, unwilling to look at one another. At length, he spoke.

'Let me explain. I have engineered this meeting for a specific reason. I'm sure each of you is familiar with your brief, so to speak. But I would make it clear that this operation is not simply a matter of individual efficiency.' He turned again to the Americans. 'We are in Ireland, gentlemen, and while I wouldn't dare to suggest that our purpose may be thwarted by spirits or leprechauns, I would stress that this is a country where the best-laid plans are apt to founder, faced with the almost unnatural capacity of the people for intrigue and deceit. Our aim is to utilize this very factor. It is therefore important that those involved at top level share complete confidence and understanding. Their must be no danger of misapprehension.'

The Commander paused. Wilson sensed the Americans'

impatience as the Commander spoke again.

'Now to business. There are, as you know, a considerable number of sectarian forces at work here. But, in the last analysis, we are dealing chiefly with two groups.' He continued, with no trace of overt hostility. 'The Provisional IRA has been indulging in open acts of terrorism for many years, and there is no need now for us to elaborate on their activities. Their tactics are familiar and predictable to us. And, of course, you chaps will make full use of that in weeks to come.'

Wilson watched while the Commander, with a typically precise gesture, tapped the file on his table. 'At the opposite extreme lies potentially more consistent opposition to our joint political endeavour. I speak of those Protestant activists who have gathered under the name of Emerald. I have, of course, a file containing all the pertinent information, but I want to take this opportunity to allow Wilson here to give us the benefit of his first-hand experience.' The Commander sat back in his chair. 'Sam, if you could be brief and to the point.'

Wilson glanced at the mercenaries beside him. Then, without further hesitation, he began to speak in a cultivated Ulster accent.

'I personally hold the rank of Lieutenant Colonel in the organization, and I expect to be promoted on my release from a short prison sentence that I have been serving for my duties in the name of Emerald.'

He rested his large hands on his knees and continued fluently.

'The organization was formed originally in reaction to the failure of the British Government to find a satisfactory solution to the problems in Ulster. Members include high-ranking Unionist politicians, civil servants and senior police officers – in contrast to more notorious Loyalist groups who draw their support solely from the working classes and lack effective leadership.'

Wilson paused to gather his thoughts. He could see that the Americans were already listening with interest. 'Emerald is split into two wings, political and military. There is constant friction between them, for various reasons, and this is open to exploitation. We are also subdivided into a series of committees – strategic, financial, propagandist. Operations until now have been covert, with top priority given to the collection of information and, in the military wing at least, preparation for a provisional administration after a projected British withdrawal. To make this feasible, there is a considerable arsenal of weapons, and no shortage of funds.'

He glanced at the Commander, who was leafing through the file, before he went on. 'Any acts of terrorism are carried out by gunmen employed specifically for the purpose, though the ultimate aim is to gather all Loyalist activists under one umbrella. So there is a continual campaign to recruit members from the Protestant community, especially those who can add political muscle or serve usefully in specialist areas.'

At this point his superior intervened. He had removed two photographs from the file and now handed them to the Americans. 'Sam, if you could perhaps conclude by giving us an outline of the respective leaders of the two wings.'

Wilson altered his style of delivery. 'Head of military operations, General John Fforde, DSO, Cremorgan House, near Clones, County Monaghan. Bachelor in his early sixties. Prominent career in British Army. Retired amid speculation. Fanatical separatist given charge over headquarters in the Republic, where he cannot interfere in Ulster politics.' He added: 'It is essential that his position in the organization is strengthened in the next months.'

The mercenaries studied the photographs as Wilson continued. 'Head of political activities, Sir Cameron Smyth, Malone Road, Belfast. Widower in his middle fifties. Ex-Ulster Unionist minister at Stormont. Prominent industrialist embittered at the imposition of Direct Rule, but still loyal to the idea of the Union. Ousted from power by Democratic Unionists. Retains many contacts in Civil Service and Security Forces.' Again Wilson chose to add a personal qualification. 'This is a man whose presence in the organization is likely to hinder the progress of our operation.'

The Commander leant forward. 'That's splendid, Sam. Now, chaps.' He took back the photographs and closed the file. 'If I may add my piece. Our task is to see that the project which the politicians have been working towards behind closed doors, not only at recent summit meetings with the Republic, but in a multitude of less publicized encounters, is met with no effective opposition, so to speak. Your own sphere of activity is strictly delimited, though I hasten to add that it is concentric with other intelligence operations. As an example: we have long known that Emerald owes a great deal to its ability to recruit informers at the office of the Secretary of State. But, thanks to the work of certain colleagues, Emerald is now receiving the kind of neatly doctored information which will make our job a damned sight easier than it would otherwise have been. This is the kind of integrated exercise I personally have been trying to cultivate since I came here.'

The door opened and the secretary brought in the tea. One of the Americans, taking his cup with a cynical air, at last responded. 'OK, we get the message. Has this got anything to do with tonight?'

'Gentlemen, tonight you will be working specifically for Emerald. You will be firing the opening salvo in what we hope will be the last battle.' The Commander was plainly determined to pursue the meeting to his own chosen conclusion. 'Now perhaps you would be so kind as to tell us how such employees go about their business.'

The Americans looked at one another; it was clear that they considered a mask of reticence essential to their trade; but they were not prepared to seem subdued by any superior British manner.

'I'll keep it short,' the senior mercenary said, putting his cup on the floor. 'The building is L-shaped. Reception, bar, dining room, bedroom block. A small van left at the apex against a supporting wall'll do it. The stuff these guys use is called Co-op Mix. A hundredweight or two of nitrate fertilizer soaked in a catalyst. Nowadays they set it off with a slab of Russian TNT.' He hesitated. When the Commander encouraged him to continue, he sighed impatiently. 'OK. There's a small aperture in the side of the explosive. We put the detonator in and attach it to a timing device. They use simple gadgets, like the kind you get on washtubs. Then we load the whole apparatus in the back of the van and set the timer. When we're good and ready, it blows.'

His colleague interjected, 'No one's said anything to us about a warning. I guess you guys reckon on someone getting killed.'

'I'm afraid there must be casualties if it is to evoke a suitable reaction,' the Commander replied.

Wilson questioned the senior man. 'What about the vehicle?'

'Hijacked,' he answered quickly.

Wilson was not satisfied. 'Where?'

The American turned to face him with a dry smile. 'Shankhill Road. Protestant ghetto. OK?'

There was a short silence. The Commander watched with an air of satisfaction. 'Well, chaps,' he said finally, 'I think that wraps it up for the time being. I'm sure you all appreciate why I feel it necessary to go through this kind of ritual, if only for my own peace of mind. I've a number of similar meetings to organize over the next few days, so I hope you won't mind if I ask you to leave now. I wish you all the best of British.'

They stood and shook hands. The Americans turned to go, still without showing any conspicuous sign of amity. The door closed behind them.

The Commander finished his tea and said, 'Well, Sam, I'm afraid it's time to return you to Her Majesty's care.' He buzzed the intercom and asked for the escort to be summoned. 'How long has it been?'

'Six months, sir. Tedious until now. But, of course, tomorrow . . .'

'You don't anticipate any problems?'

'Nothing I can't handle.'

The Commander again appeared satisfied. 'It's looking good, Sam, I'll tell you that.'

'I'm glad to hear it, sir. Goodbye, then.'

Wilson went through into the vestibule and, while the secretary waited for the guard, he stood by the outer door, assuming the suitable demeanour for a recently interrogated prisoner. When he had gone, the intercom buzzed again. 'Right. Get me Moore on the phone.' There was a short pause, then an added command: 'And I'll have some more tea, if you'd be so kind.'

Chapter 3

Roy Moore lived in a spacious split-level house a mile outside the village of Templepatrick in County Antrim. He was known to his neighbours as an enigmatic figure who had inherited a thriving business in security from his father, but who had, after the onset of the troubles in Ulster, been unwilling or unable to cope with the expansion of the enterprise, preferring to involve himself in council politics and a social round of drinking and adultery. As a result, he had not only lost a succession of lucrative contracts to his rivals, but his marriage had disintegrated, leaving him with few friends and heavy alimony to pay. He spent his time wandering moodily in the acre of landscaped garden surrounding his home or carousing late into the night in the more prestigious Belfast clubs, a man with expensive tastes and increasingly insufficient funds to afford them.

On an early evening, ten days before the Commander's Intelligence meeting in East Belfast, he was sitting by the hearth, where a fragrant peat fire burned, drinking the whiskey the Governor of the Maze praised so extravagantly. His jacket had been thrown over the saddle-hide chair opposite. His tie was unfastened. He reclined with his eyes closed, listening to a Bach lute suite, while the flames threw shadows over the walls and ceiling around him.

In recent months Moore's life had undergone a transformation which was not reflected in his profile. It was not now regrets over his marriage or his business which occupied his thoughts. A complex sequence of events ran constantly through his mind. He had entered the ranks of Emerald some years before. As a Unionist councillor, he had become involved in a typical piece of corruption. The consequences would have ruined him if it had not been for the intervention of a senior politician associated with his father. Sir Cameron Smyth had publicly refuted the allegations of a building contractor naming Moore, amongst others, in connection with illegal practices. The price of Smyth's support was not made clear until after the luckless builder had been found hanging from a tree outside his home, and a statement was discovered that exonerated the councillors he had accused. Moore was then informed that he could not only show his personal gratitude, but also give valuable assistance to his fellow Unionists, by donating five hundred pounds to a secret Protestant organization which would, as a result, accept him as an active member.

Some time later, he submitted a tender to the British Army for fortifying a series of border posts. His offer was unexpectedly accepted, and he was invited to discuss arrangements at Lisburn Barracks. At that meeting, a professorial English civilian had been present for a short while, who seemed more interested in his personal outlook than his knowledge of security wire and concrete bunkers. When he was subsequently invited to dinner in the Officers' Mess and drawn into an intense discussion of Ulster politics, Moore realized that the contract was unlikely to prove a straightforward business deal.

A number of meetings followed with the bespectacled Englishman, and it soon became plain that it was Moore's involvement with Emerald in which he was primarily interested. Moore made it clear that his role was of little significance. But this was apparently known already. He was then given a list of facts about himself which could only have emerged as a result of deliberate scrutiny: his lack of familial commitments, his financial position, his pastimes, including his enthusiasm for hunting and his occasional venture into rally-driving. The way in which he had been approached pointed to a single, confidential purpose.

Sitting in his leather chair, drumming his fingers lightly on the arm in time to the music, Moore smiled as he recalled his initial sense of privilege and excitement. The Englishman's style had been so subtle. It had made him feel that he had almost a duty to impress. He had been pleased to find that, when he was forced to, he could express passionate opinions about the destruction of the democratic process in Ulster. When he had fully communicated his vision of a bleak future, in which he could see little hope of peaceful co-existence, the Englishman had responded with his own idea. He had calmly announced that the British were using the currently well-publicized summit meetings with the Republic to shield their plans for a political resolution which would guarantee the wishes of the Protestant majority. It was his personal role to secure the services of men whose activities would ensure that the plans were promoted successfully without interference. Moore had seen no reason to disbelieve him.

Subsequent encounters with the Intelligence officer had filled him with a sense of purpose and energy he had not known since his brief commission with the Ulster Volunteers. And the Englishman had pressed his case with much force. If Moore agreed to work for them his firm would receive the kind of orders from the British Government which would not only keep him in drink for as long as he was able to enjoy it, but also restore his father's name to its former position in the local community. When it had finally come to the point when he was asked to make a formal commitment, Moore had unhesitatingly signed the document that pledged his secret loyalty to the British Crown.

He took pleasure now in recalling his last personal exchange with the man who had recruited him. He himself was putting on his peaked cap, while the neutrally-dressed Englishman was standing by his car door, a thin briefcase under his arm. They had been dining at a country club near Portadown, in County Armagh.

'There are two fields here, so to speak, and it is our duty to cultivate them. The smaller must be carefully weeded of all hidden knots and pockets of resistance, and the larger pruned of all those trees and hedges bent towards the mainland by prevailing winds. This territory must become receptive and fruitful in its own right. And men like yourself must till the soil in such a way that those who sow the seed can work unhindered in your shadow. I hope you understand me.'

Moore smiled and then asked, 'And will I meet any of the sowers?'

Climbing into his car, the Englishman laughed drily. 'Shall we just say you might hit upon a bent copper on your travels. Good luck, I'll be in touch.'

The only contact since then had been limited to cryptic phone calls reinforcing the briefings he had received during the previous summer. The operation in Ulster had been scheduled to gather momentum as soon as conditions were deemed favourable. Today, Moore had been informed that the time had now come.

He finished his whiskey, and leant over to the other chair to pick up his jacket. From the inside pocket he took two photographs, which he held up in the light of the flames. Both were pictures of Mary McKee: one taken from a caravan customarily parked outside the Maze to monitor all prisoners, showing her in a riding mac, glancing sidewards as she waited at the gate; the other, a straightforward passport portrait, heightening her dark eyes, her high cheeks with their freckled complexion and her long black hair. Moore replaced them in his jacket pocket and poured himself another drink.

Glancing at his watch, he decided that he had time to wash and change before he left. He switched off the stereo cassette and went upstairs to his bedroom suite, where he showered briefly. While he was dressing, he looked at himself in the full-length mirror, noting with satisfaction that his flesh was still tolerably firm and supple. He had taken pains to keep himself fit, and though his dark hair and drooping moustache were touched with grey, and his brow was more obviously prominent than it had once been, he remained strikingly youthful and attractive for a man in his mid-thirties.

He dressed in a pair of jeans, an Aran sweater, and a black Gucci jacket. As an afterthought, he splashed eau-de-Cologne on his neck. He had few doubts of his success in at least one area of his duties.

On the same evening, Mary McKee was also sitting by a peat fire – burning in the hilly wilds of Ballymacford, ten miles or so from Moore's house. The family cottage, built in the Penal Times, when Catholics were only allowed single-storey buildings, was a long blackstone farmhouse with a thatched roof, a traditional dwelling with few conspicuous signs of modern adaptation. In their own way, the McKees had a local history of some renown, as descendants from a clan of chieftains, driven into the uplands by Scottish planters who had stolen their good land in the valleys below.

Since Mary had been forced to return to Ballymacford, her only companion there had been a large grey Alsatian dog called Silver, who sat curled over her ankles as she stared into the flames. For the last six months, her widowed father had been confined to hospital with a terminal cancer. Their house crowned a ridge over the bogs, solitary except for a few fir trees standing like sentinels to windward, and a similar dwelling on the hill opposite. The village lay a mile below. On foggy evenings there was often no sign of human activity. For a young woman who had taken the first opportunity to move into the city, it sometimes seemed a prison no less oppressive than the one where O'Mara was interned.

When the dog began fidgeting at her feet, she rose and put on a tweed jacket and long boots. Their dusk stroll on the hills had become a ritual as unvarying as the rain showers which accompanied it. The door banged as they left the cottage. Silver bounded up the high-hedged lane towards an old quarry where he could run wild sniffing out rats and rabbits.

At the top of the hill, Mary glanced down at the green expanse far below. The view of the predominantly Protestant acres never failed to arouse bitterness in her. The contrast with the bleak uplands was so marked. But she was no longer sure of her willingness to take part in the struggle to erase the difference.

Unlike Moore, with his new-found sense of purpose, Mary McKee saw herself as trapped by her own involvement in the political war. Her relationship with O'Mara, which had begun years before when he had been sent by his family to stay at the McKee's farm, had long since lost its meaning. Even though she had returned to the city with him, and quickly come into contact with what were then his young Republican friends, he had not proved to be the kind of man she had expected.

The more O'Mara had become involved in violence, and seeming, unlike most of his associates, to take a strange pleasure in killing, the less she had wanted to know him. This had not stopped her from following her own allegiance to the cause. By the time of his arrest, she had been appointed secretary and agent to a prominent Republican politician. But she had not been able to shake off O'Mara, who had continued to boast that she was his woman. And when he was discovered to have kept money for his own uses from a number of post office raids across the province, it was bitterly ironical that she happened to be with him as he lay shot above the right knee outside a bar in the heart of Andersonstown, left to the mercy of the authorities.

Her isolation in the cottage was a direct result. The paramilitaries had immediately ordered her out of Belfast. Confused and shocked by what had occurred, she had found herself agreeing to take the job she was offered at Kelly's Motor Inn. This, whilst it thrived on the passing trade of businessmen and government officials, was used for a number of purposes by the Republicans. She had become convinced that she could further serve the cause by using her contact with O'Mara to take messages in and out of the Maze. Everything that had happened to her over recent months seemed to have been beyond her control. But the last thing she might have expected was to have to return home, to the place where John McKee had reared her in the shelter of his old-fashioned nationalism, while she was tossed in the storms of the new.

She thought of this as she looked down across the valley, blurred by her uncertainties. She could see no escape from the position she was in now, with a succession of bleak and dangerous weeks stretching ahead of her. Lowering her eyes, she set off after the dog towards the derelict quarry.

Moore stepped out from his porch into the chill air. The garage doors were open. His Range Rover and a company Granada stood on either side of a small Jaguar. The latter was his pride and joy, a 1966 3.8 litre with an engine modified to full E-type specifications, which had belonged to his father. He climbed in and sat for some moments inhaling walnut and leather. Then he started up, reversed across the gravel drive, and rolled down towards Templepatrick.

Initially, he took the road to the airport. There was hardly a car on the road and he sped past the prosperous farmhouses, the wide gateways and leafy lanes. Then he turned left, towards the village of Dundrod. The landscape changed; rushes replaced grass, the houses became smaller, the sudden vistas wilder, as the road climbed into the mountains and he swung round sharp corners, dipping his lights in the gloom ahead.

A loose rock hit the floor of the car. He had to brake sharply. Then he took a map from the pocket in front of him; this was the point at which he was to proceed on foot. He cruised into a lay-by built for heavy vehicles, climbed out, and locked the car. Flint walls lined what had become almost a single track. Along the road were the broken gates of the quarry, opposite a vertical cliff of rough gorse and stones. The cottage would be just over the hill. When he reached the gates, Moore clambered over and leapt down the other side, wiping rust from his palms. The man-made hollow ran up to a cluster of derelict buildings and rotten machinery. Red mud clung to his feet as he went towards them.

It was not long before Mary heard him coming. She was leaning on the window sill of one of the old huts, watching her dog ferreting. She peered apprehensively round the corner of the building. Hidden under a floorboard beneath a pile of blankets in the same hut was a small gun of O'Mara's that she had kept since his imprisonment, in fear for her own safety. Her first thought now was that she was in some danger. She moved towards the door and then whistled softly to her dog.

'Heel, boy.'

The Alsatian immediately came beside her, low on the ground. She made out a man, walking speedily towards the hut. She prayed that he would go past, on his way to somewhere else. Should she try to recover the gun? But he had already turned the corner, it was too late.

At first Moore saw only the dog, poised on its haunches, muscles rippling, teeth bared. Then he heard the girl's voice.

'Don't come near me, mister, or the dog'll have you. Just walk away slow now.'

Moore backed off a few paces, grateful that she held the animal by the scruff of the neck. 'I mean no harm.' He peered at the girl through the gloom. The photographs were a poor likeness. With her black hair matted in the rain, and her slim body crouching over the dog, she was like a creature from a Gaelic myth.

His stare embarrassed her. 'Sure, I dunno what you're doin' here but you can get on out of it.'

He had almost forgotten the lines he had prepared for the cottage door. 'You see, my car's run out of petrol. I was looking for someone who might be able to help.'

She jerked her head. 'In the village. Over there.'

Moore asked, 'Will I find the way?'

She paused to think. She saw no reason to be afraid of him now. Her traditional sense of hospitality took over. 'Follow me.' Moore stepped forward. The dog snarled. 'Only keep back.'

She led him up out of the quarry. As they passed the cottage on the ridge, Moore said, 'I suppose that's where you live.'

Mary shrugged her shoulders. 'Maybe.'

'How far's the village?'

'Not far.'

They walked on in silence till they came down into the main street of Ballymacford. 'O'Grady's Garage,' she said, 'that's your place.'

They were standing by a single petrol pump outside a small thatched house. Gazing at her in the light, Moore again felt drawn towards her. The dog alone kept him at a distance. 'Look, you've been more than kind. Can I buy you a drink or something?'

Mary looked back at him, taking in his smart appearance, his arrogant manner. 'Sorry, I work evenings.'

'And where's that?' he asked. She didn't reply. 'There must be some way I can show my gratitude.'

'Don't worry, mister, I was out for a wee dander anyhow. I always take the dog about this time.'

She turned her back and walked away towards the cottage. Moore made himself known at the garage where the heavily-built owner sold him a can of petrol, evidently suspicious. Then he returned to the Jaguar. Tossing the can into the boot, he drove back down the winding track and turned onto the road which ran through the village and up past the cottage. He skidded to a halt outside the gate and sounded the horn. The girl peered from a window. He gestured to her. When she opened the door, he called out, 'I'll give you a lift to work.'

She could not help smiling. 'Och, you don't give up, do you?'

Moore shook his head. She closed the door again and he wandered if he had miscalculated. But a few minutes later she emerged, transformed, resembling the full-length photograph that he carried in his other jacket.

'So,' he said as she got into the car, 'where will it be?'

'Kelly's Motor Inn. Three miles along the Aldergrove road. An' it's only 'cause I like the car.'

Moore grinned to himself and drove down through the village as conspicuously as possible, while she appeared to search for something in her handbag. The short journey to the hotel was largely silent. When they arrived, Moore insisted on accompanying her inside. She disappeared into the cloakroom. On her return, her manner seemed to change. She assumed a confident, vivacious air. But, while she wore a small badge that identified her as an Assistant Manageress, he noted that she was not treated by the staff with any deference. At first, she declined his offer of a drink, but he was so persistent that she eventually agreed to stand with him at the bar. She was plainly relieved when, after a single whiskey, he picked up his car keys with a flourish and told her that he had to leave.

'By the way, my name's Moore,' he said as he turned to go. 'Roy Moore. I hope I'll see you again.'

Mary McKee said nothing, but watched him with a puzzled expression as he went.

The Jaguar pulled up again outside the cottage a few days later. It was dusk, when Moore knew that Mary McKee would be strolling in the quarry.

He went up to the cottage door, and left a single red rose with a thorny stem in the iron handle. On her return, Mary was at once irritated and intrigued. She took the rose inside and put it in a glass jar. It blossomed on the window sill.

The following Wednesday, Moore had only just come home from work when the telephone rang in his hallway. He threw down his briefcase on the stairs and picked up the receiver. The voice was instantly recognizable. The orders he was given were, in their thinly-veiled code, typically concise. He put the phone down and went into the kitchen, breathing quickly, trying to control the unpleasant sensation in the pit of his stomach.

The next evening, he set out at nine o'clock, taking the Range Rover, and drove carefully along the country lanes onto the Aldergrove road. He reached Kelly's Motor Inn on schedule and parked on the edge of the car park at the far end of the building, behind one of the conifers which had been left standing. He locked the door and pocketed the keys, then crossed to the hotel, checking his watch. When he entered reception, he immediately glimpsed Mary McKee talking to another dark-haired woman. He lingered in the doorway. Eventually Mary turned and saw him. He nodded brusquely. Her face fell. She hastily went back to her conversation and he walked in to the bar.

After an interval, she followed him. He was sitting in a corner by the window, swirling his whiskey in his glass. She approached him with a professional air and asked him if everything was all right. He looked at her so intensely that she turned round to see if anyone had noticed. Then she smoothed her blue woollen dress over her thighs, ordered her own drink and sat beside him. Moore saw that she was deeply nervous. She seemed to want to ask him something but could find no means of doing so. Shortly afterwards she left, saying that she would see him later if he was still there.

During the next half hour, as she passed to and fro, he sat in the same corner, drinking moodily. Suddenly, at ten o'clock, he rose from his seat, walked quickly through the bar, and approached her at the reception desk. He leant over the counter and said quietly, 'No questions. Just come with me.'

With an instinct common to many who lived through the troubles, she concealed her reaction. 'What's that now?' She tried to smile.

He repeated himself. 'No questions. Just get someone to fill in here and come with me. It's urgent.'

She thought momentarily of calling one of the doormen to throw him out, but then she glanced into his eyes. She was familiar with the look of a man aware of real danger. She nodded nervously.

'Sure, I'll come. Just tell me what's happenin'.'

He said only, 'You're wasting time.'

'Hold on a minute.' She went through the door behind her. Moore stood flexing his muscles, ready to run if necessary. But she reappeared within moments, her mac slung loosely over her shoulders, saying to the other girl, 'I'll be a wee while.' She let him take her arm. She had given the impression that her liaison with Moore was in the line of business.

They stepped out into the chill night air. He pressed her arm and said in a flat voice, 'We're just out for a stroll, OK?'

As they walked away, a blue delivery van pulled into the car park and crossed their path. It drew up at the apex of the building. A heavily-built man in a suit got out and, with the air of a satisfied customer, walked over to another vehicle, which was quickly driven off.

As Moore kept glancing over his shoulder, the girl, whose lips were dry now, exclaimed, 'Och no. Your head's out.'

Moore hurried to the edge of the car park some hundred yards from the van. There, his Range Rover stood under the conifer; in its branches a roost of starlings was cheeping at the tall orange lights of a strange dawn. He unlocked the back door and told Mary to get in and lie low. He climbed in after her, and closed the door. Mary sat hunched against the back seat, staring up at him with wide black eyes, as he crouched, checking his watch. He looked back at her. His whole body was trembling, he could barely control himself. Without thinking, he leant forward and kissed her. He would not forget the touch of her dry lips in the midst of his cold sweat.

As she pushed him away, a violent explosion rocked the car. The laminated glass cracked. They both held their heads while the tremor, like a fierce wind, passed through them. It was followed shortly by the sound of thudding on the roof and the ground nearby. Moore pushed open the doors. The air was thick with dust. A cloud of debris hung over the hotel. On and around the Range Rover, the corpses of starlings lay, twitching and bloodied.

Moore turned and said abruptly, 'Go now.'

Mary looked out at him. She could barely speak. 'You

bastard. Where do you think I'm goin' to go?'

He shrugged his shoulders numbly. 'Help out. I can't hang around.'

She knew that he meant what he said. As she jumped down she cried, 'For Christ's sake, what are you?'

He slammed the door, climbed into the driver's seat, and started the engine. As he negotiated a path among the vehicles in various states of destruction, he forced himself to keep his eyes fixed towards the exit. To his right, flames leapt over the pile of rubble, and people ran shouting in all directions.

By the time he had driven five miles towards Templepatrick, a roadblock had been mounted. Moore slowed down and switched off his headlights as he approached a single red lamp being waved in the gloom ahead; he was careful to observe the rule that cars coming to such checkpoints should use only sidelights to avoid making an illuminated target for any gunmen. A UDR soldier came towards the car, rifle in one hand, torch in the other. But the moment he recognized the driver, he dropped his official manner. They were regular partners at the local golf club. Moore's story that the vehicle had been stoned in West Belfast was readily accepted, and he was waved through without further delay.

As soon as he reached home, he picked up the telephone with a shaking hand and dialled the number of the BBC's central office in Belfast. A weary voice came on the line; he immediately modified his own, mimicking the accent of a Fermanagh farmer.

'Emerald's the name, Emerald, and Kelly's is just the beginning. This is to let you know we're out to put this country right.'

He put down the phone, went into the sitting room and poured himself a large brandy. He felt sick, but leaning on the mantelpiece, he managed to steady himself. Then he crossed to the stereo unit and put on the first Brandenburg concerto, a piece which never failed to calm his nerves.

Chapter 4

At the Maze, O'Mara quickly settled into his new routine in H9. He was made an orderly, posted to the bakery division to mix dough for the big rotary oven which supplied the whole complex. The work was easy and there were extra rations. It was not long before the blanket days receded in his memory, though he was constantly looking over his shoulder to reassure himself that he was safe. He had heard nothing of Mary McKee since the visit. His fears and suspicions plagued him continually. He found himself bitterly hoping that, if they were justified, she had already betrayed herself. It would save him from exacting his own revenge for the trouble she had caused him. Meanwhile, outside the prison walls, spring had begun at last – though in Ulster, it was not a season of hope and renewal.

The only intrusion on O'Mara's temporary sense of security was his cellmate, Wilson, who also worked with him in the kitchens. He could not come to terms with the idea of this large, placid-looking man in early middle age, a caricature of an ex-RUC Inspector, having, as far as he knew, been imprisoned for corruption. For days the men did not converse, though in their silence all kinds of contacts were made. Wilson had a stolid ease about him which was somehow appealing. O'Mara resisted, but in the end, it was he who spoke the first words.

They were taking a break from their kitchen work, sitting alone by the ovens. 'So you're the peeler that got itchy fingers?'

Wilson looked up from a mug of tea, with a surprised air. 'Money talks,' he said at length. 'But you'd know that yourself.'

O'Mara had not expected this. 'What are you gettin' at?'

Wilson laughed. 'That's no old war wound you're carrying.' He gestured at O'Mara's weak knee. 'And now you're pulling some other trick or you wouldn't be in here.'

The Catholic was quick to put the record straight. 'It's not money this time, man. There's other things.'

Wilson seemed taken by O'Mara's eagerness to talk. 'What

was it like over there, then?'

O'Mara merely grimaced and took several swigs from his tea as if to rinse a bad taste from his mouth. 'Anyway, how come you left the straight an' narrow?'

Wilson was also evasive. 'How do you think?'

'Sure, you were fed up with ploddin' the same oul' streets in the back of beyond.'

'I was hardly chief interrogator at Castlereagh.'

O'Mara narrowed his eyes. 'I know that, man. If you were I'd have knocked your wine in.'

Wilson stood up abruptly and walked away. O'Mara shrugged his shoulders. The silence returned. It was some days before the same impulse made him break it. It was evening, and they were lying on their bunks in the cell. He had been thinking hard about his own position; he felt so isolated he had to talk to someone about what he had done, if only to make a gesture of independence, to prove to himself that he was not scared. The big man, with his easy ways, seemed an ideal listener.

'That trick of yours,' he began suddenly, as Wilson put down a magazine he had been reading. 'I've been wonderin', what were you goin' to do with the bread? Off to the Bahamas, sure, was that the crack?'

As before, Wilson simply answered the question. 'It wasn't for my own use.'

O'Mara was interested; he sat up with the manic energy that had marked all his movements since he had left the other block. Wilson looked across at him. 'You people don't have a monopoly on illegal organizations, you know.'

'Holy God, you're not tellin' me a fella like you was into terrorism?'

'You shouldn't let appearance deceive you.'

O'Mara laughed. 'Go on then, tell us, tell us all about your darin' deeds in the UDA.'

Wilson remained impassive. 'Have you ever heard of Emerald?'

'Aye.' O'Mara nodded. 'Sleekit bastards. More money an' guns than they know what to do with.'

'OK, I'll say nothing for now.' Wilson touched the side of

his nose. 'But that's the crack, as you call it.'

O'Mara hesitated, then stood up, scratched his head and pointed. 'You know, man, I can't make you out at all. But I reckon you're cool. I reckon we've got a few things in common here.'

'Kind of you,' said Wilson, in his best policeman's manner. 'I appreciate it.'

From then on the two prisoners became involved in the kind of daily contact that could be avoided only by active antipathy. Over a period of three or four weeks, as he mellowed under the lenient regime, and the dangers of his release loomed nearer, O'Mara appeared to derive solace from Wilson's company. And Wilson was willing to encourage him, losing no opportunity to lead him into discussion, increasingly finding a sympathetic response.

They were rarely disturbed when they sat at the back of the kitchens. O'Mara talked with an urgency in keeping with his general manner. It was not long before he began talking about his past: his childhood on the Falls Road, his drift into Republicanism, and his unashamed abuse of it. Soon he was speaking freely of a training camp in the Libyan desert, of methods with explosives, of murders and escapes. They were monotonously dour, violent recollections, though through them all there ran a single thread: his attachment to a girl he never named. It seemed to be O'Mara's only vulnerable trait. When, at length, he came full circle, and his thoughts returned to his punishment by the Provisionals and his internment in the H Block, it was this thread which seemed to gather round his throat and stop him saying any more. But Wilson had, by then, fully gained the measure of his man.

It was about a month before they were due to be released that Wilson crossed to O'Mara's bed in the cell, late at night. He spoke quietly. 'Listen. I've been thinking a lot about your story.'

O'Mara, who had been lying awake staring at the ceiling, narrowed his eyes in his distinctive gesture. 'Aye, an' you keep it to yourself, man, or else.'

Wilson assumed his most innocuous manner. 'Of course I will. Only . . .'

'Only what?'

'Well, it's just that I know for a fact there are people who'd pay well to use you. No questions asked. Cash in hand.'

O'Mara grinned. 'Don't tell me.'

'Look,' Wilson said, 'whatever you think you know about Emerald, forget it. You'll be treated well.'

O'Mara paused, wondering why the big man seemed so eager. He was also mystified as to why the British had not so far sought his co-operation. He had been forced to conclude that his defection had simply been taken for its propaganda value. 'OK,' he said, 'maybe I'm interested.'

Wilson went on. 'There's enough arms and money for an army . . . you were right there. But there's a shortage of men who really know their stuff. And that's where you come in. If you're as good as you say you are, the sky's the limit. They don't care which foot you kick with, so long as you can deliver.'

O'Mara was thoughtful, sensing a side to Wilson that he had not fully recognized before. He decided to test him. 'You're tellin' me the Prods'd trust a scut like me?'

Wilson was up to it. 'You know damn well your own top man was an ex-British para not so long ago. As I said before, money talks.'

O'Mara said then, 'I'll think about it.'

'Don't take too long,' Wilson replied. 'You'll be out of this place before you know it. You're going to need some friends.'

It was a Sunday late in May. Wilson had been excused his early duties, ostensibly for a special visit on compassionate grounds. O'Mara was alone at the back of the kitchens, operating the machines with a sullen preoccupation. For days the offer had troubled him. If the British had no use for him now, what else was he to do?

He turned. Facing him were two other prisoners. One, tall and thin, carried a heavy ladle; the other, stocky and scar-cheeked, held a carving knife. They barred his path. He recognized neither of them, but he knew why they were there.

'Och, look, I can explain.' There was no response. 'I'm still with you, boys. I'm workin' on somethin' real big here, so I am.'

O'Mara realized that he was wasting his time. There was only one way out. His expression changed from one of appeasement to vicious determination. He squared his shoulders. 'OK, bastards, come away.'

He kicked out accurately. The knife flew across the tiled floor. He tried to run past the two of them, but they caught him and threw him back. His head fell against the metal oven. He struggled to get up as they came at him. He aimed a punch at the lean assailant's crotch, but missed when the other kicked out. Instinctively, he curled up, shielding his head, waiting for them to get close enough so that he could at least break the force of their blows. Meanwhile, he shrieked for the guards, though he already knew it was unlikely anyone would come to his aid.

Another kick bruised his ribs. At any moment he expected the crack of the heavy ladle, but it did not come. Yet another boot caught his head from behind. His whole body went limp. For a moment he could see nothing.

As he curled further round on himself, he heard the sound of steps from the front of the kitchen. He thought another prisoner was about to join the attack. Instead the kicks stopped. He peered through his fingers. Wilson's massive arms were locked round the tall man, squeezing the breath from his body. The other turned and ran. There was a brief, gasping silence. Wilson eventually let his victim drop, half conscious. O'Mara looked up from the floor.

Wilson smiled. 'Now what have I been telling you?'

O'Mara managed to smile back painfully. 'OK, OK. I'll leave it to you now.'

Chapter 5

Darkness was falling as Roy Moore arrived home on a balmy midsummer's evening. In the hall he found a heap of mail from the midday post, but he avoided it, went straight to the drinks cabinet, poured himself a whiskey, switched on the stereo and sank into his armchair. The only light in the room was a small spot illumining a print of a Magritte bowler-hatted man, which was reflected in mirrors flanking the fireplace. Even this was too much for Moore. He had been suffering from a hangover all day. His head was throbbing, his stomach seemed to be filled with acid. His limbs were heavy and listless. For several weeks he had been involved in the tedious task of adapting his business to accommodate the prospective British deals. Meanwhile tension in the province had been heightened by acts of terrorism on both sides of the political divide. He had turned increasingly to the cratur, as it was known locally, to rinse away the stale taste of incessant meetings with colleagues and associates. Now he wanted to suffer the consequences alone, and in peace.

As if to mock him, the telephone, in jangling discord, pierced the music. He lifted the receiver irritably. 'Yes?'

He was surprised and relieved when he heard the sedate voice of the English Intelligence officer; the more so when he realized that this was not to be a cryptic message.

'Sorry to have to leave you hanging about so long, Roy, but it's all for the best. We had to make sure there was no unhealthy interest in your affairs. Can't be too careful in the security business.'

Moore responded in kind. 'Quite so. But I hope you have something for me now.'

'Indeed we do. Your product proved highly satisfactory in our last deal. We'll be pleased to use you again.'

'Can you give me any details?' Moore asked.

'Well, first, I think it's about time you got on to that useful little secretary of yours, so to speak. I understand she's been under the weather lately, family troubles and so on. But I think she would be keen now to have the chance to give us the benefit of her experience.'

'I think that can be arranged.'

'Perhaps you could have a word with her tomorrow. As to the deal in hand, we've been working pretty hard on our clients and I'm glad to say they're ready to make their own commitment this time. So you won't be needing us when it comes to business.'

'Will they contact me personally?' Moore inquired.

'I expect you'll be hearing from them any day now. We've set the wheels in motion. You have no rivals in your particular field.'

'Tilling the earth,' said Moore urbanely.

'You have a great sense of humour, Roy, I admire it in you. But take care, we can't let this one slip through the net.'

'Any advice for me, then?'

There was a short pause. 'It's a question of scratching the right backs really. Always best to keep in with the military . . . don't let the politicians get above their station.' After a further silence the Englishman concluded, 'And it's also wise to watch out for reds under the bed. This is a delicate business. I wouldn't dance too many jigs if I were you. I'll be in touch anyway. All the best for now.'

Moore replaced the receiver and swallowed his whiskey. His caller seemed to take an academic pleasure in talking in riddles. He poured himself another drink, pleased to find that his hangover seemed suddenly to have disappeared.

A call came through to him at work the next morning from Sir Cameron Smyth, leader of Emerald's political wing. He immediately recognized the deliberately anglicized tones of the ex-minister.

'Roy?'

'Speaking.'

'Cameron here. I think it's about time we met up again, you and I.'

Moore registered surprise. 'Oh yes? Well, if you wish. When do you suggest?'

'Actually I rather hoped you might be free later this afternoon.'

Moore continued to seem nonplussed. 'Bit sudden, isn't it?'

'Something's come up, you see,' said Smyth. 'We need your services.'

Moore adopted the tone of a subordinate. 'Oh, well, in that case . . .'

'My place then. Five o'clock sharp.'

It amused him that taking orders was becoming second nature. 'Five sharp.'

'Cheers.'

Moore calculated that, even if the meeting proved to be lengthy, he would still have time to get to Ballymacford by dusk. He cancelled all further engagements for the morning and went off to Thomson's Restaurant for a long lunch.

Later that day, Moore left his office on the top floor of a small complex in East Belfast, took the lift down and let himself out by a side door. His company car was parked at the far end of the car park. He drove away, first along Corporation Street, then past the sluggish river surrounded by derelict houses and boarded-up shop fronts. Eventually, he swung into the Malone Road, with its fat well-kept homes and leafy parks, from where the slums could be seen sulking in the distance. He thought of the war cry at the start of the troubles: the Malone fiddles while the Falls burns. Minutes later he pulled in at the entrance to Smyth's home. He pressed the intercom. The electronic lock was released. As he pushed back the solid iron gates, it satisfied him to remember that he had made in profit from the security system surrounding Smyth's residence what he had paid to enter Emerald.

He travelled the short distance to the modest Victorian building and climbed out of the car. The thin, delicate politician opened the door and greeted him.

'I'm glad you could make it at such short notice,' Smyth said as they shook hands. 'It shows a true sense of priorities.'

They proceeded to a library at the back of the house. 'Tea, or something stronger?'

Moore smiled. 'Whiskey?'

'You mustn't mind if I don't join you.'

Smyth ordered tea and poured Moore a minute measure of Jameson's. Then he said, 'Smoke if you wish. I don't myself.

Bit of an old puritan all round.'

Moore looked round him at the room, cluttered with the memorabilia of Sir Cameron's political career; photographs taken with various other VIPs covered the walls. They were sitting in leather chairs facing each other across a tidy desk. Moore lit a cigar and waited for Smyth to begin.

'Anyone else coming, Cameron?' he asked when the silence remained unbroken.

'No, no. This is what you might call an extraordinary meeting.' Smyth rose abruptly as the tea was brought in, took off his jacket and hung it carefully over the back of his chair. He pushed back his cuffs and poured from the elegant china pot. Moore gazed at his sallow, almost emaciated face, then surveyed his whole appearance from the gold watch chain down to the highly polished shoes. It revealed a trim, obsessive character.

Smyth called him to attention. 'We'll be visiting the General next week. I just wanted to fill you in on some details before the old war horse gets involved.'

Moore was immediately offered a glimpse of animosity between the two leaders. He said merely, 'OK, fire away.'

Smyth sipped his tea with finger cocked, dabbed his lips with a napkin, and began. 'In spite of recent rumour and speculation, Roy, in Emerald we work in a more subtle and calculated manner than those who are involved in blatant sectarian hostilities. To this end, we have always tried to keep a man close to what's happening at the Secretary of State's office. It's not easy. All the sensitive work is fiercely guarded by the English. We Ulstermen are rarely trusted with state secrets. Nonetheless, I'm glad to say, we have so far managed to keep ourselves informed of most of the important dealings at Stormont and Westminster – even though, I must admit, these damn summits with the Republic have proved rather more exclusive. Still, our record is on the whole very fair in these matters.'

'Thanks to your good offices, Cameron, I'm sure.'

'Thank you,' said Smyth, 'I try to do my best. Now then, at present we are particularly lucky in that we are being kept abreast of a whole range of interesting developments. Our latest insight concerns a certain Russian individual called Stoyva who is at this moment living in Dublin.'

Moore suddenly appeared to have grasped the meaning of a joke which had hitherto eluded him. He coughed hurriedly, looked at his cigar, and said, 'Maybe I should follow your example, Cameron, and give these things up.'

Smyth eyed him curiously and then decided to continue. 'Don't underestimate Soviet interest in maintaining the troubled state of the province. It is all grist to the mill of dialectical materialism, comrade, the decline of western imperialism, don't you know.' Smyth waited for his listener to make some disapproving noises, which Moore duly did. 'We are now aware that he has liaised with Republican terrorist groups on a number of occasions, and in fact was heavily involved in the development of the brutal INLA. Stoyva was personally responsible for seeing that several of these men were trained at a camp near Rostov in East Germany.'

Moore said, 'I'm amazed.'

'There is an embassy in the city but the man chooses to live anonymously in one of the poorer suburbs, posing as a representative for a firm which purports to sell Bulgarian farm machinery. He is, by all accounts, a devout young Marxist who has, as a result of his spurious attachment to proletarian aspirations, developed an interest in various aspects of traditional Irish culture. He is accordingly often to be seen frequenting bars in Dublin where traditional music and dance are performed and has apparently studied the history of these islands extensively.'

Moore interrupted. 'Stout fella.'

Smyth was not amused. 'He is a communist, Roy, and therefore a menace. He is here for one purpose only.'

'I see.'

'Now, you've heard of the *flaidhs* that take place every year in Donegal?'

Moore said, 'The music festivals?'

'Indeed. We have reason to believe that Stoyva is going to be at Buncrana in a month's time. On two counts. First, to indulge in his private pastime. Second, to advance his latest assignation: the fomenting of anti-nuclear sentiment. The festival has a large influx of young people, both from here and abroad, who are only too keen to accept the wilful propaganda of the loutish elements who set up their stalls at such places, from the H Block demonstrators to these fools who have taken it into their heads to protest, not only against the sole deterrent which has safeguarded these shores for so many years, but the very use of nuclear power as our most potent source of energy.'

Moore asked, 'And Stoyva?'

Smyth sighed. 'It is in the interest of the Eastern bloc that we continue to rely on our oil supplies, surely you realize that?'

Moore said, 'Of course, I see.'

Smyth again looked curiously at him. 'The Russian will go to Buncrana with funds at his disposal and a great propensity for causing trouble. He will also be off his guard.'

There was silence. Then Smyth said, as if it were the most casual remark, 'I believe you have an interest in cars?'

Moore replied, 'I do.'

'You have in fact entered a number of rallies in the past?' Moore nodded. 'Now listen carefully. In Emerald we like to test the commitment of all our members when the opportunity arises. And we don't waste time sending them out to murder old women in their beds or blow up already derelict properties. We deal only in those matters which have genuine political significance. It is as simple as this. All Russian connections with the province are anathema. We despise nothing so much as the communist ideologies which the urban terrorists have adapted so conveniently to justify their atrocities. In Stoyva we have pinpointed one of the chief sources of Russian interference. Do you begin to understand me?'

Moore nodded. 'Go on.'

'It has been decided that you shall drive one of our employees to Buncrana, where he will have orders to dispose of Stoyva in the neatest possible way. We have recently discovered the very man for the job.'

'Really?' Moore was not surprised.

'Now, I personally have seen fit to supervise this project,

even though it is strictly outside my province. But I've been somewhat worried lately by the peculiar attitude of my military colleagues. I want this to be a straightforward operation with no complications, which is why we have chosen to carry it out in the wilds of Donegal. The simple extermination of an unwanted intruder. You see?'

Moore waved his cigar, hiding his real reaction.

'I intend the whole thing to take place in such a way that the general public hears little or nothing of it – we have had too much publicity of late – but so that the British Government gets the message loud and clear we mean business. And if they aren't prepared to do something about the state of this country, we are!'

Smyth sipped at his tea, with fastidious anger. 'At the same time the incident will be the kind of embarrassment to the Republic that they will find hard to live down. And, in the present climate, that is just what is needed.'

Moore finished his cigar and drew a deep breath. 'I take it you refer again to the Hillsborough summits.'

Smyth replied, 'Put it this way. The last time, so far as I am aware, that British and Republican politicians met formally behind closed doors was in 1922. And we all know what happened then. What is more, considering our current position in NATO, I wouldn't be surprised if other parties were involved.'

'You want to distract them then?'

'I want to bloody well destroy them.' Smyth stiffened in his chair. Then, again, he managed to control his anger. 'Anything Emerald can do in a pragmatic manner to ensure that Ulster remains where it belongs, as an integral part of the United Kingdom, I shall support to my last breath.'

This was spoken with such practised eloquence that Moore could not fail to be impressed. 'So,' said Smyth, rising and putting on his jacket, 'have you any questions?'

'You say we go to the General's next week?'

'Indeed. In spite of what I have said, John has nonetheless to agree to the arrangements. Mind you, I'll tell you this now and I don't want it repeated – be on your guard. The man is liable to get carried away at any time. He was once a sound military tactician but he's neither a wise nor patient man these days. He not only has odious personal habits but entertains an absurd belief that we could best manage our affairs independently. In short I am beginning to think he is a liability to the organization.'

Moore had already begun to calculate exactly how he should interpret his recondite orders in the context of what was likely to take place.

The politician added, 'So take anything he says with a pinch of salt. There's no way of knowing what he'll come up with if people take him seriously.'

Moore rose and said, 'OK, Cameron. I think I'll leave you now. I have some private business to attend to.'

Smyth took Moore's hand in his soft white fingers. 'Certainly, Roy. I'll contact you next week.'

Moore drove through Belfast as quickly as possible and headed off along the road to Ballymacford. The sun was falling over Lough Neagh, shading the streams where trout and salmon abounded. It was a calm, lovely evening. But Moore was so preoccupied that he noticed only the road ahead. This had been his manner almost constantly since the Kelly bombing. He had had ample time to reflect on the suffering the bombing had caused. And he had found to his surprise that, rather than feeling any guilt, he was filled with a sense of exhilaration and achievement which made him eager to be involved again in action. For some reason that he could not fully understand, this urge was associated with the Catholic girl. He had been haunted by a dream where she lay in the back of the Range Rover waiting for him to make love to her, while the small soft corpses of birds fell all around them. Strangely, something always prevented him from touching her. His legs could not move, he was in pain. The dream had so troubled and excited him that he had had great difficulty in resisting the impulse to go and see her before now.

He did not drive into the village, but took the quarry road and parked where he had done two months before. The gates still stood rusty and neglected. He climbed over them and set off towards the huts. The earth was dry and hard now. He looked round him continually to make sure that he was not being watched. The hills were deserted. When he came up to the cluster of buildings, there was no sign of Mary McKee. He decided to wait. Leaning against the wall of the hut where he had first seen her, he drank every now and then from a small metal flask of whiskey that he carried in his linen jacket.

He felt certain she would come, and he was not mistaken. When the gloom had thickened so that he could barely make out the distant features of the landscape, he heard the sound of Mary's dog running through the heather on the ridge. He bent and picked up an iron bar from a mass of debris beside the hut. He heard her calling, 'Silver, come here now.' Her whistle echoed through the quarry. When the dog appeared, it did not run at him, but stood some feet away with hackles raised, snarling. Mary McKee quickly arrived. It was not too dark to recognize him. She took the dog by the scruff, and he was suddenly sure that his journey would not be wasted.

When she had overcome her shock, she said angrily, 'You're takin' a risk comin' here.'

He still held the iron bar in front of him. 'You've had trouble?'

'As if you didn't know.' She struggled while Silver strained at her grasp. 'I've a mind to fetch someone from the village. You'd be done then.'

He replied, 'You wouldn't do that.' He jerked his head towards the dog. 'But you could do me a favour and put that animal in the hut. I want to talk to you.'

She hesitated, more ambivalent towards him now than she had ever been, knowing how he had saved her from the bombing and yet left others to perish. Eventually, her desire to find out what he might have to say made her pull Silver towards the hut. He stood watching warily, as she closed the door behind the struggling animal.

Moore threw down the bar and looked into Mary McKee's face. Her dark-ringed eyes and worn complexion testified to what she had been through since he had last seen her. She glared back at him. 'What do you want?'

He said quietly, 'I want to know if you're alright.'

She laughed bitterly. 'Sure you do.'

He asked what he already knew. 'I take it you've not said anything?'

She exclaimed, 'What, like I went out with this Prod who just happened to walk in on the night the bomb went off, and he saved my life?'

He pressed her. 'What about other people?'

'The dead can't talk.'

There was a long silence broken by the dog's whining. Moore was suffused with the same thrill of violent recollection. At length he said, 'At least you're not one of them.'

'Aye, an' I want to know why.' She stood facing him with her hands thrust into the pockets of her summer smock, looking frail and confused. For a moment he felt genuinely protective towards her. He made a show of speaking sincerely.

'I can't tell you what you want to know. Either you believe it was part of the plan, or I acted on my own initiative. Whichever it was, you ought to be grateful.'

Mary hung her head and muttered, 'So I am.'

Moore took the flask from his pocket and handed it to her. 'Here, have some of this.'

She took three gulps and wiped her lips with her fingers. Moore gazed over her head. Darkness filled the quarry now. They were quite alone. Mary shivered as the whiskey warmed her stomach. She gave the flask back, looking into his eyes. 'Christ, I'm sick of all the killin'.'

He paused, and then said, 'That's why we mean to put an end to it.'

She was so tired and febrile that the drink began to affect her almost immediately. She said morosely, 'I would've hated you once. Not for what you did. Just for what you are.' She looked down at her feet and added, 'It's not the same any more.'

There was another silence. She turned away from him. Moore drank eagerly from his flask, reflecting that his visit had been perfectly timed. She had clearly reached a point when her sense of shock and fear, and her resentment at the interrogations both by the police and the Republicans, had lost their immediate edge and left her vulnerable. He nodded slowly, glancing at her profile. Then moved towards her.

'You'd be wrong to look on me as an enemy,' he said. 'You're in a difficult position. I think I can help you.'

She looked up expectantly. She saw a kindness in his expression and sighed involuntarily. He watched tears gathering in her eyes. He gave her the small flask again, and she finished the whiskey. When he put out his hand to take it back, he held her fingers. The tears spilled onto her cheeks. As she struggled to contain them, her lips quivered.

He pocketed the flask and said, 'It must be hard for you out here on your own.'

At this, she began weeping outright. He put his arm round her; holding her against his shoulder and running his hand over her neck.

At length she drew back. A sense of shame forced her to mumble through her tears, 'It's my father. He's awful sick. Sure, they reckon there's only a few weeks now.'

He said nothing but lifted her face and put his lips to her eyes, kissing the tears from her cheeks. When he touched her mouth, she tried to draw away. But his own urge passed quickly through her, and the ache of her loneliness found another outlet as she returned his kiss, holding him against her.

When they separated, she walked away from him, staring at the ground as if in deep thought. It had grown so dark he could barely see her. She returned after a while and immediately began questioning him in such a way that he had to answer. He admitted he had a firm political commitment to the British cause in Ulster. She was not surprised. It had been publicized that Emerald was responsible for the bombing. But she did not seem interested in any wider implications, only in what he himself knew about her. He was determined to convince her that he should be trusted. So he said – as was the case – that his knowledge of her was confined to her role in the political wing of the Republican movement, and that it was this experience which could be used to her advantage. He was at a loss to understand why it should be so important that he knew nothing of her personal affairs. But it seemed she had chosen to make another of her swift decisions – this time in his favour.

She said: 'OK, so I look on you as a friend. Now what happens?'

He could not help smiling. In spite of the whiskey and the balm of midsummer, it had grown cold in the windswept quarry. He could see she was shivering. 'It's getting chilly here,' he said. 'Can't we go up to the cottage?'

The way she looked at him left him in no doubt that the nagging desire he felt for her was reciprocated, and that, knowing what she owed him and how he might be able to help her further, she had decided that she had no good reason to resist it.

She told him to follow her at a distance and to wait among the conifers on the ridge until she had made sure it was safe. Then she set off over the hill alone, taking her dog again by the scruff of the neck.

The animal sullenly accepted his presence once he was inside the cottage. It lay in the pantry doorway and eyed him suspiciously, before it grew bored and slunk off to its den by the Aga. Mary was careful not to put on the lights, even though the hills were so silent that it would be hard for anyone to approach unheard. She sat beside Moore on a long couch facing the hearth where she had stoked the peat fire into a healthy blaze. She put a half-finished bottle of white wine and two glasses at their feet. The bright flames played over their faces.

After a few desultory exchanges, neither had an impulse to talk further. Moore leant back, stroking his moustache. He found himself thinking of the trip to Buncrana with some trepidation. He was grateful for Mary's soft warm presence. He pulled her towards him, running his hand through her thick hair as she leant on his chest and stared into the fire. He could not know that she, in turn, was making her own calculations. Since her last visit to the Maze on the eve of the bombing she had come to realize that the pressures on her would be doubled when the vindictive and unpredictable O'Mara was released. For whatever reasons, Moore seemed determined to offer her a way out; and she was not so disturbed by her memories of the bloody scenes at Kelly's to refuse it.

It was now she who turned her face towards him and lightly

touched his lips. He tried to respond in kind, but he was so roused by the crude imagery of his dreams, that he could not prevent himself from kissing her fiercely, pulling at the buttons of her dress with impatience. She did not seem to be offended; she arched her body willingly towards him as he ran his lips over her small breasts, pressing his face against her. For a moment she did seem to recoil, but then she lay back on the couch as he pressed his fingers between her legs. Her hands moved under his shirt. When he entered her with the same haste, Moore could not help but wonder why they had not gone to bed in the normal way but chosen to lie like this in the firelight. It was as if neither of them wanted to be held responsible. For all its vigour, their lovemaking was not satisfying.

She held on to him when he had come too quickly, but to no purpose. She lay running her fingers into the curve of his hips while he fell away within her soft, damp embrace.

When they had risen and clothed themselves, he stood and leant on the mantelpiece, gazing moodily into the flames. He glanced round to find her looking up at him curiously. She seemed about to tell him something. Then, with an almost imperceptible shrug of her shoulders, she stood up and took his hands.

He said, 'I'd better go. I don't want to push my luck.'

She answered, 'There's no one about now.' But he could not conceal his eagerness to leave. 'Will you find your way then?'

He nodded, picked up his jacket and kissed her briefly. 'I'll be in touch.'

She laughed, 'You'd better.' Then opened the door for him and watched him go out into the night.

He hurried over the ridge into the quarry. In the pitch dark and without her guidance, he slipped several times as he made his way across to the gates. When he reached his car, he slammed the door and drove off at speed. The evening had troubled him more than he was prepared to admit.

Chapter 6

On Thursday 29 June O'Mara was released from the Maze Prison. At his own request, and with the Governor's approval, the date had been put back by 24 hours, to avoid any possible Republican reception committee.

Principal Officer Black pushed him out into the chill early morning air. The great gates slammed behind him. His only possessions were the clothes he had had with him when he was arrested – the bloodstains on his trousers faded now to a dull brown – a few oddments in a kitbag, and a £30 grant from the prison welfare. With a glance back at the grey walls and the empty eyes of the guard towers, he started walking towards Belfast along the small rural lanes around the Maze. When he came out onto the main road, he caught a bus for the city. It was 8.30 a.m.

Wilson had been released the previous day. O'Mara had a telephone number where Wilson could be contacted. He fingered the torn paper in his pocket with a sense of reassurance.

It surprised him that no one seemed to take much notice of him on the bus, but he knew that this was a feeling common to all ex-convicts. He noted that the fares had trebled. When they reached Belfast, he stayed only for half an hour; just enough time to buy a hot dog and a newspaper, and to visit a camping shop, where he spent most of his capital on a waterproof jacket, a sleeping bag, and a sheath knife. In the street again, he found a black taxi and asked to be taken to Ballymacford. As they moved off, he ran his fingers along the blade of his new knife.

The city seemed to have changed very little. British squaddies were still in evidence at gates, roadblocks, houses and shops. If a street was not patrolled by soldiers, it was covered by police. He could not help but feel pride at the work that he and his associates had done over the years. In spite of the odds, they had still managed to wreak havoc in the area. The taxi crawled through the grey waste of West Belfast with its faceless housing estates, roads littered with rubbish, windows bricked up, and walls covered in sectarian graffiti.

The few pedestrians he saw seemed as drab and hopeless as the prisoners he had left behind him. He felt again the need, a single need, to take care of himself, to survive this desolation.

He was relieved when the Glen route broke from the confines of the suburbs into the country, twisting and climbing towards Ballymacford some ten miles away. The driver had been chatting intermittently about the recent upsurge in terrorist activities, but O'Mara had heard little of what he said. He drew on a cigarette and watched the sprawling slums vanish in the haze.

As they drove, he became aware of a particular thirst. It occurred to him for the first time since he had been released – though in jail he had often thought of nothing else – that no drink had passed his lips for many months. The car was approaching the spot where he had often stopped in the past, at Mac's Bar. He tapped the driver's shoulder. 'Hey man, slow down a minute, will you?'

The driver made no attempt to oblige. 'Ballymacford, wasn't it?'

O'Mara grabbed his shoulder and said, 'I'm tellin' you to stop now.'

'Go easy, fella, I hear you.'

The old diesel taxi juddered to a halt. The driver sat trembling, waiting for some violence. O'Mara half-considered christening his knife, but then looked closely at his victim – the drab suit, the badly cut hair, that same hopelessness in his shallow eyes. He pocketed his weapon.

'Och shite, I'm only out today, man. I'm not goin' to bother with the likes of you.' He thrust his few remaining pounds into the driver's jacket pocket and got out of the car. 'Will you wait?' he asked ironically. In response, the taxi sped off and rattled away again down the valley.

O'Mara walked towards the pub, a dark box with no advertisement. The steps down to the locked door were strewn with crates of empty stout bottles. He knocked and waited. Some minutes later, a large tousled head appeared at the grille. The eyes in the head widened. Then Mac stood back and let him in.

He had a broom in his hand. 'Holy God, it's you, Pat

O'Mara. Sure, I've not set eyes on you for ages. I thought the Brits had you in jail.'

'They did. But I'm out now an' I've a terrible thirst on me, so give me a drink there, will you, Mac?'

The fat landlord eased himself behind his small bar and reached for a bottle of beer.

'Jeez, man, I don't want that piss. Give me a rosiner an' don't take all day.'

With a shrug of his shoulders, Mac took down a bottle of spirits and poured his visitor a large Irish, then gazed at him in open admiration. 'Sure, you've done your bit an' no mistake. If there was more men like yourself, we'd have them bastards out of this in no time, no time at all.'

O'Mara looked from the stubbly vacant face, the ill-fitting dentures and dull eyes, to the waxy belly bulging where the shirt buttons were missing. He felt like spitting. 'Sure, Mac, an' we owe it all to glypes like you.'

He asked for another whiskey, took his glass and sat on a barrel in a corner. The alcohol was already affecting him like a poison; after a third shot his head was spinning, and he could barely listen to Mac rambling on behind the bar. He looked round him at the drab interior and he remembered the times he had sat there with Mary McKee all those years before. He felt that he should move on quickly; the McKee farm was still two miles off. But he did not move. His eyes drooped, the dim bar disappeared. When he opened his eyes again, he half-expected to find himself in the prison cell. Instead, he was face to face with the fireside nationalist who had given him whiskey and who was now gazing at him only a few inches away.

'Here, are you alright, Pat?'

O'Mara recoiled. 'Sure I am. Now don't be an oul' quilt an' give me the bottle by the neck.'

Mac went back to the bar and fetched the whiskey bottle. 'You know, Pat, we've been behind you boys all the way, never mind what they've been tellin' you.'

O'Mara drank in silence. The fat man changed tack. 'Anyhow, sure you'll be glad to get back to your Mary, won't you lad?' The gunman continued to ignore him. 'Now there's people been puttin' their neb in, sayin' she's been a bad wee girl while you was away an' all, but don't you believe it, Pat. She's salt of the earth, that one, you can be sure of that.' Mac wiped the sweat from his face.

O'Mara made a grab at him but missed completely and lurched forward over a table. Mac stood back. 'Och, look, there's no need for that. I'm on your side, Pat, don't touch me now, come on.'

O'Mara stood up, kicked a chair into the corner and left without a word. Mac did not trouble him to pay. Outside O'Mara reeled in the bright mountain air, and sat down at the roadside. Eventually, he walked off with a heavy stagger up the steadily inclining road towards the village.

As his weak knee began to lock, the long thatched house came into sight, smoke trailing from the chimney. O'Mara was touched with a moment's fond recollection. It only made him more bitter.

The farm turned out to be empty, the door locked. He limped to the pantry window. The catch was as loose as it had ever been. He clambered into the house. Inside, he took a long drink of cool spring water from a jug, then lay down on the battered sofa. Within minutes he was asleep, snoring drunkenly.

Mary had waited almost a week for Moore to return. Now there was nothing left to eat in the cottage; she had been forced to go down to the local stores. On her return, before she could open the door, the dog began to whine. She left it tied to the gatepost, crept back up to the house and looked through the open pantry window. In his sleep, with his clipped hair and old clothes, O'Mara looked exactly as she had known him before his imprisonment. She gasped, turned and ran, untied the dog who bounded ahead of her, and did not look back till she had reached a gap in the hedge along the road. There she crouched, nervously stroking the animal's head, waiting for the lean figure to come limping over the brow. The breeze shivered in the heather, the bog eased and swelled. O'Mara was still snoring the cottage.

She went down hurriedly to Ballymacford, to the telephone

box at the corner, and looked for Moore's office in the directory. She dialled the number. His secretary, whether acting on orders or her own initiative, said that he was engaged in an important meeting and was not in any circumstances to be disturbed. Mary asked if she could leave a message; the assistant noted it with evident suspicion and promptly rang off.

Mary stood in the phone box while Silver whined outside. She finally decided that her only possible course was to turn to her neighbours. She went to the McLeans', to the cottage on the ridge opposite McKee's farm, and called out at the open door.

Dympna McLean, a stout young woman who had once been her schoolfriend, welcomed her in with matronly warmth. 'Sure, the family's all gone to the market, love, there's just meself,' she said, bending low over a stove. 'But sit yourself down an' we'll have a wee jaw.'

Mary left Silver in the doorway and sat down by the fire. Dympna cleaned two mugs on her apron, set them on the table and made tea with water from a great kettle boiling on the range.

'So what brings you here? You must have some kind of trouble, for we never see you from one week to the next since you've been back.'

Mary was in no mood to pretend. 'Pat O'Mara,' she said. 'He's come back an' I can't see him.'

'Is he out already? Sure, I thought . . .'

Mary interrupted. 'I don't understand it either. The last time I saw him he was still on the blanket. Och, if he's gone an' sold out or somethin' there's goin' to be hell to pay.'

The other woman took it all in her stride. 'Well, don't you get mixed up in it, that's all I say.' She laid her arm round Mary's shoulder. 'Your man's always been trouble, sure he has. An' as for you, well, you've hardly been goin' out of your way to make things easy for yourself, with the kind of company you've been keepin'.'

Mary avoided her eyes, breathing deeply. 'There's nothin' private in this place.'

Dympna laughed. 'Sure, you didn't think there ever would

be, did you girl?' She withdrew her arm with a brief hug of reassurance.

Dympna then talked for an hour or more, with barely a pause, about her amorous exploits with the local smith. Mary found it difficult to listen. The net around her seemed tighter than ever. She fell asleep.

Dympna covered her in a shawl and resumed her household chores. When Mary awoke, it was to the sound of the McLean family returning from market. She left with Silver for the quarry, in the hope that Moore had received her message and would meet her there as she had asked. But though she waited for over an hour, there was no sign of him. At last she returned to the McLeans' and agreed to stay the night.

When O'Mara woke it was already dark. He decided that he could not afford to wait any longer at the cottage, no matter what he wanted. After he had rummaged through the rooms, he hurried down through the quiet streets of Ballymacford to the same telephone which the girl had used that morning. He took the paper from his pocket and dialled the number Wilson had given him.

'Yes?'

He heard a voice he did not know and was about to put down the receiver when he thought better of it. 'Wilson,' he said simply.

'You mean Sam. Hang on,' came the reply as if the call had been expected.

Then his former companion came on the line. 'Who is it?'

'Me, Pat, Pat O'Mara.'

'Where are you?'

'Never mind. How do I reach you people?'

'You're sure about it, then?'

'Aye, I'm sure.'

Wilson gave him an address in Newry. He took it down slowly, in a mess of capitals. Then he left the phone box and waited in the shadows until night fell thick over the village. He walked casually to O'Grady's Garage, kitbag over his shoulder, cigarette in hand. There he knocked at the door, and as O'Grady shuffled inside, he took out his knife. He brandished the knife in O'Grady's face and demanded a car to take him to Belfast. The dour old man obliged with an ancient estate he was repairing for the McLeans. O'Mara climbed in and sped off towards the capital. The inhabitants of Ballymacford had learnt for certain that he was on the loose again.

At McLean's farm the next morning Mary heard that O'Mara had gone; with apologies to the McLeans for their car, she left and crossed over to the McKee ridge with Silver at her side. Inside the cottage she found that O'Mara had stolen the savings she kept in a wallet at the back of one of her dressing table drawers. To her surprise, the cottage had not been ransacked. This implied that O'Mara would not be satisfied with paltry acts of revenge. Mary became still more determined to put herself out of his reach.

This time when she phoned Moore's office, he himself answered. He had received no message, he said. When she told him that things had become dangerous for her at the cottage, he said he would come as soon as he could. She took this as a sign of solicitude.

He arrived at the quarry that evening. She had carefully prepared her story: Moore's visit to her had not gone undiscovered and she was under serious threat if she did not reveal his identity. For a moment he seemed genuinely perturbed. He questioned her further while he considered what he should do. He was reluctant to assume any specific personal responsibility. Yet he could not pretend that his employers would thank him if he allowed her to disappear from the scene before the time had come to gather the information that they required from her. So he stood by the huts, equivocating, as darkness deepened around them.

At length, she decided that she had had enough interrogation. 'Och, look, I'm tellin' you, I can't stay here now.'

He said nothing. Nagging him, beneath his other considerations, was a private interest that he did not want to recognize. As he looked at her waif-like features, her face fraught with uncertainty, he found her hard to resist.

She chose that moment to add, 'Sure, why don't you take me to your place. Wouldn't I be safe there?'

He stroked his moustache, frowning. This contingency must have been foreseen, but he had been given no brief. A Catholic girl at his home would scarcely enhance his standing in Emerald. He felt almost as if he might be walking into some kind of trap.

Yet he found himself saying, 'What about the dog?'

Mary's face relaxed into a smile of relief. 'Sure, he knows you now, an' he's a fine guard dog an' all.'

Moore shook his head, sighing heavily. It was he now who appeared to be forced into a quick decision. He reasoned that a few days sheltering her would not necessarily be such a risk. He would then at least have time to get a satisfactory brief. After a few moments he nodded and said, 'Get your things, then.'

She hurried off over the ridge. Not an hour later, the Jaguar was pulling into the drive at the large house near Templepatrick, and Mary McKee was still voicing her gratitude.

To Mary's disappointment, the next evening, he telephoned to say brusquely that he had to travel to the Republic to make arrangements for a business deal, and would not return that night. She was to keep hidden, and not to answer any more calls. There was everything she needed in the house.

Later, she could think of nothing better to do than to tidy up Moore's bachelor territory, reflecting that the house was more like a modern museum in a foreign country than a private home in Ireland. As she lay in his bed staring at the ceiling, she wondered about the kind of man who would choose to live in such a place.

Chapter 7

An hour after he called home, Moore was crossing the Irish border into County Monaghan. That morning, while Mary had still been sleeping soundly, he had received another call, inquiring as to whether all was going according to plan. He had hurriedly alluded to his 'useful little secretary', but had merely been told that he shouldn't allow himself to be distracted from his work. Before he could reply, the line went dead.

Moore glanced across at Cameron Smyth at the wheel of his Rover. They were already late for the meeting with General Fforde and his associates. Smyth was driving fast. After they cleared customs, four or five miles of dangerous winding country road brought them to the Fforde estate. It seemed that Smyth was taking a deliberately tortuous route.

As they neared the estate Smyth said, 'Can't be too careful about this place, Roy. You see, only the committee members come here with any regularity.'

Moore wondered how much he should believe. They turned between a pair of rusted iron gates along a road, through the dense forest of the demesne, unpaved and covered in grass.

'No security, you'll notice. We've done our level best to attract the least possible attention from the local population. John has the place registered as a club for retired army officers. Hence the regular arrival of Ulster registration vehicles.'

'Where is the house?' asked Moore.

'Still about a mile away.' Smyth negotiated the rough track, grimacing as loose stones struck the chassis.

Moore sat in silence. Eventually the woods thinned. He glimpsed acres of uncultivated land; there was no sign of any livestock. 'Has the General no cattle, Cameron?'

'All rustled over the border years ago.'

'Is that so?'

'The family has never been liked here, you see. They have long had a reputation as negligent landlords. The locals have given them a hard time. Poaching their rivers, rustling their herds, vandalizing their property . . .'

'If they've proved negligent, I would have thought that was inevitable.'

Cameron glanced briefly at his passenger. 'I'm surprised to hear you say it, Roy. There is no creature more irrationally ungrateful than the Irish peasant.' Moore said nothing. 'You don't agree? Well, perhaps I should qualify what I say. The Irish peasant and the English minister. John has learnt this only too well. You see, Cremorgan was a present to the family from Cromwell for services rendered. Once upon a time it was the hub of an estate which stretched halfway across the county. Over the centuries, the tenants have deserted and most of the land is mortgaged or gone to seed. The General – quite rightly in my opinion – blames the British Government for failing to support him with hard cash, and the Irish peasantry for the rest.'

'Why doesn't he sell up and leave?' Moore inquired.

'Again you surprise me. You sound like a member of Sinn Fein.' Smyth pouted at the wheel and Moore could tell he was beginning to be irritated. 'Whatever happened, he would never do that,' Smyth went on. 'To his credit, he would have to be shot first and dragged away. No matter that he leaves something to be desired in other departments.'

'Spoken like a true politician,' said Moore aloud.

Smyth pretended to ignore him. The house came into view beyond a bank of thick foliage, a huge three-storeyed edifice set in an expanse of weed-covered gravel. Flaked pillars graced the doorways and crumbling chimneys festooned the rooftop. General Fforde himself stood in the doorway like a craggy statue, waiting for them.

Cameron Smyth parked the car beside two others and fiddled with a briefcase full of papers. Moore climbed out and shook the old soldier's hand. Though he was a tall, tanned man with an impressive frame, his sharp beak of a nose and the loose strands of white hair pressed over the crown of his head gave him something of a clownish appearance.

'Glad to meet you, glad to meet you, even if you are late,' the General declared. 'I'd just popped out to see if there was any sign.' He continued to shake Moore's hand vigorously. 'Now I know who you are, old chap, Roy's the name, isn't it? I'm John.'

Smyth greeted his counterpart with reserve. Then the General clapped a hand on each man's shoulder, much to the distaste of the politician, and the three of them went in to the house.

The General took them to the dining room where the meeting was to be held. Facing each other across a long oak table decked with decanters of whiskey and port and cut Waterford glasses were two other inner committee members; four chairs stood empty. Moore greeted, in turn, the Reverend Malcolm Fadden – responsible for propaganda – whom he had last seen at a Loyalist rally in Lisburn; and Terence Wylie, a merchant bank director – head of finance – who had, after Moore's recruitment, taken responsibility for Moore's business account in Belfast. Fforde and Smyth took seats at the respective heads of the table.

'Is there someone missing?' asked Moore as he sat down.

Fforde replied, 'Yes, yes. One of my best chaps is coming in to tell us about your fellow operator on the project in hand. Actually he's just been doing a bit of time at Her Majesty's Pleasure, on our behalf. And as a result of his sacrifice, I have it in mind to tell him that he will be promoted this very evening, if we can get the thing through before he arrives. So let us proceed, shall we?'

Moore sat quietly while the various formalities were conducted. The release of the absent member from jail seemed rather too convenient to be mere coincidence. He would be very interested to meet the man who had sacrificed so much for the Unionist cause.

Eventually Fforde moved matters on. 'Right. Now then. As you are aware, this is not a full committee meeting. We have simply come together to assure the smooth running of an operation for which Cameron has chosen to assume responsibility, but which I personally feel needs one or two minor amendments in order to make it fully effective.'

Smyth tutted and waited to hear what Fforde might have to add. But the General did not immediately oblige. 'You, Terence,' he went on, 'are here to ensure the provision of adequate funds so that the appropriate equipment may be used. And you, Malcolm, to organize whatever publicity we see fit. I believe Cameron has an idea that only certain strategic sources are to be put in the picture. However, no doubt he will tell us what he intends. May I take the opportunity to introduce you formally to a young man who will be involved in the operation personally. Roy, welcome to active service.'

Moore nodded, feeling their eyes upon him. Fforde continued, 'As is so often the case, we are indebted to the good offices of our informant in the English camp at Stormont. But I will allow Cameron to do us the courtesy of explaining exactly how he has helped us in this particular case.'

Cameron Smyth tilted his half moon spectacles and began in his parliamentarian's voice. 'I don't need to add to what John has said about the value of having loyal members of the organization in positions close to the Secretary of State. I shall now show you a memo of the information we have been supplied regarding Victor Stoyva, the subject of the operation.'

As the sheet clipped together with photographs of the Russian was circulated, Smyth prepared to speak further at length. But before he could continue, a large placid-looking person was ushered in by Fforde's batman, who himself remained posted at the door. Moore gazed at the newcomer as he came to the table.

'Ah Sam, how very good to see you!' Fforde exclaimed, taking him by the shoulder. The whole company stood up. 'We appreciate what you have done for us all.'

Smyth added his response, 'Hear, hear.' The others joined him.

Fforde was in his element. 'So much so, it is my duty to inform you that it has been agreed that you should be promoted to the rank of Colonel. The appointment will be properly ratified in the near future.'

The man shook hands with each of the other members and took his place.

Smyth returned to his speech. 'I'm sure Sam will understand if we press on. I shall now hand you details of the plan. Then I shall ask Sam to say a few words about our absent employee.'

There was silence while they perused this second sheet. It was broken only by the sound of clearing phlegm. The Reverend Fadden appeared to suck a never-ending stream of small liquorice throat pellets that he took from a silver box he carried in his jacket pocket.

At length, Wylie said, 'I see no problems here. It all looks tight to me.'

Fforde enjoined, 'Well then, I think it's about time I put forward my own little scheme, don't you? It won't take long.'

Smyth pouted. Fadden took his silver box again from his pocket and popped a pellet in his mouth, saying absent-mindedly, 'Come on then, John, tell us what you have.'

'Well,' Fforde began, 'I have it in mind that while our two operators are busy at Buncrana, my man Mitchell, whose credentials I have no need to confirm' – he waved a hand at the batman standing silently by the door – 'takes himself off to Dublin and turns our Russki's pad upside down.'

Smyth glanced briefly at Moore. He then exclaimed, 'For heaven's sake, man, what do you expect to find in his apartment? Blueprints for Armageddon?'

Fforde was undeterred. 'Something rather more pertinent to our own designs, I would hope.'

'Do you seriously expect that a Soviet agent is going to secrete anything of the slightest importance on his premises?'

Moore could not help but smile. Cameron Smyth took it as a sign of support. Fforde retaliated. 'Why the deuce not?'

Smyth ran a hand through his sleek hair. 'If you need me to tell you that . . .'

The Reverend Fadden interrupted, his deep voice booming above the others. 'Come on now, John, be sensible.'

Fforde leant forward. 'Look, I may not be a bally politician but I'm damned if I don't know a thing or two more about Intelligence than either of you!'

Moore was astounded at how quickly the meeting had degenerated into a slanging match. Then he recalled various council meetings that he had attended. He decided to intervene. 'If I may be permitted to say something; I think John's addition to the plan is not without merit. If it proved successful it would add a certain bite to the operation. Anyway, what is there to lose?' Fforde gazed at him with approval. 'Is there anything to lose?' Moore repeated.

Wylie seemed unwilling to answer, fiddling with a corner of his papers while the two Ulster politicians looked at one another sullenly. Then Smyth said, 'As I perceived it, the whole point of taking the man at Buncrana was to avoid this kind of risk.'

But Fforde ignored this and turned to the man who had remained silent until now. 'What do you think, Sam?'

'I think,' said the big man humbly, 'that it sounds like a good idea.'

Smyth, who knew he was outnumbered, shook his head dismissively to imply that they might well come to regret their decision. He said no more. At the same time, Moore wondered if he did not have some more convoluted motive for so readily allowing Fforde to have his way. 'Well, I suggest we move on,' the politician muttered at length, 'and let Sam speak.'

All assented. The newly promoted Colonel recounted his activities in the Maze Prison, culminating in his sharing a cell with a Provisional prisoner he did not name, who had defected from the IRA and would lend his services to Emerald for a suitable fee. Moore listened with calculated attention.

At the point when it became clear that the other man at Buncrana was to be a defector from the enemy, Fadden bawled incredulously, 'You mean to say this man's a good for nothing Papist?'

'Should assassination be the sole religious property of the Presbyterians, Reverend?' the big man calmly retorted.

The Reverend Fadden, for once, was speechless. He glared across the table, then looked to Cameron Smyth for support. But he was disappointed. 'Malcolm,' said Smyth, 'you surely understand the nature of this kind of work. There is one factor which is decisive, and that is money. It is capable of ensuring greater loyalty than any sectarian commitment.'

'Well, it's a fine day when the loyal men of Ulster look to a Fenian to carry out their work.' Fadden yet again took out his silver box and popped a liquorice pellet into his mouth.

In the silence which followed, Smyth seemed to have recovered his composure. At length he said, 'It should be emphasized that we are not so catholic in our recruitment as Malcolm might wish to imply.' There was a murmur of laughter. 'The reason we have not seen fit to allow this man, who, in deference to the Reverend's feelings, we shall refer to henceforth as Paddy' – there was further laughter – 'to attend a meeting such as this is that he must first prove himself efficient and reliable. The outcome of the Buncrana project will act as sufficient measure.'

He fell silent, to nods of agreement. Fforde, who sat staring into his whiskey, was keen now that his own contribution should not be forgotten. 'I must say I'm glad anyway that my little addition has proved acceptable. It's not enough, you know, to eliminate opponents. Our policy must be at all times to try and reap political rewards.'

'So speaks a military man,' said Smyth.

'Political rewards!' Fadden returned to his customary obsession. 'It's the Papists we're after and it's the Papists we'll get.'

Wylie now came out openly on the soldier's side. 'Malcolm, would you calm down for a moment. It's quite clear that what John says is true. If we had exerted more pressure in political circles in the past, things could look very different now.'

Smyth rejoined, 'Terence, are you trying to say I have failed in my personal capacity as head of political affairs?'

Before Wylie could reply, Moore again intervened. 'Cameron, you yourself have expressed concern about developments on your own front. Had things been handled, shall we say, more sensitively in the past, would we now for instance be witnessing these clandestine meetings between the Republic and the English which bode such ill for the province?'

'Exactly!' said Fforde, 'Exactly, Roy! If you had spent most of your life fighting for the bally English as I have, just so you could watch them try to pull out of a sinking ship and leave us to the mercy of the green seas like the poor Rhodesians or any other of the loyal allies they've sold out along the line, you'd waste no opportunity in trying to put whatever pressure you could upon them to ensure they didn't get away with it.'

'Hear, hear!' said Wilson, timing his moment of support.

'Gentlemen, gentlemen!' Smyth cried in a tone of moral superiority. 'Don't let's get carried away! John has got what he wanted as usual. Stoyva's apartment will be searched, and anything found there brought back to Cremorgan. Now can we stick to the matter in hand and not waste our breath on empty rhetoric?'

'You consider nothing we have said to be of any substance, Cameron?' interposed Moore.

There was a sudden silence. Again Fforde, with an effusive smile, showed how much he appreciated the young Unionist councillor. 'Well said, old chap.' He then stood up melodramatically and intoned, 'These meetings are vital for the maintenance of morale at the highest level of the organization, so that morale may be passed down to all ranks.' He spoke as if rallying the troops on the eve of battle. 'It is imperative we recognize that our aim is to combat both terrorists and traitors, with equal resolution. It is my private dream that the opportunity will come when we can kill these two vultures with one stone.'

Smyth said drily, 'Perhaps the Reverend can arrange some divine intervention.'

There was a muted chuckle around the table. But Fforde, with his tone of passionate intensity, was on the point of winning his battle. 'And I hope and trust that that day will not be far away.'

Smyth was not deaf to the General's euphoric tone. 'You talk as if you know something the rest of us do not. Is that the case, John?'

Fforde was jokingly evasive. 'Surely, Cameron, you don't imagine I could possibly know something you yourself were not aware of?'

Smyth persisted. 'That's no answer.'

Fforde retaliated once more, decisively, as if he had been holding his best card in reserve. Moore recalled Smyth's warning; the General may not have been patient or wise, but he was still a skilled tactician.

'Alright then,' he said in a new tone, 'I had determined to

keep this under my hat until I was sure that something useful might come of it.'

Smyth's style had changed. He leant one arm on the back of his chair and picked his nails. 'Well?'

'I received a message from Belfast some hours ago. I have had my man decipher it. It appears now that Stoyva may be more precious to us than we have so far thought.'

Smyth was silent, wondering if Fforde could be bluffing. He had means of checking, but it would be a great embarrassment to have to admit to such discordance at the highest level of the organization. He said curtly, 'Evidence?'

Fforde shook his white old head. 'That is not yet available. All we know is that it is likely that Comrade Stoyva may at present be involved in something a good deal more serious than anti-nuclear propaganda.'

Smyth's mind continued to race. He could see the General was soused with drink; he had begun to slip into his familiar affected stutter. That there had been some kind of communication he could not doubt. But the old man was clearly exaggerating the import of the message which, conveniently, would have been destroyed as a matter of routine. He resolved to do what he could to find out the truth, the moment he returned to Belfast. He inspected the faces of the others at the table. Only the two non-committee members betrayed any trace of disbelief. Even Fadden was so driven by the blind ambition to destroy his enemies that he was prepared to believe Fforde was intimating some kind of vital breakthrough.

He was taken by surprise when Roy Moore said impertinently, 'I wouldn't be too sceptical if I were you, Cameron. I must say, before I became involved with the organization, I was continually astounded by revelations of various Intelligence activities on this island. One has only to think of the Littlejohn brothers and their MI6 allegations, and the disappearance of Captain Nairac. There are countless examples.'

Fforde beamed at him again. 'Precisely. My plan to search Stoyva's premises is therefore essential. In times like this, as we ought to be fully aware considering our own activities, official premises are the last place on earth one would try to keep anything secret.'

Smyth turned in his chair so that he no longer faced the General. He shook his head. Fforde continued, 'As I say, it seems to me that we could be on the point of an enormous success. Now, gentlemen, I suggest we adjourn the meeting and have a drink in peace.'

They stood in the middle of the dining hall drinking Fforde's port, except Smyth, who sipped at a cup of coffee. It became clear to Moore that the General was probably involved in Emerald as much for the opportunity of dominating other men as for the hope of realizing an independent Ulster.

'Well, gentlemen,' he declared at one point, 'the evenings are drawing out, what. Longest day of the year last week.'

Moore was the only one who bothered to answer. It was time to take his role a step further. 'There's nothing I like so much on a pleasant evening as a good shoot. How about you, John?'

Fforde's eyes immediately brightened. 'What, you shoot, do you, Roy?'

'I do. Though I doubt if I'm in your league.'

'Don't worry about that. There's just enough light, old boy. What do you say?'

'There's still a long way to go to the season, surely?'

'Damn the season, Roy. They're my bally duck.'

Moore readily agreed, while the others declined Fforde's offer. With an eager cry to his batman, 'Come on, Mitch,' the General took Moore by the arm and led him outside, across the gravel to a shed hidden among the first trees which served as his gunroom. There the old soldier grabbed boots, jackets and guns with a child's feverishness and held them out to his companions.

The batman had yet to say a word all evening, and as he climbed into his boots, Moore asked him about his shooting prowess. The small wiry man gazed back at him, silent.

'Open your mouth, old chap,' Fforde cried. Mitchell did as he was told and opened it. Moore recoiled. 'Captured by the Japs at Mandalay in '43,' said Fforde. 'They said he talked too much, you know, trying to keep up morale up among the POWs. So they made sure he wouldn't talk again.'

'I'm sorry,' Moore said.

Mitchell seemed totally unconcerned. He merely went back, with military precision, to equipping himself, and then stood waiting. Fforde nodded to him as soon as he was ready. Then, when the batman had gone back to the house to fetch the retrievers from the kitchen, he said, 'Damn good man for the job, see?'

Moore said, 'I'm sure he is.'

They went down through the woods, along the River Finn, to a windswept lake surrounded by rushes. The dogs ran on ahead. All seemed deserted until suddenly a mallard jumped ten yards ahead. For a moment the drake was a green ball accelerating against the darkening sky; the next, it was dead. Fforde had fired one shot with his Purdey, his swing and timing perfectly executed. The dogs swam in competition to retrieve the bird, which was soon dropped, limp, at their master's feet.

'Fine shot, sir,' said Moore.

'That was nothing.' Fforde opened the gun, put an unused cartridge in his belt and walked on. 'If you want to learn to shoot, my boy, India's your place. Bengal Tent Club. Those were the days, what. Tigers, boars, leopards, you name it, I bagged it.'

Mitchell, who was walking behind them on the narrow path, turned and fired into the gloom. Within minutes, another drake was lying at their feet. The batman betrayed a hint of a smile as he strapped a second warm corpse to his belt.

Moore asked, 'So Mitchell was out there with you?'

Fforde nodded. 'Yes indeed.'

'Then you, too, were captured by the Japanese?'

Fforde said only, 'Don't talk about it any more, old chap. Rough times, rough times.'

Moore followed the General along the path which had turned back towards Cremorgan House. He felt he had begun to get the measure of his man. They shot four more birds. Moore himself managed to kill two, to the General's warm approbation. When the night drew in, they shouldered their weapons and returned to the house.

It seemed that the others had retired to their rooms. Only Sam was left drinking in the dining hall, and when he saw them he said, 'I was just waiting to say goodnight and thank you, John.'

Fforde stepped close to him. 'Jolly good of you, Sam. Sorry there's not much to do in this neck of the woods for a chap like you.'

The big man smiled and left, nodding to Moore and Mitchell on his way. The batman followed him out of the room. Moore was left alone with the General. The latter poured them both large whiskeys and motioned his guest towards a small sliding door, hidden by a bookcase, which opened into a sitting room. Mitchell was raising a peat fire with an ancient pair of bellows.

'Sit down, Roy, and let's have a good old natter, eh?'

Moore stretched his legs by the fire. Within minutes they were talking volubly, like old friends. Moore sought for suitable memories from his duty in the Ulster Volunteers to match Fforde's pert anecdotes from the British Army in defence of its ailing empire.

'Well, well,' the General declared at length, when Mitchell had replenished their glasses from a new bottle of whiskey, 'I don't suppose we'll ever see the like again. Damn shame, damn shame, I say.' He paused to drink. 'I tell you, my boy, when I die, bury me at the Bengal Tent Club and I'll be a happy ghost, what.'

Moore smiled. He sensed with the instinct of another kind of hunter that Fforde was ready to be chased. 'Tell me, John, all this must seem rather a poor show in comparison. As a humble member, I can't say I've seen anything which makes me feel operations have proved particularly effective.'

Fforde nodded sagely. 'Ah but you must understand, Roy. The essence of any guerrilla movement – and alack the day I would have to say it, but that's what I'm in charge of here – is the capacity to remain inconspicuous. Strike secretly and run. The less people hear of what you get up to until you're on the verge of victory, the better. Do you read me?'

Moore swallowed his whiskey and asked, 'How does that tie

in with more recent activities?'

Fforde replied, 'You shouldn't believe everything you hear, Roy.' He leant forward confidentially. 'It is my belief that someone, either within the organization or without, wants to push us into the open. Make no mistake about it, I stand by what I've just said. But if my information is correct, they may be doing us a great favour. As I inferred at the meeting, I have good reason to think we are at a vital point in our history. If that is so, we can afford to come out with colours flying.'

Moore looked appropriately impressed. Then, after a pause, he resumed his more sceptical attitude. 'But say such a victory did happen. I can't believe we have the capability to capitalize on it. I mean, say we were for instance to declare UDI in the province; how on earth could we defend it without English help?'

The General smiled. 'Roy, tell me' – he spoke with drunken intimacy – 'tell me with complete honesty, right. Tell me what your vision of a perfect Ulster would be.'

Moore paused for thought. Then he said with equal intensity, 'A country governed by those of its citizens most suited for government, owing allegiance to those who provide the substance of its wealth, and keeping in their place those whose intentions are merely destructive.'

Fforde seemed much moved. 'Bravo, my boy! And beautifully put.' He stuttered on. 'I tell you, I was born an Anglo-Irishman and I shall die one. People don't seem to understand what it means to have such blood in your veins. But make no mistake, Roy, we have our own history, our own traditions, and our own future, which is precisely the kind of state you have outlined. And we'll fight for it till the last drop of blood is spilt.'

Moore said then, 'It's a shame there has to be so much internal disagreement, don't you think?'

Fforde rose, poured them both another whiskey, and remained hovering over Moore's chair. 'Ah, you mean Cameron. He's a snake, my boy, and I don't trust him an inch. The only reason his own types slung him out was because they never knew which way he'd turn. It's as much as I can do to stop the whole business from deteriorating into his blessed Unionist pragmatism.' Moore carefully reminded Fforde of his original hypothesis. The old man steadied himself on the mantelpiece. 'Yes, ah yes. Well, I don't mind telling you, Roy, I've taken a real shine to you, my boy. And I have no doubts you will carry off this business at Buncrana with no trouble at all.'

Moore grew impatient. 'Sir, you can depend on me to do my bit. But . . .'

'Exactly,' Fforde declared, 'exactly what I'm getting at is this.' He was following his own inebriated logic, as he stepped back to survey the subject of his favour. 'You're asking me if we could ever consolidate an initial victory, right? You're saying, how would we fare without English support, and by this I imagine you mean both political and financial commitment. Well, let me tell you, Roy, in the last analysis there's only one thing which counts in a struggle such as ours. And that's the gun, Roy, that's the gun.' He waved an arm and said, 'Come with me.'

Moore stood up. Whether he had lured the old fox into the open or whether he was about to have to resist a homosexual advance, he did not know. But he followed the General to the kitchens, where he took a torch from the shelf, made a sign to Mitchell who was cleaning the shooting gear with the dogs at his feet that no one else should be allowed to come after them, and went out into the night. They made their way round to the back of the house where the desolation was more marked, and then among the barns and stables in various stages of decay to a long, walled garden. Fforde ducked through a low entrance.

'Mind your head, Roy,' he said, in a theatrical whisper as he stumbled along a track through high grass and sprouting shrubs.

At the end of the track, covered in ivy, stood a large slate-roofed outhouse, secured by a heavy padlock. Fforde opened it and beckoned to his companion. Inside were various farm implements stacked apparently at random. Fforde pushed his hip against one of three heavy milkchurns and asked Moore to help with the others. Once they had been pushed to one side, they stood over a concrete trapdoor, also padlocked. When he had opened this, the General said buoyantly, 'Righto, down we go,' and clambered feet first into a long stone shaft. In the light of the torch, Moore could see a steel ladder which appeared to be relatively new. He followed the General's white head down the shaft. At the bottom of it they stood facing a solid oak door, which the General unlocked with a third key. Behind it was a vaulted chamber stretching among shadows on all sides. The whole area was packed to the roof with cases, boxes and cartons.

Moore whistled through his teeth. 'Is this what I think it is?'

'The old cellars my ancestors used for similar purposes, actually. I've made some adaptations.' Fforde chuckled at his own joke, then grew immediately solemn. 'Roy, you are looking at the main Emerald armoury, my boy. Wait till I find the light.' He stepped to one side and pulled a switch. A number of dim lights shone through the cellars. 'Come over here.'

He led the way through a narrow gap between the cases to a neat metal rack of long boxes, clearly eager to display his intimate knowledge of the arsenal. 'All new SLR here. Splendid rifles. Designed by *Fabrique Nationale* of Belgium. We've nigh on a million rounds of 6.762 ammunition.' He pointed to another rack. 'Old Lee Enfields there, rechambered for the new NATO rounds. I like to keep the weapons standardized. There's nothing so infuriating in times of crisis as a hotchpotch of small arms all requiring different kinds of ammunition. Invariably the wrong stuff gets delivered.' The General added, as he moved to a third collection, 'Though I'll admit I was glad to get my hands on this lot. Kalashnikov assault rifles. Poached from the opposition, you might say, thanks to certain former colleagues of mine. Any slight inconvenience they might cause is vastly outweighed by their strategic value.'

Fforde droned on, pointing to case after case of arms; specifying the kind of ammunition, the exact size of mortars and grenades, even the type of uniform, which he insisted was essential for the establishment of discipline and morale. At length he came to a number of large crates and announced, 'Here lies our pièce de résistance, Roy. Blowpipe missiles.

Used to great effect in a recent little colonial skirmish, you may recall. Wire-guided, fired from a hand-held launcher, suitable either for ground to air or ground to ground attack. We would only consider their use in a full-scale campaign, I might add. Nonetheless, we are highly privileged to have them.'

When it seemed that the brief tour was over, Moore ventured, 'May I ask where all this came from?'

The General turned squarely to face him. 'It's no secret, Roy. We bid on the international market like anyone else. Though you might be surprised to know that there are times when our men are forced to team up with the Republicans to make bulk purchases at competitive rates. Of course, the sale is split before being transferred to the island.'

Moore expressed surprise, then said, 'But isn't it dangerous to be so heavily involved in this kind of business?'

The General replied, 'Guns have been coming into Ulster since the First World War when the German shipment sailed into Larne. The Loyalists have always been well armed.' He smoothed his white hair over his crown in a typical gesture. 'But I must admit I did consider it prudent some years ago to have a gunsmith brought here to the estate. He's been busy adapting indigenous weapons ever since – dab hand at the Bren gun, would you believe.' Fforde stifled his own amusement. 'Don't misunderstand me now. There are chaps in the UDA and UVF who think nothing of turning out a homemade Sten on a lathe. It only requires high grade steel for the breech and barrel. I'll have you know I find this kind of conduct unsatisfactory to say the least. I'm a professional soldier, Roy, and it's my duty to prepare for a serious armed struggle. Every weapon in this store is regular issue and I won't have it otherwise. I trust from what you've seen tonight you'll agree my strategy is pretty sound.'

Moore assented. 'I had no idea the armoury was so impressive.'

The General was gratified. 'Ulster will fight and Ulster will be right,' he intoned.

Moore said carefully, 'Carson was a born leader, John. Do you think our men really will fight now?'

Fforde exclaimed, 'Fight now! Fight now, my boy? I tell you, we already have a highly disciplined army of volunteers at our disposal.'

Moore continued along the same line. 'And will you stand in Carson's shoes?'

Fforde smiled. 'I shall stand, Roy, wherever I am needed.' With which he shut off the lights and locked the door behind them. They climbed from the cellar, secured the trapdoor and replaced the milkchurns.

As Fforde tested the final lock, Moore asked carelessly, 'This is the only entrance then?'

Suddenly the torch was shone fully in his face. 'What kind of a fox do you think I am, old boy?' The General tramped off without waiting for an answer.

Back at the house, Mitchell greeted them with cups of cocoa. To Moore, it seemed a last surreal touch. He felt very tired now and his head was spinning. He quickly said goodnight, leaving the two old soldiers together.

Next morning, by the time he went down to breakfast, the new Colonel had disappeared, due to return within the hour, with the hired gunman. Left to his own thoughts, Moore had spent a restless night. Since witnessing the intense commitment and the considerable military potential of the Loyalist organization to which he belonged, he felt an urgent need to have more precise knowledge of the British plan at his disposal; to understand how his role linked in with that of more prestigious operators; and, more important, to discover if there was anyone he could contact without breaking his own cover. He was no longer attracted to the game of solving abstruse riddles. He was anxious for hard facts. While the others at the breakfast table discussed the latest item of news from across the border, he brooded silently over his coffee, with an uneasy sense that events had lately begun to move out of his control.

At nine o'clock the big man came back to Cremorgan. With him was a lean, unshaven character in a waterproof jacket and stained trousers, introduced as Paddy. Moore felt a further tremor of unease as he rose to shake hands. The defensive leer with which Patrick O'Mara had greeted the others remained firmly in place.

Moore said, 'I believe I'm going to be your driver.'

O'Mara turned to the man beside him. 'Hey, Wilson, do I have to be workin' with someone else?'

There was a shudder of disapproval, as if he had broken wind or exposed himself. Then Fadden stormed out of the room. It was Smyth who spoke, with his usual fastidiousness. 'Please, under no circumstances are surnames to be used. It may only be a formality on our part, but it is one you shall respect.'

Moore was momentarily grateful to the Catholic. In the midst of his worries, the thought recurred to him that there was perhaps sufficient circumstantial evidence concerning Colonel Sam Wilson to hope he had even now come across a fellow traveller.

O'Mara held up his hands. 'OK, OK. Sam, then. What's the crack anyhow?'

Fforde, resplendent in a scarlet dressing gown over a pair of Indian pyjamas, took O'Mara aside and, with the aid of the photographs and information sheets, explained the Buncrana project to him. The others waited in silence. Eventually he could be heard saying, 'So why don't you sit down now and have a cup of coffee with us?'

O'Mara sat at the table in Fadden's vacant chair. He swallowed his coffee in three gulps and said, 'So your man's good, is he?'

Moore spoke for himself. 'If you're good yourself, there should be no problem.'

O'Mara glanced dismissively at him, then turned back to Fforde. 'OK. So let's talk about bread.' He was clearly in a hurry to leave his present company as soon as possible. Every action, every word was designed to convey his distaste.

'Right,' said Fforde, doing business without posturing. 'I take it you mean money. One hundred down. Four hundred when the deed's done.'

O'Mara nodded. 'And Sam said you'll take care of me for a wee while, is that right?'

'There's a small cottage near Bettystown just north of

Dublin. You can have it for a month to start with. Food, bedding, the lot.'

O'Mara could not help but show his appreciation. A safe house was more valuable to him even than the fee. He had only one further question. 'And what about a weapon?'

Fforde continued to prove expert at this kind of dialogue. 'You'll have an ordinary firearms licence for a shotgun in the name of my batman. That way there can be no possible legal interference. You and Roy will pose as a couple of sportsmen on a weekend trip to Donegal who happen to come upon the festival and decide to stay over for a night.' He smiled at his own invention.

O'Mara did not share his amusement. 'Och now, a bloody shotgun?'

Fforde remained in control. 'Loaded with a specially primed buckshot. It would stop a moose. I don't believe Russians are so thick-skinned.'

Wylie and Smyth were enjoying the manner in which the Catholic was being treated. O'Mara regretted his brief moment of gratitude. He said curtly, 'And when's the hit?'

Fforde replied, 'In two weeks' time. You'll rendezvous with Roy at St John's Church outside Bettystown, Saturday July 15, twelve hundred hours sharp. Any more questions?'

O'Mara shook his head and stood up. 'No. Just tell me how I get to this house and give me the bread.'

'Sam will look after you,' said Fforde, and deliberately turned his back on the gunman.

Wilson led O'Mara out. There was a general sense of relief when he had gone. Smyth said, 'Well, he certainly looks the part, doesn't he?'

Fforde crossed to the window and watched them leave in Wilson's car. 'He'll do the job. I can tell a killer when I see one.'

Wylie agreed. 'He seems straightforward enough.'

Moore was only listening half-heartedly, staring into his coffee cup. Smyth turned to him with a mocking smile. 'Not nervous are we, Roy?' Then he dabbed his lips on a napkin and pointedly left the room.

Some minutes afterwards, Fadden returned, carrying his

overnight bag. 'Terence, it's time we were going.' He stalked out into the morning air.

Wylie called after him, 'I'll just fetch my things.'

For a moment, Moore was once again alone with the General. He waited for some sign of his former familiarity, but it was as if the evening before had not passed. Eventually he, too, fetched his belongings. When he returned, the others were standing in the decayed porch, arguing desultorily about the gunman's employment.

Smyth said, 'Well, I don't think there's really anything to be gained from this. Goodbye, John, and thank you for your hospitality.'

Fforde bade them all goodbye, again offering no particular gesture to the man with whom he had been so favourably impressed.

Not long afterwards, Moore and Smyth were driving back into Ulster. On the journey, the politician had said little to his passenger. To add to his uncertainties, Moore wondered if he had antagonized Smyth by his behaviour at the meeting rather more than intended.

At last, as they neared Templepatrick, Smyth said, 'So you think you have equipped yourself with the appropriate attitudes, Roy?'

Moore replied, 'I'm not sure I understand you.'

'Then I shall speak precisely. Let me warn you. If you are considering any kind of union with the General, don't. He is not what he seems in terms of the organization. One should choose one's allies with care. Do you understand me?'

It would have been possible to understand Smyth's warning in any number of ways. Moore said, 'I'll think about it, Cameron. The meeting has taught me a lot of things about Emerald I didn't know before.' He answered more honestly than the other had reason to believe.

'Let's just hope your commitment remains in the right direction,' said Smyth, as they pulled into the driveway at Moore's home.

They came to a halt outside the house. Moore sat, waiting for any further advice, but Smyth, like Fforde before him, chose to remain distant. Then the last thing he had either expected or desired happened. Mary McKee came out to greet him.

'Who's that, Roy?' asked Smyth as she came towards the car. 'I thought you were divorced.'

Moore sighed in exasperation. 'Just a bit on the side, Cameron. I'm no celibate.'

Smyth was not satisfied. 'Local girl?'

'Sort of.' Moore opened the door as if he had no qualms at seeing her.

Smyth watched with interest. 'Hallo, Miss . . .'

Moore hoped that she would not take his bait. 'Hallo there,' she said simply, putting her head on one side.

But Smyth noted the accent and was anxious to draw her into conversation. 'And how long have you been staying here, my dear?'

'Long enough to know I don't like it much,' she replied.

He smiled condescendingly. Moore cursed them both. 'I'll be in touch, Roy,' Smyth said. 'Goodbye, young lady, I hope we meet again.' Then he reversed and drove off along the drive. He glanced in the mirror at the couple standing in a weak pool of sunshine. There were two pieces of investigation that he must order now, on his return to Belfast.

Chapter 8

On the day of the trip to Buncrana, O'Mara was up before dawn. He had spent a fortnight at the cottage near Bettystown, a holiday home on a deserted lane a hundred yards from the sea. There was little furniture: a couple of hard chairs, a table and a bed. But this suited the ex-prisoner well. The local population treated him with indifference; the house was known to belong to a Northerner, and strangers were regular visitors. For his part, the gunman had temporarily dismissed from his mind all thoughts but those concerned with the job in hand. Whatever had happened to Mary McKee, he would have to deal with her later, once he had proved himself to the Protestant organization and achieved a more permanent bill of safety with sufficient money to give him freedom of movement. Meanwhile he lived in a state of manic excitement. This was the first hit he had undertaken in a long time. He felt almost as if it was his first.

By eight o'clock he had eaten a light breakfast and checked his kit for the hundredth time: tent, sleeping bag, knife, cans of food, shotgun with ammunition and case. He had twice reassembled the double-barrelled Browning, which had been shortened by Fforde's gunsmith to 24 inches, with the chokes opened to aid manoeuvre and increase the spread of the shot at close range, though not so conspicuously as to arouse suspicion. He had also examined its innocent-looking shells, which had been reloaded to magnum power, so that instead of the dust-like pellets of number 6 shot, they now contained $1\frac{1}{4}$ ounces of ball-bearing sized rounds known as SSG. O'Mara had overcome his initial distaste for the weapon; it would be a novel way of despatching a victim. He loaded everything into his army-style kitbag and went outside. O'Mara hoped that Moore would prepare his own part no less scrupulously.

He spent the rest of the morning walking up and down the sea shore, chain smoking, trying to force himself to be patient. But there seemed to be so much at stake that he found it impossible. The rendezvous was for midday. As it was, he arrived half an hour early and waited in the dark interior of the church, pacing up and down the aisle as if his soul was in torment. With a few days' growth of beard, a woolly hat pulled down over his head and his anorak matched with a pair of waterproof trousers and wellingtons, not even the most vigilant priest would have recognized him as a criminal who had terrorized the streets of Belfast.

Moore arrived punctually, driving a two litre Fiat fitted with Eire numberplates. He sounded the horn in the lane outside the church. O'Mara hurried out to meet him. From the outset of the journey it was clear that, while neither man had any knowledge of the other's character, a sense of distrust existed between them. O'Mara had no communicative impulse to satisfy, as he had had in the H9 Block cell. And though Moore himself had a particular set of questions he was anxious to put to the gunman, he realized that this could only be done later on in the trip, when they had more reason to talk. Their silence remained unbroken as they drove diagonally across Ireland.

Along with various hunting accoutrements, Moore had been furnished with leaflets about the *flaidh* in Buncrana. O'Mara scanned them without interest. It appeared that every kind of traditional activity would take place, from the All Ireland Fiddle Championships to step-dancing exhibitions for four years olds. They were not interested in these innocent festivities. Another, less professionally produced information sheet listed a number of meeting places for those engaged in less generally acceptable pursuits. O'Mara studied this carefully. To all appearances, the Russian would be a sitting target.

Once they had traversed the difficult mountain roads and crossed into Donegal, Moore, who had studied the route maps with similar care, began the long descent towards the north west coast. He glanced at his passenger and said, 'Best get rid of the political leaflet now. I hardly think we're meant to look like activists, do you?' Without a word, O'Mara screwed up the paper and threw it out of the window. Moore drove on.

Eventually, they came in sight of Buncrana and its winding estuary, caught in a flurry of late afternoon showers. They followed the coastline for some distance, past a series of little quays and flaked boats bobbing in the tide, before coming into the resort itself, set on a promontory where the river met the sea. The streets were still relatively peaceful. Workmen were putting the finishing touches to hoardings and platforms. There were clusters of Gardai at the corners. Moore counted 20 or 30, in normal circumstances an inconceivable number for a Donegal town. But none appeared to be armed, and they were chatting light-heartedly. No serious trouble was expected.

'Well,' said Moore, cruising along the main street, 'do you fancy a drink?'

O'Mara kept his distance. 'This is work, man. Just find the campsite.'

Moore pulled up beside a young policeman and asked the way. Even O'Mara appreciated the irony. Within half an hour they had pitched the gunman's tent and arranged their belongings.

O'Mara seemed to relax for the first time. He sneered at his companion. 'So where's your dossbag?'

Moore avoided his eyes and said, 'If it's OK with you, I'll sleep in the car.'

'Suit yourself, Or'ngeman. You wouldn't want to get contaminated, would you now?'

They waited through the early evening while the site filled steadily with young people, the men invariably bearded, the girls in patched denims and parka jackets. Their initial purpose was to be seen by as many festival-goers as possible in their role as a pair of sportsmen diverted to the *flaidh*. Both men settled easily into their parts: the Protestant in his green plastic cape striding about with an air of enthusiasm; his less ebullient companion checking their equipment by the tent. Moore had even brought a cassette of traditional dances which he played loudly on the car recorder. The showers continued to fall. Everything was as it should be.

As he sat on the bonnet of the Fiat smoking a thin cigar, Moore reflected on how pervasively he had become involved in the art of appearances. Over the days since his return from Cremorgan, his attitude towards Mary McKee had been flagrantly harsh and insensitive. Repeatedly, she told him that she had meant no harm in coming out to meet him. She had never thought that he would bring anyone intrusive to his own home. But he suspected that she had planned his welcome in order to ensure his close identification with her and so his commitment to look after her interests. As a result, he had gone out of his way to make clear that she was at his home strictly on sufferance. He had even insisted that she sleep in one of the spare rooms, and locked his door at night to make certain that the distance was kept between them. She had reacted strangely, looking at him without expression, lying listlessly in bed for hours at a stretch, eating very little. He had once or twice been on the point of relenting, but her sullen acceptance of his behaviour seemed only to harden him. While he vented the anxiety and frustration he was experiencing in his unofficial activities, she appeared to be preoccupied with some inner tension, as if perhaps she was ill. Whatever the reason, it meant that he could at least be certain she would not, in any circumstances, touch the telephone.

He had received just one call during this time. It consisted of a pert inquiry as to whether he had solved the riddle set him, and a coded statement that the success of his present assignment was, in some undisclosed manner, vital to operations in the capital of the Republic. He had answered brusquely that the Red would be the one to do the dancing, and then prepared to undergo another inquisition. But, as before, the line went dead without warning. Moore was certain it must have occurred to the strategists that his commitment would by now have been severely tested. They must have had a rare confidence that he would continue to oblige, or else his contribution was a great deal more insignificant than he wanted to believe. Either way, he was no nearer to finding out exactly where he stood. These last days had proved an awkward interlude. He resolved to put them out of his mind.

O'Mara meanwhile, now that he had escaped the confines of the car, seemed to be in his element, among fellow Republicans all gathered to celebrate the arts of Celtic tradition. As the Protestant watched him, he opened one of his cans and greedily swallowed spoonfuls of cold beans, sitting in the entrance to the tent, without once offering to share his food. He was clearly determined to remain cool towards his companion.

Eventually he threw his tin across the wet grass and said, 'It's time we went into town now.'

Moore's irritability spilled over. 'Look, if we're going to do this thing properly, I suggest you stop talking to me as if I were some kind of appendage. My name's Roy, alright?'

O'Mara glanced up at him, thought for a moment, then said, 'Sure. But it works both ways.'

Moore nodded tersely. 'I agree. The sooner we swallow a few prejudices and at least look as if we know each other rather more than we do at present, the better, Paddy.'

O'Mara gave a hollow laugh. 'Sure, there's a fucken Prod all over.' He zipped the tent closed and stood up. 'You can cut out the Paddy. Me name's Pat.' Then he looked across with narrowed eyes. 'Look, I don't want to know you, understand? I don't want to have nothin' to do with you. If I had my way I'd be here on my own, but I've got to follow orders. So you get this straight, man. We're here to do a job and nothin' else. There'll be no messin' about, right?'

They left the site and crossed the bridge over the river. Moore noticed for the first time, as O'Mara struggled to keep pace, how he walked with a marked limp. After they had reached the main street, he slowed down. His companion did not appreciate the gesture. He glared and went on ahead.

It was remarkable how swiftly the town had been transformed. The fringes of the festival ranged all over, in pubs, streets, shops and greens, marked by groups of youths with rucksacks and musical instruments strapped to their backs. A girls' accordion band was practising in the square. Other musicians, with flutes, fiddles and banjoes already freed from their cases, had composed the first of the impromptu sessions which would continue for three days.

At the top of the main street, the two sportsmen came upon the first sign of other activities. A mock-up prison cell had been constructed from wood smeared with brown paint, under a banner proclaiming: SMASH H BLOCKS. O'Mara quickly turned down a side street, while Moore listened to a newly elected Republican MP, dressed in a neat suit with trimmed beard and piercing blue eyes, vehemently denouncing the antics of the British Government through a faulty PA. He was handed a leaflet, which he pocketed with a sympathetic smile. He did not expect to set eyes on Stoyva himself. But at a small distance from the H Block dais was a stand unmistakably proclaiming the relevant cause: a cardboard mushroom cloud towered over an atomic power station. A couple of students were busy setting out pieces of literature on a table under the canopy. Moore watched them for some moments and then walked on. There were two or three other stalls on the brow of the hill, but he had found what he wanted, and retraced his steps. He reflected how subtly such movements were arranged to appeal to those who would only be alienated by any signs of bureaucratic organization. It was another example of appearances.

He followed O'Mara down the side street into an old commercial hotel. The gunman went to the bar and ordered himself a pint of Guinness.

'I thought this was work,' said Moore under his breath. Then he called aloud to the barmaid, 'My round, love.'

'It is,' O'Mara replied, taking his drink from one of many lined along the bar.

Moore ordered a whiskey and surveyed the dilapidated lounge, full of discarded beer mats and torn plastic seats. Some of the locals had gathered to avoid the influx of tourists. The street outside was comparatively quiet.

'We start here,' said O'Mara.

'You mean we look for Stoyva now?'

'In all the bars.'

'That way we get seen, I suppose.'

'Right in one.'

They stood at the bar for some time. Moore tried to instigate various conversations which O'Mara listlessly avoided. He could still see little or no chance of being able to sound out O'Mara about his time in the Maze for some clues to the identity of his fellow prisoner. Eventually, they left the Central Hotel and visited one by one the town's more lively bars, on a circuitous route back to the site. By the time they had reached Sean Maloney's in a cul de sac on the outskirts, the sessions were in full swing. Hundreds of Ireland's most renowned traditional musicians had gathered to swap jigs and reels with a genius and fervour only the Irish possess.

When O'Mara caught sight of him, the Russian was hemmed in between a genial old fiddler and a young boy with a crooked back playing a piano accordion. The man was clearly immersed in the complex rhythms of the reel. Behind a pair of round spectacles, his eyes were closed; thick locks of black hair shrouded his forehead. Both in appearance and attitude, he was typical of the young enthusiasts to be seen in every bar. A fiddle case lay unopened under his chair.

'Well now,' said O'Mara softly, 'how's about ye, Russki?'

Moore looked and saw nothing but the usual fervent crowd. At a second glance, he focused immediately on Stoyva's pensive features. 'I suppose,' he said with deliberate casualness, 'he had to be somewhere.'

'Sure, and maybe he'll give us a tune or two himself.'

They had jostled their way into at least ten other bars to find him. Now they leant against a wall and appeared to listen as intently as the Russian himself to the music. As more people packed into the narrow room, Moore struggled to the bar for a bottle of whiskey. When he returned, he found O'Mara pressed behind a couple of tall girls with the yellow hair and blue eyes of Scandinavians. They were shaking their heads in time with a passion more appropriate to a rock festival than to a session in a Donegal taproom.

O'Mara swigged from the bottle and cried, 'Jeez, could you lassies stop flaffin' your heads, youse makin' me dizzy.'

Moore laughed. Both men had drunk enough now to be infected with the spirit of the *flaidh*, and the sight of Stoyva had had its own inebriating effect. The Scandinavian girls turned together and smiled, as if the mere possession of an Irish accent was a sufficiently charming credential.

As the frantic thrum of reels quietened to the more docile tempo of a hornpipe, the girls began swaying their hips. Moore leant back as the small denim buttocks of the girl in front of him brushed against his thighs. He glanced at O'Mara who was similarly enjoying the hornpipe. 'Still work?' he asked.

O'Mara's mood had quite evidently altered. 'Christ, now I've seen your man meself I'll not be botherin' me barney.'

They kept offering the girls as much whiskey as they wanted, careful not to drink more themselves. By the early hours of the morning, when the whole bar had been roused into a common feeling, the dancing of the girls had become no more than a gentle leaning motion against the two Irishmen behind them. Airs were being played soulfully on the fiddle. A tall young Cork man sang unaccompanied songs in Gaelic in a mellifluous voice. Stoyva's instrument remained humbly in its case. Meanwhile, the two sportsmen went out of their way to make their dissipation obvious to the whole gathering; locking their arms round the waists of the young girls, and hooting encouragement to the musicians.

It occurred to Moore that there was probably nothing that he needed more than to satisfy the lust that had been frustrated by the problems at home. He was by now quite lost in the part he played; a lithe figure in Aran sweater and long riding boots, holding a slim girl who kept gazing round with glazed eyes, stretching her arm for another tot of the cratur. For his part, O'Mara seemed merely to have forgotten his recent painful experiences. The music was familiar to him, the Gaelic comprehensible. He had no need to pretend.

They all four ambled back to the site, couples arm in arm, like many other pairs rolling drunkenly to bed.

'See man,' said O'Mara as they crossed the bridge, 'it's all part of the crack.'

Moore answered in the brogue he had readily assumed, 'Aye, sure it is.'

The girls looked at each other, thinking of the Irish tales they would tell when they eventually returned home.

When they reached the Fiat, O'Mara showed the first sign of unease. He turned to Moore, 'What now, man?'

Moore made no answer. He was whispering in his companion's ear. A smile broke over her face. She talked briefly to the other girl, who nodded. Then, without further hesitation, she took Moore's hand and disappeared among the tents. O'Mara stood by the car and watched them go, while the handsome and eager girl looked at him expectantly.

An hour or so later, after promising to meet the girl again the next evening, Moore returned to find the gunman sitting alone at the entrance to the tent, moodily fingering his sheath knife. He stepped up to him. 'Hallo Pat.'

O'Mara grunted. Moore had the air of a satisfied man. 'Yours wouldn't, I take it? Oh well, you can't win them all, I suppose.'

Leaving the car door open, he sat in the passenger's seat and smoked his last cigar of the day. It was very late now, but the revellers were still returning from the session in droves; singing, shouting and vomiting in the dark. Moore smiled elatedly; he almost seemed to have forgotten why they had come.

O'Mara was unimpressed. 'Anyhow,' he said sullenly after a while, 'we didn't come all this way to go whorin'.'

Moore continued to be facetious. 'No, I can't say we did. On the other hand we might as well do the thing properly.'

His companion threw the knife into the earth where it quivered. He looked up. 'Christ, you rile me, man.'

Moore looked at the knife and said, 'Shame. We seemed to be getting on so well back there.'

Their silence was broken by yet another band of youths reeling back to the camp. O'Mara stood up, walked round to the other side of the car and climbed into the driver's seat. Moore grew wary. The smile disappeared from his face.

But the gunman was not concerned with him. 'Tell me what happens tomorrow.'

Moore put out his cigar. 'Tomorrow?' He took a breath and concentrated. 'Tomorrow we drive down into town, round the side streets to a point within watching distance of the stalls.'

'Central Hotel.'

'Fair enough.' Moore went on, 'We wait for Stoyva to arrive, if he isn't there already.'

'He'll be there.'

'I get out and ask him for a quiet word. I don't say who I am or what I want. I just tell him I know who he is and what he does and that I want to talk to him privately. Whatever happens, he won't blow his cover, he can't risk it. So either he'll come with me or get out of Buncrana double quick.'

O'Mara said, 'OK, go on.'

'If he agrees, which isn't likely, I drive up to the mountains and you do your stuff. If he doesn't, we wait for him to leave on his own steam. The only road out of town follows the estuary towards Letterkenny. There's a lay-by just outside Buncrana. He drives a blue Skoda. I know the registration.'

O'Mara seemed satisfied. 'You know your business anyhow.'

Moore relaxed again. He pressed the cassette; the dance tunes, to him indistinguishable one from another, filled the night air. Someone whooped from a nearby tent. He said, 'I hope you know yours.'

O'Mara replied, 'Don't you worry on that score, man.'

The moods of the Catholic were so unpredictable. Moore sensed that if he wanted to question O'Mara, it would have to be now, when the prospect of the operation seemed for a moment to bring them together.

'Pat,' he began, without the supercilious tone he had used before, 'would you mind if I asked you a personal question? You don't have to answer if you don't want to.'

O'Mara scowled. 'What do you want?'

Moore said, 'It was Sam who got you into this, wasn't it?'

'Aye,' said O'Mara, 'you know that, man.'

'Well, what made you trust him?'

O'Mara answered brusquely, 'You think I had a choice, do you?'

Moore was not interested in the gunman himself. 'No, what I mean is, what was it about Sam particularly, why do you think he was the one who . . .'

O'Mara interrupted. 'He was in the same fucken cell, what else do you want?' He paused. Moore thought he had missed his chance. But the gunman grew suddenly reflective, as if the image of the cell itself was enough to stir some sensitive memory. He went on, 'He was good to me anyhow. Sure, he's not what he seems, Sam, he's a powerful fella.'

Moore said quietly, 'I know what you mean.'

Then O'Mara broke off abruptly. 'So are you done askin' questions now?'

Moore seized his opportunity. 'No. I've just one other. What was he inside for?'

O'Mara was already halfway out of the car. He put his head back inside and sneered, 'You people don't like it when your own pigs get dirty, do you now?'

'You mean he was a policeman?'

O'Mara shut the door behind him. Moore, recalling words from an allegory he had never forgotten, tapped his fingers on the dashboard in time to a jig, relieved that he had solved at least one of his problems.

What happened the next morning put an end to any short-lived thoughts of relief. Moore woke in the car with a stiff neck and a dry throat. O'Mara had been up since dawn, packed everything including the tent into his kitbag, and was hovering round the Fiat with an air of purpose. Once Moore had thrown some water over his face and exchanged his green cape and shooting hat for a leather jacket and flat cap, they drove to the layby on the road out of Buncrana where they might later have to wait. The gunman prepared his weapon. It was a bright summer's morning and the waters in the estuary glittered in the early sun.

They drove back through the town's side streets and parked a few yards from the Central Hotel. With a glance at O'Mara's narrow eyes, Moore got out and walked towards the anti-nuclear stall, which he could see in profile at the end of the street. He tried to appear as carefree as he had the day before, but the pit of his stomach turned, and he looked as if he was suffering from drink.

Stoyva was vigorously campaigning against nuclear power among four or five similarly dressed colleagues. He had his back to Moore, but his bearing was unmistakable. As he came closer, Moore found himself shirking the stall, pretending an interest in the H Block display. Then he looked back down the side street at the Fiat. He could see O'Mara watching his every move.

He turned back towards the anti-nuclear stall. Stoyva cast a careless glance at him, perhaps vaguely recognizing him from the night before, then returned to an intense dialogue with a girl in a T-shirt and shorts who was holding a bicycle. Moore hesitated, then stepped up to the Russian and said, 'Excuse me, I wonder if I could have a word?'

The expression on Stoyva's face was inscrutable. Within the mask of the young intellectual was a calculating stare; his eyes were a dark, intelligent grey. He made the faintest of gestures to a large bodyguard, dressed in a donkey jacket and jeans, whom Moore had not even noticed in the crowd; then said in a Dublin accent laced with Slavic vowels, 'Do you want to join the movement then?'

Moore's lips were dry as he said quietly, 'Viktor Stoyva, I know all about your work. If you wouldn't mind, I'd like the opportunity to talk over a few things with you.'

The Russian frowned exaggeratedly. It was evidently impossible to decide if Moore was a Republican seeking help, a policeman, a hostile agent, or a mere crank. He persisted with his Irish impersonation. 'Now I don't reckon that'd be awful convenient at this minute. Some other time maybe.' Then he took Moore's hand and said, 'Anyway, I'm glad to meet youse.' He turned with a swift decisive nod to his bodyguard.

Moore moved fast down the side street. Only when he reached the car, where O'Mara was sitting with the window wound down, did he look back. The large Russian quickly spotted the gunman waiting. Moore jumped in and started the engine, reversed past the Central and sped off towards the estuary.

They had waited no more than a few minutes in the layby when the Skoda roared past, the large man at the wheel, the slight figure of Stoyva beside him. Whether the Russians had been expecting a squad of British Intelligence men to descend on them, or were merely anxious to avoid any interference, they drove out of Buncrana as if they were prospective victims of a Stalinist purge.

'OK, man, here's your chance.'

O'Mara uncovered the gun as Moore pulled out. They drew up quickly and kept a reasonable distance without any trouble. The southbound lane was almost clear; most traffic was still heading into Buncrana. Only the Skoda, a white Ford truck, and a car full of German tourists drove ahead of them along the coast. A few miles from the town, the Skoda turned abruptly into the car park of a small guesthouse.

'Drive on,' cried O'Mara, 'drive on man.'

Moore did as he was told. The route climbed into the gorse-covered hills, then turned back on itself and ran parallel with the sea.

O'Mara snapped, 'Stop here.'

They pulled into a small clearing, where a rocky rise dropped sheer to the guesthouse grounds. The gunman stepped out and peered over the edge. The Skoda was still in the car park. There was no sign of the Russians.

'They're inside,' he said as Moore joined him. 'They're goin' to wait.' Then he lit a cigarette and looked round. 'For Chrissake, wise up, man. The only thing you'll get for fretting is a bullet in the head. You can drive, can't you?' Moore nodded. 'OK, so that's all you have to do.'

Moore was for a moment moved to defend himself. 'I'm afraid I haven't made my living from killing.'

O'Mara retorted, 'You've just started then, haven't you?'

It was not until early afternoon that the Russians reappeared from the guesthouse. O'Mara spotted them. 'Sure, they've gone an' had themselves a good feed. An' here's us eating out of oul' tin cans.'

Moore came across from the car. At least this time O'Mara had shared his makeshift meal. The Protestant was grateful for the beans and corned beef. It had eased the knot in his stomach.

'Right,' said O'Mara, once it was clear that the Russians were going to continue along the Dublin road and not turn back to Buncrana. 'Are you fit?'

They returned to the car and waited. Again it was not long before the Skoda came into view. No sooner had they pulled out than the Russians accelerated. With another glance at the determined eyes of his partner, Moore accelerated hard in pursuit. They ran along above the sea and then climbed higher into the hills. The needle touched 70 as they spun round the rocky bends. The Skoda was no match for the big Fiat. Moore used all his knowledge and experience; they were soon on the Skoda's tail; the haze from its exhaust, indicating the engine was well worn, flickered across their windscreens.

O'Mara's voice was measured. 'Steady now. When there's a chance, get up beside them.'

Moore said nothing but scanned the road ahead. A junction was approaching which would give him his opportunity. He eased forward, only to see the Russians' car screech round the bend and set off along the minor road.

Moore was quick to respond, and skidded after them. 'Right, Pat, we'll have them now.'

They were now on a deserted side road, running through moorland into the mountains of Donegal. O'Mara leant from the window. They were closing fast on the Russians. There was a metal crack in the bonnet.

'What the hell was that?' cried Moore.

'What do you think? Now don't fucken sit here an' let him take pot shots. Get up there, man.'

A change occurred in Moore then. The fear which had numbed his limbs left him and was replaced by aggression. All he could think of was to succeed in what he had undertaken. With a surge of speed, he steered steadily round a long bend until he was within a few feet of the Skoda's boot. He swerved one way and another on the short straight which followed. There was another crack in the metal structure of the Fiat. He swore. O'Mara had the gun on his knee, poised. As the road widened, Moore realized that the moment had come. Ahead of them was a sheer bluff. On the near side, a rock wall ran round the next bend. He could either squeeze through on the inside or risk the bluff. He knocked the Fiat from fifth into fourth gear; it bounded forward, inching its way through at almost 80 miles an hour. The right wing of the car grazed the rocks pocked with heather. Moore could smell the pungent odour of burnt rubber and metal.

O'Mara lifted the shotgun to the window and squinted down the barrel. The bulk of the other Russian stood between it and Stoyva. The right-angled bend loomed only yards away. Moore drew level. Stoyva leant over his driver, aiming his small revolver. The rock wall towered over them. Moore braked. There seemed to be a moment's stasis, and in that moment O'Mara fired, before the Russian. Stoyva took the full load of buckshot in his head and neck. Then the Skoda disappeared over the bluff. The Fiat skidded into the rock face, threatened to overturn but merely scraped along the surface. Moore struggled for control as they scorched round the bend and emerged onto another short stretch of straight road. Again they threatened to overturn, but he held the car steady. Eventually he brought the car to a halt in the middle of the road, both men straining against their seatbelts.

O'Mara climbed out, shaken, and walked back to the bluff. The Skoda had crashed through a small copse and lay crushed some 20 feet below in a glistening bog. The engine was smoking. There was no sign of life.

Moore came and stood beside him. They watched in silence for some moments. Then O'Mara said, 'You made a pig's arse of that, Or'ngeman.'

Moore said, 'We got him, didn't we?'

'Aye, aye, we got him.'

'Shouldn't we make absolutely sure?'

The gunman sighed. 'Och, your head's a marley. What we do is get the fuck out of here. Is the car fit?'

'It'll drive.'

'Right. They'll be a few hours before they sort this one out.'

'I suppose they can't trace the gun or anything like that?'

'Only if they get hold of the empty shells. The hammer leaves a wee mark on the cap. Only they'll not be gettin' hold of them, will they?'

Moore took a last look down at the battered car, then lifted his eyes to Errigal and the other towering mountains of north west Ireland. He shook his head and followed O'Mara back round the corner. They looked at one another over the roof of the Fiat, in a quiet broken only by the metallic clicking of its cooling exhaust, then climbed in and drove off. Moore was glad he had studied the local roads so thoroughly. By the middle of the afternoon, he had taken them through Derry, and back across country to a rendezvous some ten miles from Cremorgan. There he handed over the car, the hunting equipment and the gunman, to one of Fforde's employees on the estate. Then he took his own Jaguar and headed back across the border into Ulster.

Chapter 9

The evening after the murder at Buncrana, Fforde was alone at Cremorgan. The big house creaked emptily around him, but he was not suffering from loneliness. There was a satisfied smile playing at the corners of his lips. He had just been informed that Stoyva's death had been confirmed by the Eire authorities. After ordering the remaining commission to be delivered to O'Mara at Bettystown, he had decided to retire to his library, the centre of the house in both traditional and operational roles. He had need now to consult the vital strategic information contained within it.

Only two aspects of the affair diminished his sense of satisfaction. First, through some decision in Fadden's department, Stoyva's death seemed to have received enormous publicity. He himself did not object to this: all suspicion aroused between the British and Irish Governments was to Emerald's advantage. The thought that the Russians would be at once disjoined and enraged pleased him greatly; there would be serious repercussions. Nonetheless, Smyth's orders had been explicit. Someone somewhere had either ignored or disobeyed them. In a clandestine organization, this should always be cause for concern.

His more acute worry was that Mitchell had failed to return from Dublin. His small Scots batman was quite capable of looking after himself; he excelled in unarmed combat and possessed other fighting qualities. But he, too, was past his prime. A lifetime involved in various uncompromising pursuits, from gamekeeping to petty larceny, had taken its toll, even without the tortures that the Japanese had inflicted on him in the course of the war. Fforde was deeply attached to his man. It distressed him to wonder whether Mitchell might have come to some harm.

The General bent his head in thought and climbed the oak stairs which swept up from the hall and continued along the gallery. There, the pale areas on the dirty walls bore witness to how the family portraits had been bartered to satisfy the demands of modern democratic society. Gaps in the Georgian bookcases in the library itself marked the depletion of a once treasured collection. But in the library was evidence of considerable adaptation to the age. A Bell & Howell 16 millimetre projector stood on the large table, surrounded by telephones, a reel-to-reel tape recorder, a number of decoding manuals and various pamphlets and reference works. A telex machine ticked away in one corner. Fforde locked the door behind him and removed a three volume collection of Swift from a bookcase, to reveal a safe set in the wall behind. From this he took a small box file and crossed to an armchair. He opened the clip and took out the contents. It was his belief that they comprised a weapon more powerful than any he had stored in the cellars.

The value that the leaders of Emerald placed on having a mole at the office of the Secretary of State had recently been confirmed by a series of important leaks. During the last few months, a number of these communications had been received at Cremorgan, which Fforde, in accordance with the rules of the organization, should have passed on immediately to his colleagues. He had, instead, seen fit to withhold these, for reasons that he would find hard to explain if his strategy was not successful. But, since no personal contact was permitted with the informant, he could continue to do this with impunity, until such time as it would be appropriate to act upon his information. The General considered that the time was at hand, which was why he had made his intimation at the meeting.

The three papers that he now held contained, to all appearances, the most potent information yet to come out of Northern Ireland. They were enlargements of Minox photographs taken in the office of the Secretary of State, which had been received only a few weeks before the Buncrana meeting. The General was aware that throughout the island there were others with sensitive documents in their possession; there were many at Stormont and elsewhere willing to leak state secrets for a reasonable reward. But he had been led to believe that only one other interested party had gleaned any substantial knowledge of these particular facts; and he had been eliminated.

A map of Ireland would at first sight have seemed

unremarkable. On closer scrutiny two British flags could be seen on the west and north east coasts. There were explanatory paragraphs beneath the rugged outline. Reading through them never failed to turn Fforde's cheeks puce.

In typically bureaucratic language, it was explained that the flags represented prospective NATO bases for conventional forces to be held in the name of Great Britain. In the north east, Ballykelly (an airfield used as a combined RUC and Army camp, with long distance rifle ranges and other facilities, situated on the Magilligan peninsula) would provide convenient access to mainland Britain by both air and sea. On the west coast the Union Jack would fly, more controversially and with greater strategic value, over the Black Head peninsula south of Galway Bay. It was easy to infer that both bases would be used to monitor activities on the island, and could give notice at once should any hostilities occur. NATO would thus be able to ensure that, no matter what emergency might arise, there could be no second Cuba in the western world.

The document did not need to state what exactly the British Government had in its possession which it would be willing to trade for the use of such facilities. Fforde reflected that it was no mere concern for conventional security which necessitated the absolute secrecy in which recent summit meetings had been held. Arrangements for a political bargain were clearly well under way.

The precise location for these conferences was Hillsborough Castle, County Down. Once the seat of the rich and powerful Hills family, but in the wake of their decline in the early part of the century sold for the use of the new Northern Ireland Government, it had been largely ignored since the demise of Stormont, except for such meetings. In Fforde's hand was a second map: a detailed plan of the interior and exterior of the building that was not a souvenir for tourists, but a design incorporating details of security arrangements, meeting chambers and sleeping accommodation, including the Secretary of State's private apartments. By now Fforde considered that he had a satisfactory picture of the way these summits functioned.

Each time he consulted the document, he tried to memorize a further detail.

Only a third disclosure was needed to complete what, to the old soldier, was an obscene vision. Fforde had this in his possession, too: a list of VIPs with a vested interest in a United Ireland, ranging from a number of Irish American senators, through various British and European politicians and civil servants, to leading Republicans on both sides of the border. The list was headed with a reference to Hillsborough; and the date of the next summit was noted as 11 August, between the notorious sectarian anniversaries.

Over the next weeks, it was probable that many other private negotiations would be taking place at various rendezvous, of which Emerald would be informed, but would be unable to do more than make generalized allegations. Fforde believed that it had fallen to him alone to ensure, somehow, that the crucial summit never took place; or if it did, that the implicit resolution would never be implemented.

Until the evening of the Buncrana meeting, he had had no sound reason to suppose that his task was ever likely to be one he could sensibly achieve. The unseemly behaviour of which Smyth was so censorious was a sign of his reaction to the knowledge with which he had been burdened. He had, for many days, wandered his estate, drunk miserably alone or with his batman, and reflected long and bitterly on a family loyalty to Britain which had spanned centuries up to the present. His own father had perished on the Somme, and he himself had been forced to endure the barbarities of the Japanese. Again and again, he would rise in the night and sit, as he was sitting now, with the documents in his hands, striving to visualize a credible means of resistance. But he had failed. Short of trying to storm the castle, he could think of nothing which would avoid a long and bloody rebellion after the deal had been announced.

Then had come news of Stoyva. Apparently the Russians had, through their own Intelligence network, learned the substance of the Hillsborough conferences. Their agent's presence in Buncrana was doubtless only an aspect of his customary duties; but he could not have been unaware of the imminent summit. The Russian interest in a neutral, if not sympathetic, island on the Atlantic flank of Europe was such that they must somehow make attempts to forestall its implementation. It was inevitable that their agents in the field would be employed in some destructive capacity; though it was impossible to predict the extent of the risks they would take. Whatever the case, the thought that various outsiders were taking action to decide the future of his country had filled Fforde with a desperate determination. He had, almost through sheer effort of will, concluded that the opportunity was at hand to thwart their intentions. It did not for a moment trouble him that his conclusion rested so heavily on the information provided for him.

With a heavy sigh he put the file back in the safe and turned the combination lock. He flicked through the telex paper without great interest, telling at a glance that the messages which had arrived sporadically throughout the day contained no vital code words. Then he left the library, locking the door behind him. He was once more in the ancient desolation of Cremorgan. There he stayed, as he trudged along the gallery to his bedroom, undressed, and lay down to sleep.

He was woken in the early hours of the morning by the opening of his bedroom door. He put his hand beneath the pillow and gripped the small Smith and Wesson revolver that he always placed there. Then he smiled to himself.

Mitchell crossed the room and switched on the bedside lamp. Fforde knew him by his step. The batman sat on the edge of the bed. The General stretched out a scarred hand and pressed it against his cheek. The small Scotsman returned the gesture. All was well.

'So,' said Fforde when he was fully awake, 'have you made a report?'

Mitchell put a hand in the pocket of his tweed jacket and produced a cheap notebook bound by thin metal rings; he tore out five pages and handed them over.

'You're priceless, Mitch. What would I do without you?' While Mitchell crossed to the window and stood gazing out over the tranquil landscape, Fforde bent his head to read.

Sunday, 16 July. Dublin mission. Mitchell for John. I arrived at Dublin station at 1800 hours. I walked to O'Connell Street and caught a bus for Rathmines. The tenement house where Stoyva lived was five minutes by foot from the stop. I entered the building and climbed to Stoyva's apartment on the third floor, gaining entry without trouble.

The apartment consisted of two rooms, a bedsitting room and a kitchen. The former was in a state of considerable disorder. Books were open on every surface. Various articles of clothing were discarded everywhere. The kitchen was also in a mess. However I was able to search the contents thoroughly, though this took me longer than expected and I could not be a hundred per cent certain that I did not miss anything. By this time I had begun to despair of success. There was nothing of any value bar one or two industrial documents from Bulgaria. As I was concluding my search someone knocked at Stoyva's door. Whoever it was must have known Stoyva was not there. I did not answer but remained silent. It was then I discovered, in my haste to search through the mess in the apartment, that I had overlooked the pile of mail from today and the day before, lying in a wire basket hanging on the door. In the postbox were two bills, a letter in English from a CND co-ordinator – not of any importance – and a card from an instrument repairer near Grafton Street. I cannot say why, but something about this last item aroused my suspicion. It was also the only correspondence with a private address attached. I resolved to visit the repairer's workshop without delay. Naturally I have retained this card.

Fforde flicked his fingers. Mitchell knew exactly what he wanted, came forward and handed him a small circular:

CHRISTY O'LEARY
(Quality instrument repairs)
Your violin is now ready for collection.
Please call at your convenience.
C.L.

Fforde returned to the notes:

> I left the apartment at 2000 hours. Since I was in need of sustenance at this point, I adjourned to a nearby pub for some light refreshment. At 2030 hours I took a number 15 bus to Grafton Street. I found the instrument shop without trouble, though it was not in fact a shop but a small personal domicile where Mr O'Leary carried out his repairs. However, it was situated in a prominent position and I felt I should wait until such time as I could enter unobserved. For this reason I adjourned again to a pub for further light refreshment. At 2130 hours I returned to the said premises. The street was not crowded now and I managed to gain entry by a side window overlooking a small alley. The workshop was situated on the ground floor. There were three banjos, one mandolin, and what I think is called a hurdy gurdy, in different states of repair. But O'Leary's speciality was violins. There were seven in the workshop. I was at this point unaware that Mr O'Leary himself occupied the room over the shop. There was no sign of his presence when I entered.
>
> After I had ascertained that there was no way of identifying Stoyva's violin, and that it was also impossible to ascertain whether any of the instruments concealed anything of value without destroying them in the process, I decided to go ahead. I loosened the strings on three of the violins, placed them one at a time over my knee and broke the neck from the body to reveal the interior structure. Then I heard a noise above me, as of someone rising from a bed or chair and crossing the floor.
>
> I immediately concealed myself behind the workshop door. I heard footsteps on the stairs, then the door was opened. I waited while an old man entered the room and switched on the top light. I still held the violin which I had been in the process of investigating when I was disturbed. I took the broken neck in one hand and the body in the other. Once the old man had seen what had happened to the other two instruments I realized I would

have to silence him. This I did by stepping forward at the moment he was about to turn and looping the metal strings over his head and around his neck. I then crossed the neck of the violin over the body and pulled tightly until the old man stopped struggling. I allowed him to fall onto the floor. Then I went quickly upstairs to find out if he was the only person present. There I confirmed his identity and made a quick but thorough search of his personal belongings. I also took the opportunity to remove my gloves. When I returned downstairs I put on my gloves again, moved Mr O'Leary under the workshop table and continued to investigate the violins. It is my pleasure to announce that the sixth violin, a model bearing the inscription of a Kerry instrument maker, yielded considerable dividends, which may be divided into two parts. Within the body I discovered a small metal canister, neatly glued to the inner surface of the soundbox. This I also have in my possession.

Fforde did not pause this time but continued to read.

There was nothing to be found concealed in the neck. However, since I knew this was no ordinary violin, I persisted in my investigations. To my pleasure I discovered that one of the tuning pegs was hollow. Within it I found another smaller cylinder containing a piece of microfilm. This too I have retained.

Further thorough investigation of the instrument revealed nothing else. This is not open to doubt. With the aid of Mr O'Leary's tools it now resembles a heap of matches rather than a musical instrument. I also took the precaution of destroying all the other instruments in the workshop in search of further evidence, though by this time I was certain I had in my possession whatever had been intended for Stoyva. The destruction of the hurdy gurdy and its ornamental handiwork was a matter of some regret to me, and since it was my brief to discover what I could concerning the property of one man only I shall admit my efforts were not as complete as they might have been. I was also becoming anxious to leave the scene. At

2300 hours I made ready to leave the premises by the way I had come in. When I had reached O'Connell Street on foot, I weighted my bloodstained coat with a brick and threw it into the Liffey from O'Connell Bridge in a moment of excitement. This was quite foolish and unnecessary.

I walked on to the station and caught the train to Clones, collected the bicycle I had left there, on which I arrived some 25 minutes ago, and made ready my report.

Fforde beckoned. Mitchell, with a small nod, came over and sat again on the edge of the bed.

'Some 25 minutes ago! You old rascal! Give me the bally stuff and hurry up.'

Mitchell took a thick wallet from a deep, concealed pocket in his jacket. The General inspected its contents gingerly. Then they both grinned with relief and delight, and clasped one another, while Fforde continued to murmur affectionately, 'You bloody old rascal, Mitch, you bloody old bitch!'

By dawn, Fforde had in front of him in the library, with the help of the projector, a massive Russian lexicon, and his code manuals, an accurate translation of the information on the microfilm. He had placed the larger cylinder in the safe. Now, as he penned his final draft, he was glad he had done so.

1472.
Jacob Creutzfeld virus. Highly virulent variety. Immune to all insult. Recommended administration: ingestion by mouth. Tasteless, odourless.
Transfer to 1021, contact Hillsborough 3347. Deadline 11 August.

It was not until Fforde read the complete message that he felt its full impact. Mitchell, who was gazing over his shoulder, shook his head in disbelief. Fforde was silent for some moments; then let out a long sigh which seemed to drain the last breath from his body.

Mitchell put a hand on his shoulder as if to try and calm him. But Fforde began prattling like a small boy, 'Well, someone's for the high jump now, what. By Christ, Mitch, they'll have the wind up. There's no need to worry about 1021 anyway, they'll have him out in no time. Thanks to you, Mitch. And they won't dare get involved now, not when they know someone's got hold of this, by Christ. Oh yes, someone's for the high jump now!'

There was silence now that Fforde's immediate fervour had been released. At length he stood up and turned to his companion, hands on hips, and exclaimed, 'But do you see it? Hillsborough 3347, Deadline 11 August.' He paused to look at the message again as if he might have made a mistake, then cried, 'We've got it, Mitch! By Christ, we've got it!'

Mitchell grinned from ear to ear. Fforde suddenly began pacing up and down the library, rubbing his forehead. Meanwhile the first daylight eased through the window, filling the room with a dull grey. A lone fox barked in the woods.

'Now here's what we do. I'll have to contact Smyth straight away. Hell, I can't wait to see the look on his face. And I'll need a medical man to fill us in on the background to this thing. We may be able to use him in another capacity if we can get hold of the right man.'

Mitchell stood and listened, smiling at Fforde's return to his customary zeal. The General was prattling again. 'Right then. As far as the others are concerned, we shall arrange another inner committee meeting for Monday week. If you could just go up to Belfast at some stage and contact Sam for me, I'd be jolly grateful. I want him down here then.'

Mitchell nodded. Fforde paused in the middle of the room as if he had forgotten something, then crossed to the safe, turned the lock, and, wrapping his hand in a silk handkerchief, took out the small, innocuous-looking metal cylinder he had put inside it some hours before.

'I don't know what it is,' he said at length, 'but I'll get it into that bally castle if it's the last thing I do.'

Chapter 10

Fforde spent the following day organizing his own summit meeting. It had not taken him long to decide which medical man to contact. Emerald had on its books an ex-RAMC Major who had risen in the Ministry of Health to the post of Principal Medical Officer. Fforde, like Smyth, possessed files on all prominent members of the organization, and did not hesitate to make direct contact.

He dialled the DHSS office in Dundonald House and announced, 'Doctor Harry Balkwill, please. I wish to speak to him urgently.'

He was answered by an irritating whine. 'Who is it speaking?'

'Tell him it's a close friend, would you?'

There was silence. The secretary checked with her superior. Within moments, Balkwill himself was on the line. 'Hallo?'

'Harry? John here. How are you?'

'Oh. John. I see.'

They exchanged pleasantries as if they were in fact close friends. Then Fforde's impetuousness got the better of him. 'Well, Harry, to tell you the truth, the reason I rang you is that you can do a couple of favours for us, if you would be so kind.'

The civil servant was not surprised. 'Well, I must admit I was wondering if my services were ever going to be of any use.'

Fforde ignored this. 'The first I would rather talk to you about in person, so I'd be jolly grateful if you could attend a small meeting next Monday at my place. I'll have you picked up of course.' Again Doctor Balkwill seemed eager to oblige. Fforde went on, 'In the meantime I'd also appreciate it if you could gather all the information available on what I believe is known as the Jacob Creutzfeld virus. Does it mean anything to you, offhand?'

Balkwill replied with medical evasiveness. 'Only to a degree. Creutzfeld Factor. Yes. It's usually a disease contracted in middle age. I suppose you'd have to call it an illness of the brain. It has been suggested lately that it might be of viral origin. I believe there's been some research in various countries.'

Fforde was impressed. 'And what's the general prognosis?'

'Very poor. But you shouldn't go on what I say off the top of my head. I'll see what I can do for you by Monday, though I must admit it's a rather unusual request.'

Fforde chuckled. 'You're a credit to your profession, old boy.' He then gave the doctor details of his collection and return, which were noted with enthusiasm.

Again Balkwill said, 'Well, I must say I'm glad at last to be of service.'

Fforde replied, 'Yes, yes, but let's say no more about it just now, old boy. Never know who's listening in, do we? See you.' Then he hung up.

Balkwill, in his spacious office overlooking Belfast's sprawling grey mass, immediately contacted one of his junior colleagues and ordered him to collate all recent research into the Jacob Creutzfeld Factor; meanwhile wondering what possible use it could be to the Loyalists of Ulster, among whom he counted himself.

It was with similar impetuousness that Fforde dialled the number of Cameron Smyth's office in another quarter of the city.

'John here, old boy.'

Smyth said, 'Well, well. I was on the point of contacting you myself. You've saved me the trouble. You see, I have a rather disturbing piece of news.'

Fforde took little notice. 'Yes, I'm sure it can wait, Cameron. Nothing can be as vital as what I have to tell you.'

The politician sighed. 'Really?'

Fforde was playing with his rival. 'Can't divulge over the wire, old chum. If you could make absolutely certain you attend at Cremorgan next Monday. It will be the most urgent meeting we have ever had, Cameron. The co-operation of the political wing is of fundamental importance at this time.'

Smyth rejoined, 'John, if you are still obsessed with Bulgarian interests, I suggest you control yourself. I have personally made inquiries about the likelihood of our late friend possessing any essential information and have been firmly assured that we know all there is to know about him.

The man's work is over.'

Fforde grinned. 'Is that so, Cameron? Well, I'm afraid I've no time now for arguments of this nature. You must attend on Monday for the sake of all we value.'

Smyth then inquired, 'And have you no interest whatsoever in what I have to tell you?'

'Is it something you can't handle yourself, old boy? I am rather busy just now.'

Smyth paused for thought and then said, 'No. Nothing I can't handle myself.' Again he paused. 'So long as I have carte blanche to do whatever is necessary.'

'Yes, yes,' the General said impatiently, 'that goes without saying.'

'Fine.' Smyth sounded pleased with himself. 'I'll see you on Monday then. I can't wait to hear what it is you've hit upon.'

Fforde muttered, 'I'm sure you can't, old boy.'

They both hung up simultaneously, each thinking that he had the satisfaction of the discourtesy.

While Fforde went on to contact the other members of Emerald's inner committee, Smyth sat thinking at his desk. He found it hard to believe that the disturbing piece of news of which he had spoken could be outweighed by anything discovered by Fforde. The old General was, as usual, blowing his own trumpet.

The mood of Smyth himself was diametrically opposed to that of his military counterpart. Following his investigations, he was now sure that there was something sinister taking place within the organization. It had fallen to him to find out exactly how far it had gone, and how it could be stopped.

It was the chance meeting with Mary McKee which had proved crucial. On his return to Belfast, Smyth had decided that the simplest and most effective way to discover more about the girl would be to have one of his henchmen break into Moore's home when Moore was in Buncrana. On the night when Moore himself was making love to his Swedish friend in a small tent, Mary McKee, sleeping alone in his bed, heard the alarm system signalling the presence of an intruder. Her first thought was of O'Mara. She was unable to move.

Then, after her dog's barking had died down, she quietly inched her way downstairs and reached the masterswitch, which turned off the alarms and simultaneously put on all the lights in the house. She found that, whoever the intruder was, he had not been interested in Moore's possessions. All that had been stolen from the living room was her own handbag, and a letter she had been writing to her father in hospital. The fact that the break-in coincided with Moore's absence pointed immediately to some kind of betrayal on his part. It put his recent behaviour towards her in a new perspective. She sat in his armchair and resolved that she would force him to show his true allegiance as soon as he returned.

When Smyth came to examine the contents of the handbag, he, too, was greeted with a new perspective. Besides the usual feminine paraphernalia were two salient pieces of information: a medical card with the girl's particulars, and a visitor's pass to the Maze Prison. He realized at once that he had no time to waste.

The next afternoon he sent the same employee off to Ballymacford to find out all he could about Ms Mary McKee. It was in the early hours of the morning, when Mitchell was locked in his master's embrace, that Smyth learnt of a certain Mac's Bar, where the proprietor had been unduly forthcoming about the girl's recent history, and the subject of her prison visits. When he heard the name of the prisoner, he had been unable to suppress his anger. The luckless informant, instead of being rewarded for his work, found himself the object of a politician's invective. It was not an experience he would easily forget.

After another night of anxious calculation, Smyth received Fforde's call. The opportunity that Fforde gave him to keep the whole matter to himself for the time being was not unwelcome. There would be a more propitious moment to announce a conspiracy: when he had discovered all the answers, and in the process could look forward to humbling the soldier.

His first step was to contact Sam Wilson on the other side of Belfast. He was determined to trust no one, but he intended that Wilson should be put in a position of particular responsibility. In a brief meeting at a house off the Cavehill Road, he simply instructed the Colonel to visit Moore at his home and tell him that Emerald was not prepared to tolerate sexual liaisons with Catholic women. Incidentally, he probed his subject for all he knew about O'Mara. Wilson merely replied that he had come to share a cell only by chance, and that O'Mara had spoken little, if at all, and never about himself. Smyth resolved to observe carefully whether in fact the warning was delivered, and how Moore reacted. If, in the meantime, he could discover that Wilson knew more than he had admitted about the connection between the two operators at Buncrana, he would be perfectly placed to exploit his position of responsibility.

This clearly left him one further option. He himself would have to tackle the Catholic gunman in such a way that he must confess his own part. And this he determined to do as soon as possible.

When Mary McKee told Moore of the intrusion on his return from Buncrana, and he checked that his more private possessions had been undiscovered, they argued intermittently throughout that night and the following morning. Moore answered all her outbursts with an air of dismissal, but found that his own resistance was diminished. The scene of the Russian's death loomed continually in his mind. He wanted to sleep, and this she denied him. Only the irrational nature of her accusations protected him. If at any time she had held a single cogent line, he would probably have found himself telling her a great deal more than he should. But she kept leaping from one supposition to another, which made it easy for him to infer that she was becoming paranoid; and if this was her normal behaviour, she should perhaps seek some medical advice. In fact, it was clear to him that her ordeals over the previous weeks had taken a heavier toll than he had thought. Her expression was vacant and worn. She seemed to have lost her firm, slim vitality. Time and again he tried to placate her, but she refused to believe anything he said.

When it became plain that he would make no concessions, she tried her gamble. She knew what danger awaited her at

Ballymacford; but in order to test his disposition, she demanded that he drive her back to her cottage and leave her there. At first he firmly declined. But she persisted, sensing the personal reaction she had hoped for, before she realized that she had made a terrible mistake. For Moore found himself considering that if Smyth – and he had no doubt that it was Smyth who had been behind the robbery – was out to attack him through her, it would be easier to defend himself if she were gone. Also, it would give him time to re-establish his position. He would have to find some way of getting through to Sam Wilson in his real guise. As to the girl, irrespective of his feelings towards her, it was clear she was placing him unnecessarily at risk. Until he knew exactly what he should do with her, it would be wiser to live alone. It was with these thoughts running swiftly through his mind that he unexpectedly agreed to her demand; and once this had happened, there was no way she could withdraw it.

By the time dusk had fallen, Mary McKee was once more alone in the cottage with her dog. Had she known that Fforde, meanwhile, was drafting his speech for Emerald's next committee meeting, and Cameron Smyth was speeding down to Bettystown, she would have felt even less secure than she did. But had she been aware of other preparations taking place throughout Ireland, she would probably not have felt it even worth her while worrying.

Smyth arrived at O'Mara's holiday cottage with a revolver in his pocket and a dry determination to succeed. His only course was to take O'Mara by surprise. Having been generously praised and rewarded for his exploits, the Catholic would hardly expect a threatening visit from his new employers.

When Smyth knocked discreetly at the door, O'Mara was in the middle of another of his makeshift meals of corned beef and beans, his hunting knife on the table beside his plate. He called out. Smyth announced himself. O'Mara rose, unlocked the door, and then unceremoniously resumed his meal. He was still high with the thrill of his own success. He assumed that Smyth had come merely to add his congratulations.

The politician knew he should not delay. 'I thought I'd come down personally to offer my compliments,' he said.

O'Mara laid the knife on the table and shovelled a forkful of beans into his mouth. 'Aye, well, I could've done with another driver.' The Catholic could sense his visitor's unease, but he put it down to the same sectarian distaste he had experienced at Cremorgan. He was astounded when he looked up from his plate to find a Walther aimed between his eyes.

'What the fuck . . .'

Smyth controlled his nerve. 'Actually, I've a few questions to ask you about the very man you speak of.'

O'Mara responded with the instinct and experience of one accustomed to the sight of a gun. 'You an' all? Och, you fellas are full of questions about youse own.'

Smyth was impressed by his indifference. 'I must admit I've no real intention of using this. You see, if I wanted you killed I wouldn't dirty my own hands.'

O'Mara nodded. 'No, you wouldn't do that now, would you?'

'On the other hand, I have, as all of us have in the higher echelons of the organization, some elementary training in the use of small firearms. So I suggest you take me seriously, Paddy.'

The gunman, in his turn, was impressed. There was nothing he knew about his driver at Buncrana that he could want to conceal, especially with a gun at his head. 'OK,' he said. 'Only the way you blether, don't blame me if I don't get your meanin'.'

Smyth's delivery became deliberate. 'Who's employing you?'

'You are.'

'You have no further connection with any Republican groups?'

'They'd eat my ass.'

There was a pause while Smyth watched O'Mara's eyes. O'Mara asked impertinently, 'Do you mind if I finish my tea before it gets cold, man?'

Smyth stepped forward and removed the knife from the table. 'By all means.'

O'Mara went on with his meal. 'OK, keep goin'. An' watch that fucken thing don't go off, now.'

Smyth privately considered he was dealing with something like a domestic animal or a mental defective. He continued. 'What, then, is your precise relationship with Roy Moore?'

O'Mara stopped eating suddenly. 'Moore?'

'Apart of course from your partnership at Buncrana.'

The gunman shrugged his shoulders. Smyth grew impatient. 'Don't stall, Paddy. I know about yourself and Mary McKee. I also know she has been staying at Roy Moore's house recently. And from what I can gather she's been seeing him for quite some time.'

There was a long silence while O'Mara stared wide-eyed into the distance, slowly trying to accommodate an unacceptable idea. Smyth did his best to accelerate the process. 'Well, I'm waiting.'

The gunman remained speechless; it was not beyond him to sense, as the politician had before him, a conspiracy at work. 'Holy Mother!' he said at length. 'Holy fucken Christ!'

Smyth wrinkled his nose. 'Tell me what is going on.'

O'Mara's eyes narrowed and he responded as if he had no interest whatsoever in the man standing over him with a gun. 'You tell me.'

'You mean to say there is no particular relationship between yourself and Moore?'

'Mary fucken McKee.'

'I know that much.'

O'Mara looked up again. 'Och, leave it out, man. Go point your pistol at someone else. I'll tell you this, an' I won't tell you again, so listen, right? They said there was some Or'nge guy, just before Kelly's got done. If I'd had a chance I would've got to him when I came out, right? But I needed the cover you fellas'd give me. There's a lot of people after my skin.' He paused, with a further incredulous stare, then said, 'So then youse send me halfway across the fucken country with some guy called Roy, an' there's no way I'm goin' to take it into my head he's the cunt who's had my woman, is there?'

Smyth could not doubt the man's sincerity. O'Mara went on, 'So now you come down here tryin' to tell me I'm some kind of plant or somethin'. Well, I tell you, the only guys I'm workin' for is youse. An' you know the next job I'm gettin'? Fucken right you do.'

Smyth gave a ghost of a smile. He said quietly, 'Someone, somewhere, is using you, Paddy, and I'm going to find out who it is.'

O'Mara looked down at the remains of his supper and pushed the plate away. 'How do I know,' he said after a moment's thought, 'it's not you fellas tryin' to double-cross me?'

Smyth said simply, 'The same reason I know you're telling me the truth.'

O'Mara nodded. There was silence. They could hear the sea in the distance, a light wind coming up over the east coast. The gunman said at last, 'So how much do I get for your man?'

Smyth paused to consider. 'Nothing. Yet. If you kill Moore there's no way I can be sure I'll get to the bottom of this. I need him where he is. No. You get the girl, and I pay you. No one else is to know about it. I should add that someone is warning Moore this very evening, so I don't expect she will be at his house much longer. I imagine you will know where to find her. Her father is at present confined to the City Hospital, is he not?'

O'Mara said, 'Aye, he is.' He felt not the faintest qualm; he had until now been unsure what exactly he should do to her, but the certain knowledge that Mary McKee had betrayed him in more ways than one left him no choice. Whatever tenderness had once existed between them merely fuelled his anger. He said, 'Two hundred. Now.'

Smyth hesitated. Then, still holding the gun, he took his cheque book from his inside pocket. O'Mara made no move. He hung his head in his hands, muttering to himself. Smyth decided to put down the gun. He wrote the cheque and handed it across.

'Now then, Paddy. I've written this for a special account we use. Any branch of the Irish Alliance will cash it, if you tell them to phone the number on the back and check it out. Do you understand?' O'Mara pocketed the cheque with a nod. 'So. I can't say I'm exactly overjoyed to find you temporarily on my side. But Ireland has known stranger allies in her time. You see, I believe you're a straight man, you do a good job and you ask just recompense. I can respect that.'

O'Mara scowled. 'Och, you're too kind, mister.'

Smyth pocketed his gun. As he opened the door into the late evening, he said, 'Let me just warn you in advance. Stick at what you know. Whatever may happen, don't be tempted out of your depth, do you hear me?'

O'Mara had come to the door. He was about to shut it. 'Cut the shite, man. You're as screwed as anyone or you wouldn't be trustin' the likes of me.'

Smyth said in parting, 'That won't be the case for long.'

O'Mara locked the door behind him. Then he took out the cheque and stared at it, wondering if it went any way to easing the fury in his heart.

Colonel Sam Wilson arrived at Moore's home later that evening. Moore was drinking whiskey and listening to baroque music, unsoothed by his former pleasures. When he saw the big man's silhouette in the doorway, he felt inclined to slam the door. But he sensed that he had been allowed to drift this far alone. Some relief was at hand.

He resolved not to ask for any advice until the other had made clear how much he was prepared to give. 'Come in, Sam,' he said, 'and have a drink.'

Wilson followed him and sat down in an armchair, while Moore poured their drinks. Like Smyth, he was not in a position to waste time. 'Cameron asked me to come, Roy,' he said. 'I think you know what it's about.' His normal amiability had been replaced by a more determined air. He added, 'You certainly seem to have turned him against you.'

Moore decided he could risk a small provocation. 'That was the idea, wasn't it?'

Wilson merely said, 'Was it?'

Moore exclaimed, 'Cameron can get lost anyway. I don't appreciate burglars.'

Wilson replied blandly, 'Even though you've made your living from them.'

Moore did not acknowledge the joke. He stood stiffly in

front of the mirrored fireplace and asked, 'What do you suggest I do?'

'Whatever you want. I'm only here to deliver a warning. The Catholic girl is a liability. You can't afford to get any more involved with her.'

Moore realized what was happening. Wilson would do his utmost to preserve the illusion of his cover in Emerald and yet contrive to communicate on another level. He felt he had had enough dissembling for the time being. 'A liability? How exactly?'

Wilson persisted in his double role. 'Whatever you want from her, get it as soon as you can. Then I suggest that you both take off, out of the way somewhere for a while, to let things cool off. When you return, you will be given precise instructions as to what should be done with her.' He added, 'That's sound advice, Roy.'

Moore thought for some moments and then said, 'What if I don't take it?'

'I imagine Cameron will get very nasty.'

Wilson sat, waiting, drinking his whiskey. Moore watched him. Ever since he had decided that Sam was the 'bent copper' once described to him, he had longed for some opportunity to seek his counsel. And now that Sam sat before him, his large hands resting on his thighs, he could find no questions to ask.

Wilson stood up abruptly and said he would have to leave. It produced a predictable reaction. 'No, no, have another drink, Sam. I can't let you come all this way just for an argument.'

Wilson smiled. 'No, I suppose that would be childish.'

Moore poured the whiskey with his back to his visitor. He felt the same nervousness that he had felt at the stall at Buncrana. Then he turned and said simply, 'I'm fed up with this, Sam. For God's sake, I may not be on your level but I surely deserve some respect.' Wilson gazed at him curiously. Moore continued, 'I think I've a right to a full idea of how things are being organized, don't you?'

Wilson quietly inquired, 'Were those the terms of your engagement?' He could still have been talking of Emerald.

Moore admitted, 'No. Maybe they weren't but . . .' He shook his head then exclaimed, 'The fact of the matter is I need some kind of reassurance.'

Wilson came across to him and picked up the glass which his host had forgotten. 'Roy,' he said, 'this will probably be the only chance you'll get to prove yourself to your fellow countrymen. There's unlikely to be a war of any significance so long as the balance of power remains as it is at present. Why don't you just put your head down and get on with it?'

Still, infuriatingly, he shielded behind his cover. Moore stared into his wide brown eyes and said, 'In a war at least a soldier knows exactly what he's fighting for.'

Wilson looked back candidly and said, 'Does he?' There was an intense, questioning silence, counterpointed with the strains of Bach. Then he turned away, saying quietly, 'There's no place on earth more confused and chaotic than a battlefield.'

Moore was not to be distracted by abstract images. He followed his visitor to the hearth and faced him again. 'You're a man of some rank, Sam, I know that much. In this game I'm a novice. Now I'm telling you straight, as a subordinate, if you like – I haven't so forgotten my own military service that I don't know what that means – if you leave here without answering one or two questions, I'm going to find it difficult to continue carrying out my orders.'

Wilson eyed him carefully. Coincidentally, the Bach suite reached its climax, and the cassette clicked off. This time the silence was entire.

Moore shivered involuntarily, thinking for a single instance that he had made the worst possible mistake. He had to say, 'I take it you understand me?'

Wilson was frowning, as if carefully weighing a decision. Then he replied, 'I understand you.'

Moore sighed deeply. 'Thank God for that.'

The big man said, 'I'd appreciate it if you would turn the tape. Walls have sharper ears these days than ever before.'

Moore hastened to oblige. He asked quietly as another suite began with a sequence of strong chords. 'You think this place is bugged?'

'You had a burglary two nights ago? I'd be surprised if it wasn't. Don't worry though, it can be seen to.'

It was the first sign of any common commitment. Moore smiled. 'As you would say, I'd know all about that.'

Wilson returned his smile. 'Yes, of course you would.' He then became serious. 'I'm afraid I can't answer any specific questions. But I've been told I am at liberty to inform you of this much, and believe me, I am not myself aware of a great deal more . . .' Moore was going to interrupt but Wilson put a hand on his shoulder. 'No matter how small each man's personal contribution may be, the whole of this operation is on a previously inconceivable scale.'

As Moore was aware, Wilson still chose his words so carefully that they could refer to activities within the Protestant organization of the kind Fforde was always intimating.

'As far as you are concerned, you know what your tasks have been, and you will continue to be informed of them in the same manner. I'll say no more about the girl. I think you know where you stand. Of the Russian, I can only tell you that his removal was in itself vital, but you were quite right in what you said at the meeting: a certain bite had to be added to the operation.'

Moore succeeded in interrupting. 'From what I could gather, John was certain that something fairly important was going to come his way.'

Wilson smiled. 'When someone wants something badly enough, they often seem to get it. They don't discover till it's too late that, no matter how close its resemblance, it was never the real thing.'

Moore was genuinely shocked. The language was still ambivalent, but he understood what Wilson was saying. 'Sam, it will all have been worth it in the end, won't it?'

He received no direct answer. 'I myself am not in possession of all the facts. As I have said, all I can tell you is that this is no parochial exercise we are involved in. It is essential that we all play our parts conscientiously if we want a permanent solution to the problems here. If any of us were to prove inadequate now, it would be, to say the least, a considerable inconvenience.'

Moore felt suitably chided. There was something very

impressive about the stolid man standing there. He now chose his own words carefully. 'And how are inconveniences dealt with?'

Wilson looked at him with a trace of sympathy. 'Appropriately, so to speak.' Saying which, he put down his glass on the mantelpiece and stood in silence. In spite of what he had said, he seemed to be waiting for Moore to continue pressing him with questions. It was perhaps a test. Moore deliberately said nothing else. The big man smiled at length and said, 'Now I must go.'

Moore showed him to the door, where he turned, again silhouetted in the late evening. 'By the way, where is the girl?'

Moore said, 'She's gone.'

He nodded and left. Moore closed the door and returned to the hearth. He felt like an animal, weak with hunger, who had been thrown a bone heavy with meat.

Chapter 11

Although she halfheartedly planned various means of escape, Mary McKee remained alone at her father's cottage for three days, with little money, and a sense of persecution. Nothing seemed to have changed there. Though there were patches of summer colour on the bleak ridge, the prosperous valley below seemed still more of a contrast. A hundred yards away in a small, stonewalled field, Dympna McLean's cows grazed obliviously. As she sat gazing from the cottage window, Mary's thoughts were dominated by a single sobering awareness. Throughout her experiences over the last weeks, she had not once been to visit her father in hospital. Until she had returned to the cottage, this had troubled her only slightly. But surrounded again by the evidence of his lifelong struggle to support her, she was pained to think that she had neglected him. The hours passed in a series of penitential reflections, which made her more and more reluctant to leave the seclusion of the cottage until, as once before, the need for provisions forced her to go down to the village.

On this occasion, O'Mara arrived in Ballymacford on foot. He had no wish to be seen. He did not reach the cottage while she was away; but only a few minutes after her return, he came over the ridge and crouched by a hawthorn bush. The sight of smoke from the chimney did not now fill him with any fond recollections.

This was not the contract agent who had chosen his moment so coolly in the hills of Donegal. His hands were shaking, and his eyes were filled with a desire for revenge. He was dressed only in an open shirt and jeans, with his beard well-grown and his hair ruffled in the wind. He was a man who had come to kill only for his private satisfaction. He drew his knife from its sheath and fingered its sharp edge. The sun glinted along the surface as he crouched on the ridge. He could see his prey moving in the pantry below. He eased himself down over the rocks until he stood at the side of the cottage. He could hear the dog whimpering within as he came round to the front and kicked at the door. It remained fast. He swore and kicked again until it shook on its hinges.

Inside, Mary had been roused from her reverie by Silver's alarm. Again her first thought was of O'Mara. She looked round her. The pantry was a small room, with a double gas ring beside the sink, and thick shelves fixed to the stone wall. The only weapon to hand was a long-handled iron pan. She lifted it from the shelf and called the dog, who had run into the parlour. Then the kicking came at the door. She crouched by the dog, holding its hackles as the door shook under the force of the blows, and screamed out, 'Go away, go away!'

O'Mara's blood rose. He had been steadying himself on his weak knee and it could hold no longer. He limped round the other side of the house to the pantry window with its faulty catch. Mary saw his face appear above her, contorted with hatred. The dog leapt from her grasp and threw itself at the pane. O'Mara recoiled momentarily, then pushed the window open. As the dog continued to leap and snarl, he held the hunting knife poised, and as Mary watched, lashed out in a single movement. The blade caught the dog across the forehead, biting into the furrow of its eyebrow and slicing one ear. It rose again, blind with shock. The gunman brought the hilt of the knife down hard on the crown of its head. It fell to the ground, stunned, while blood poured from the wounds.

The sight of her beaten defender was enough to rouse the girl, but by now O'Mara was already halfway through the window. She ran at him, brandishing the pan, but even if she had not been as weak as she was, she would have proved no real threat. He lashed out again with the knife. The blade itself missed her arm by inches, but the force of the blow knocked the pan from her grasp. As she clutched at her bruised wrist, he clambered down and stood over her.

Again she screamed, 'Go away, leave me alone!' If he had come simply to kill her, as he had been paid to, these would have been her last words. But now he could touch her, O'Mara was in a frenzy. He put the knife down on the ring and took hold of her shoulder in one hand. With the other he ripped open her blouse. She began to spit and yell, to wriggle from his grasp. He bent his head to her breasts. His teeth sank into her flesh. With his free hand he was fumbling with himself, parting her legs with his knee. She could hear the dog whimpering beneath them as he tore away the strips of cotton from her shoulders. When he brought his head up again, she did what he himself would have done, without thinking: she saw his nose in front of her and brought her own forehead hard against it, cracking into the bridge, then burst past him into the parlour.

Within moments he followed her. She had reached the door when he dragged her back, naked to the waist, closing his arm round her neck. She began to choke, her eyes watered and swelled. She dropped to her knees, and his grip loosened; she grabbed his little finger and twisted it with all her strength. Through her screaming she heard him cry out in pain. He released his grip and the air rushed into her lungs. Then he brought his elbow hard down on her skull, twice. She let go of his hand. Her head was spinning and pounding; she could barely see. A heavy black shape hurtled through the air and hit O'Mara full in the chest, sending them both sprawling on the floor. It was the dog, wild with fear and pain.

The man now crouched trying to protect his face. Silver tore a strip of flesh from his back, matted with his nylon shirt, striving to get a grip on his throat. The knife was still in the pantry and O'Mara struggled towards it. The dog sank its teeth into his shoulder. He grabbed its hind legs and tried to tear them apart. Meanwhile the girl got to her feet and began hitting out at him, though as many of her weak blows fell on the dog's wounded head as on the gunman himself. The dog had already lost a great deal of blood and was quickly tiring. Mary stood back and realized she had a few moments to make her decision. She could either make use of the opportunity that the dog's loyal defence had given her to escape, or she could try in vain to protect them both.

She had run 20 yards or so in the direction of the McLeans' when she heard a single howl, and knew that O'Mara had broken free long enough to reach his knife and sink it into the dog's heart. She began to moan, broken, but she continued running towards the McLeans' ridge.

In the cottage, Silver lay dead. O'Mara stumbled to the sink and poured water over his wounds. He had no mind to chase the girl; he could chase no one. He inspected his body. His shirt hung in tatters. He could see the white bone of his shoulder exposed through the flesh. Blood flowed freely from lacerations on his back and abdomen. A shallow tear across his cheek stretched to the border of his left eye. His nose, and possibly his finger, were broken. He grabbed the knife again in impotent fury, ran outside the cottage and yelled over the bracken at the receding figure of the girl, 'I'll have you, I'll have you, you fucken whore!'

Mary was climbing quickly to the other cottage. At the echo of O'Mara's shouting, Dympna McLean came to the door. She saw the half-naked figure of her neighbour and rushed back inside for a shawl. This she threw over Mary as soon as she reached the gate, helping her inside.

'Holy God, Holy God!' the fat woman kept crying. 'Mary McKee, what's goin' on?' Mary could only continue her low moaning. 'Come on now. Was that Pat O'Mara over there?'

Mary whispered, 'Aye.'

'Well, he'll know better than follow you here. All the boys are up behind in the field. I've only to call them down.' Mary shook her head and buried it in Dympna's breast. 'Boys a dear, what are we goin' to do with you, love? What's been an' happened now?'

At last, Mary found her voice. 'I can't tell you. Just do me one wee favour, would you? Go down to the telephone an' call the number I'll give you. An' later get a couple of your brothers to go over an' bury my dog.'

Dympna cried, 'I'm not leavin' you like this. Look at the state of you. By all the saints, woman, you look like you've just been raped.' A deeper expression of horror came over the woman's ruddy face. 'Sure, Mary love, you've not been raped, have you?'

Mary suddenly appeared unnaturally calm. 'No, Dympna, I've not been raped, not yet. Now would you do what I ask you?' She repeated the telephone number until it was remembered. 'Don't give up till you speak to Mr Moore himself. An' don't mention O'Mara whatever you do. Just say I've been beaten an' ask him to pick me up at O'Grady's Garage in an hour's time.'

Dympna exclaimed, 'But, love, sure, you can't just . . .'

Mary's momentary calm gave way. 'Christ in heaven, Dympna, would you just do as I ask you!'

The other girl hesitated, then bundled Mary onto the sofa, took her purse and hurried out, locking the cottage door behind her. She was badly out of breath by the time she reached the telephone. She had no difficulty in getting through to Mr Moore.

'Well, I'm Dympna McLean of McLean's Farm at Ballymacford,' she shouted into the receiver, 'an' Mary McKee's told me to tell you she's in an awful bad way on account of gettin'a lacin' an' she's up at our place now, only she's askin' for you to pick her up at O'Grady's Garage in one hour's time.'

She had even less trouble in achieving the desired result; the Protestant agreed immediately. When she returned to the cottage, Mary was curled up on the sofa, shivering.

'Now I'll get you somethin' to wear, girl.' Dympna went through to the back of the cottage and returned with a long, baggy sweater. 'If you ask me, you should stay with us,' she said, as she watched Mary disappear into it. 'But if it's Prods you want, it's Prods you shall have. Now wait here. I'm goin' to take you down to the village meself an' I'm goin' to bring this with us.'

Dympna went to a cupboard and took out her father's shotgun, not dissimilar to the one O'Mara had used on his hunting trip to Donegal. Brandishing the weapon with the look of one familiar with its use, she led her bruised companion down to Ballymacford.

There was no sight of O'Mara. A number of villagers stopped in the street or came out of their houses, but Dympna would only say to them, 'Now you can stop rubberneckin', it's nothin' to do with you.'

Moore was typically punctual. He got out of the Jaguar and put an arm around Mary McKee. The villagers gathered agitatedly around them. O'Grady himself turned to the assembled company and cried, 'You can bet it's all down to this Or'nge bastard.'

But Mary turned and said, 'Why can't you people just leave me alone?'

Moore quickly helped her into the car, as Dympna stood waving the gun ambivalently in the face of the small crowd. Then they drove off, leaving the inhabitants of Ballymacford to fight among themselves.

This time when they drove to his home, there were no expressions of gratitude. Moore was genuinely shocked to see her bruised and scratched, with the shock darkening her eyes as she sat dumbly beside him. He helped her out of the car and took her straight to his bedroom, removed her clothes and soon eased her into a hot bath. He washed her gently himself. Then he attended to her wounds as she shivered on the tiled floor. It was not until he was drying her with his thick bath-towels that it occurred to him he had not bothered to ask her exactly what had happened. Apparently she had not been exaggerating the danger she was in from her own kind.

Once she was dressed in a pair of his silk pyjamas, and sat in his bed sipping a large brandy, he began, 'Mary, I want you to understand. It's never been my intention you should come to any harm. Think of the Motor Inn. I mean it.'

Her shivering had calmed. She now sat looking back at him from a great distance. 'But it was foolish to let that man in the car know you were living here. It's put me in a difficult position. And it hasn't helped you either.'

His words appeared to strike some chord in her. She continued to look at him as he went on, 'There is a way out, though, for both of us. It means that I use what you can tell me, now, to bargain with. There's nothing to be gained from stalling any longer.'

She said nothing. He hesitated, then concluded, 'You have to trust me, that's all. I don't want to see you like this again.'

At last she spoke. Her voice was, once more, unnaturally calm. 'That's it, is it?'

He was momentarily taken aback. He could not meet her eyes. Instead he crossed to the window and gazed out over the lawn. He said without expression, 'You must give me all the names and addresses of the people you know involved in legitimate political activities who are members of Republican terrorist organizations.'

He did not turn as he waited for her answer. There was silence. A pair of curlews flew over the house. He watched as the sun was briefly eclipsed across the lawn. Then he heard her quiet voice behind him. 'I'll do it. Sure, I'll do anythin' after today.'

He sat down beside her on the bed and held her face between his hands. 'Then I can guarantee I'll get you a fair deal. In the meantime, the best thing we can do is get out of the way until things are sorted out here, OK?'

She shrugged her shoulders. A week before it might have meant something different to her. Now, in a daze of shock, she believed him, but with such a strange insensibility it hardly seemed to matter.

He took the brandy glass from her hands and set it on the bedside table. 'You're still cold. You should try and sleep. We'll talk later.'

She slid down until her head rested on the pillow. He kissed her cheek, then looked into her dark eyes. When he returned an hour later, she was in a deep sleep.

Later that evening, the phone rang as he was shelling prawns in the kitchen for his evening meal. He was quick to answer.

'Good evening.' The caller was in an amicable mood. 'I believe you've made a friend.'

He sighed, 'Yes. And I can't say it wasn't before time.'

'You should take it easy, Roy. There are no real problems. Your work has been satisfactory so far.'

He could not help but feel gratified. 'I'm glad to hear it. But I can't help feeling I should have had a better idea of the whole package before I got working on my part of it.'

'I think you understood the principles involved.' There was a pause. 'Now then, I wanted to catch you before you take your holidays, to make sure you get a few things cleared up before you go. How's it looking?'

Moore guessed rightly at the meaning. 'It's looking fine. If you tell me where I can leave the details, I believe I can let you have everything by tomorrow morning.'

'Good show!' Moore wondered if he did not detect a moment's genuine recognition. 'I believe we both bank with the Irish Alliance, do we not?' Moore confirmed this. 'Fine. I tend to avoid the central branch myself, but there's a small bank in Royal Avenue I've found suitable for my purposes. I suggest you visit it tomorrow. Tell them who you are and ask for the manager in person. He looks after a certain deposit box. Give him everything you have, and he'll keep it safe until I can get down there, so to speak.'

'Are you sure that's wise?' asked Moore. 'I don't need to tell you of some of the bank's more illustrious connections.'

'My dear man' – the voice betrayed a cynical amusement – 'there are still one or two incorruptible individuals in the province.'

Moore said, 'Then I should take a holiday, you think.'

'Quite so. Until certain other matters are resolved.' Moore realized this could mean anything, but he did not pry. 'Anyway, we'll know where to contact you in the event of our needing your services.'

'You know where I'll be?'

'The west coast is lovely at this time of year. Try the Glencar House hotel in Sligo. I think you'll find it's run by very friendly people.'

Moore understood that this was more an order than a recommendation. 'So that's that for the time being then?'

'Indeed. Goodbye, and good luck.'

He put the receiver down and went back to cracking the pile of pink shells; glad, for reasons he could not fully understand, that he had made no personal statement concerning Mary McKee. When he had finished preparing the meal, he telephoned an associate to tell him he had private business in the Republic, and that he would return as soon as it was completed. Then he sat down with a drink and waited for his dinner to cook.

He ate at ten. Afterwards, he took a tray up to the bedroom. Mary McKee was still asleep. He put the tray down beside the brandy glass, undressed, and eased himself into bed. She seemed, instinctively, to turn away from him, then half-awoke and leant back into his arms. He held her still, listening to her breathing. Soon he felt himself drifting into sleep. His hands began to move across the silk pajamas, fondling her breasts, easing over her limbs. He slipped the trousers from her legs. She turned towards him and opened her eyes, gazing at him mistily. He said, 'It's alright, I'll make you warm.' She seemed to be lost in the same strange indifference, as he parted her thighs and slowly moved into her. He made love to her as gently and carefully as he could, while she lay, barely moving, sighing, still in her strange way half-sleeping, yet holding him, keeping him close.

Eventually, he lay back and stroked her hair. The silence was broken only by their breathing. For the first time in recent days the dreams which had once troubled him constantly passed through his mind, affecting him with the same sense of painful impotence, even though he had come inside her hardly minutes before. Then she began to speak, as if still in her sleep. The whole surface of his back shivered.

'Sean McGeehan, Falls Road. Michael Doherty, Falls Road. Peter McCafferty, Ballymurphy.'

It was uttered in a soft monotone, like a penance. He lay still beside her, breathing deeply. After she had continued through some ten names and addresses, he found himself switching on the lamp and getting out of bed.

'Christ! What the hell . . .'

She looked at him distantly. 'It's what you want, isn't it?'

'You bitch. What's the matter with you?'

She persisted. 'Isn't it what you want?' She resumed her litany. 'Eamonn Connolly, Turf Lodge.'

As he shouted at her to stop, he experienced another of those moments when he wondered if with her too, he could possibly have made a dangerous mistake. He muttered, 'I wouldn't believe it,' then sat down beside her and held her fiercely by the shoulders. 'Have you got something else you ought to tell me?'

She seemed suddenly to respond to him genuinely, looking away with a new fear in her eyes. He waited breathlessly for her to speak. A flicker of a smile spread across her face.

'I'm three weeks late.' She put an arm round his neck. 'It must have been at the cottage. Sure, I meant to tell you it was a bad time, but I didn't think . . .' He remained staring at her in silence. She said, 'It's never happened before.'

He rose and crossed the room, went to open the door, turned back and opened the window instead. He gazed out over the grounds without a thought in his head, feeling the blood pulse through his body like a flood straining to burst out into the night.

Chapter 12

At the next meeting of Emerald's inner committee, Moore's chair was taken by Doctor Harry Balkwill, MD OBE, the senior civil servant originally from Ballymena, whose small rotund figure faced the cumbersome bulk of the Reverend Fadden. Wylie sat beside him. As before, the two leaders confronted one another from the heads of the table. Sam Wilson had again delayed his arrival.

Fforde was in full flow, detailing his personal involvement in Emerald from its conception, listing his successes, lamenting his failures, as if he had been about to resign. In fact, he was painstakingly preparing the ground for an announcement that he knew the others would find hard to accept. Smyth had already interrupted several times with sardonic comments.

Wilson made his entrance a few minutes before Fforde intended to reveal his discovery. Like the others before him, he was introduced to Balkwill and appeared to be intrigued by the presence of a medical adviser. Smyth glared at him but Wilson avoided his eyes. Once he had taken his place, Fforde continued.

'Now that we are all present and correct, I shall come quickly to the reason why I have called this meeting.'

Fadden, chewing on his liquorice pellets, and in unusually high spirits, declared, 'Good man. I hope you will.'

Fforde said, 'As you will have gathered, I have seen fit to acquire the services of a medical expert for a specific purpose. I have now simply to tell you why he is here.'

Smyth fidgeted impatiently in his chair. He was still brooding over O'Mara's abortive attempts at Ballymacford, for which he had lost two hundred pounds, and the upshot of his attempt to frighten Moore. He had also made inquiries concerning certain arrangements within the Maze Prison and found nothing to allay his fears of Wilson's possible duplicity. His suspicious anger threatened at any moment to take control of him.

Fforde was evidently unconcerned. 'Gentlemen,' he said, snapping his fingers towards Mitchell standing at the door, who disappeared immediately in the direction of the library, 'in what I am about to show you lies the future of our organization. Thanks to my activities on the Buncrana project, we can now be absolutely sure that the Russian was engaged in highly important Intelligence activities in our island.'

Wylie interrupted, 'Surely we knew that?'

'Terence, we could never have known the scope of his activities, for we were unaware of the operation he was ordered to penetrate.'

'What do you mean?' Fadden inquired.

Fforde finally decided that his moment had come. 'Gentlemen, the prospective outcome of the Hillsborough summits justifies the worst of our fears. It is none other than the barter of our province for military facilities on both sides of the border. The decisive conference is to take place on 11 August.' The disclosure was intended to shock, and it did. Fforde went on, 'The Russians had as much reason as anyone to try and prevent this outcome. Gentlemen, the means which they intended to employ are now at the disposal of the organization.'

Wylie was the first to speak. 'Will you tell us exactly how this is supposed to have come about?'

Fforde replied, 'I will.' He delved into a folder in front of him and produced a wad of typescript. 'Here are copies of my man's report which I will pass among you . . .' Mitchell now made a timely return, wallet in hand. 'Ah, but first things first!' cried Fforde. He opened the wallet to reveal the sealed canister and the small cylinder of microfilm. 'Here, gentlemen, is the means.'

There was further silence, and then Smyth exclaimed abruptly, 'How much longer are we expected to take part in this charade?'

Fforde ignored this. 'Now then, Harry,' he said, turning to Balkwill, 'tell us, if you would, all you know about the Jacob Creutzfeld Factor.'

Balkwill sat up nervously. He had quickly realized the meaning of Fforde's announcement. He was so startled and incredulous that he was loath to add any element of scientific authority to the charade, as Smyth called it. But he was committed to the task. He opened his notes and coughed.

'Well,' he began timidly, and then assumed his best civil servant's manner of delivery, 'I have gathered all facts appertaining to what John rightly refers to as the Jacob Creutzfeld Factor.' He paused to collect himself before launching into what was clearly a prepared speech. 'If we live long enough, we all of us decline into some state of senility sooner or later.' It appeared that no one was in a mood for any facetious response. 'In the right context, it is no cause for concern. However, there are several forms in which it can occur prematurely. Jacob Creutzfeld's disease embodies one of these forms. It is a virus impervious to insult from either chemicals or extreme heat, contracted usually by ingestion, which in the early stages is marked by an inability to concentrate or make decisions. This quickly develops into a more clinical state of acute confusion. Most intellectual tasks prove unmanageable. The memory suffers, language becomes a difficulty. In effect, the brain becomes spongy and ineffective.'

Fforde himself listened with particular interest. The appropriateness of the Russian plan seemed perfect to him.

'We have reason to believe Creutzfeld has a direct parallel in a tropical disease called Kuru, discovered in New Guinea, which, I have been informed, could have resulted from the consumption of human brains by cannibals on those islands. Pathologists are now very wary of working with tissue affected by the Creutzfeld syndrome in case of personal infection. Nevertheless, a great deal of research has been taking place, in the last ten years particularly. Leaders in the field are the Swiss and the Russians.'

No one had yet interrupted the speaker, in deference to his air of medical expertise. But at this juncture, Fadden exclaimed, 'Excuse me, Harry, but I haven't come all this way for a lecture on cannibalism.' He alone, with his customary myopic ebullience, had failed to make the obvious link. The others were silently waiting to see exactly how Fforde would try to convince them that he was to be taken seriously.

Balkwill cut short his prepared speech. He concluded with

renewed nervousness, 'No, well, I'm only doing as I was asked. I shall simply add that to all intents and purposes, this kind of disease belongs to that range of illnesses which modern medicine has generally neglected in favour of more popular afflictions which appear to affect the young particularly: smallpox, polio, etcetera. The Jacob Creutzfeld Factor is potent by virtue of its comparative obscurity. An effective diagnosis would not be likely before the disease had reached its more severe stages.'

Fforde asked quickly, 'And if the virus were to be isolated and refined into an especially concentrated and virulent strain and find its way into, say, a hotel or a hospital?'

Balkwill replied, 'It would cause considerable harm. All who ingested the infected substance would, within days, develop the initial symptoms. Within weeks, they would be afflicted with premature senility.'

At last Smyth responded openly. He spoke with an unexpected calm, like a doctor offering a negative prognosis. 'This, I'm afraid, is the last straw. Over recent months I have done my utmost to overlook what I have believed to be a serious infirmity in our military command. However, the time has come for me to speak my mind. John, you are not fit to hold your present position. This preposterous business is the final proof. I am entirely disappointed in you.'

Wylie nodded ambivalently, while Fadden finally understood what was happening. 'Have I got this right?' he cried. 'You're trying to tell us that the thing there contains this virus?'

Gesturing towards his batman at the door, Fforde said only 'We have Mitchell to thank for this. His work in Dublin was exemplary.'

Wilson sat quietly and waited to see what would happen next. Balkwill, who had unwittingly been enlisted on Fforde's part, felt it is duty to add, 'There is no medical reason why the virus could not be treated in this way.'

Wylie said petulantly, 'I'm afraid we're not discussing medical empirical method.'

Smyth agreed. Balkwill thereafter remained silent. 'Indeed we are not. John expects us to believe that a Russian agent in

Dublin had in his possession an obscure germ with which he intended to infect a whole conference. Either he thinks we are all as palsied as he, or he trusts that our desire to ensure Ulster remains free from Republican influence will blind us to the excesses of his own ambition. It is my opinion that this is a device he has engineered to put us in a position of false expectation to cover his own deficient leadership. I am more interested in how and why he has kept what he knows about the Hillsborough conference to himself until now.'

Fforde replied furiously, 'I would have thought that was blatantly obvious. It is only now that we can do something about it. May I also point out that the germ was not actually in Stoyva's possession, as you will discover when you read the report. Furthermore, it was not Stoyva himself who was going to carry out the project. The Russians had another man actually working at Hillsborough.'

Wilson seemed to be privately enjoying the open feud between the two leaders. Fforde had the determination of a righteous old campaigner. Smyth was cool, superior, like a headmaster. He could not predict the outcome, but it was clear which temperament was more appropriate in the wooded groves of Ireland.

The politician continued as if Fforde had not spoken. 'Therefore, before it goes any further, I suggest we draft a mandatory resolution to censure this reprehensible act.'

Wylie again seemed to assent without committing himself. His reverend companion was less ambivalent. He said, 'I'm afraid we can't just dismiss something like this out of hand, Cameron.'

Smyth looked at Fadden with open disdain. Wilson continued to remain aloof. Fforde now declared with solemn majesty, 'I, sir, would no more dream of misleading the organization than I would strangle an infant in its cradle.'

Smyth was ready for this. 'Then may I suggest that you yourself are being deliberately misled.'

The General was momentarily silenced. Wilson inquired with his familiar air of humility, 'What makes you say that, Cameron?'

Smyth turned on him. 'If you need to ask, I shall tell you.'

He paused to ensure full attention. 'I too, have come to this meeting with certain revelations to make. I'm afraid I have to inform you all that a serious conspiracy is at work among us.'

Fforde exclaimed, 'And you accuse me of excess and palsy!'

Smyth went on, 'There are a number of factors which I will not now go into. But I shall tell you this. I have identified at least one source of corruption and am hot on the trail of others.' He glanced pointedly at Wilson and said no more.

Wilson was forced to retaliate. 'I find these histrionics extraordinary. I was ordered to come here to take part in an urgent meeting, and so I have. My loyalty to the organization is unquestionable.'

Smyth said bitterly, 'Why is it then, as a direct result of my ordering you to warn Roy about his illicit relationship, I discover that he and his woman have left the province?'

Fforde intervened. 'What's all this about, Sam?'

Wilson sighed, 'Apparently Roy has been seeing a Catholic girl. Cameron asked me to warn him about it, which I did. I don't see how it casts any detrimental light on me that they have subsequently disappeared. Far from it.'

Fforde grinned. 'I hardly think that amounts to evidence of a conspiracy, eh Cameron?'

Smyth scratched his cheek irritatedly. Still he refused to reveal all he knew. 'There are other factors, as I say. However, I am not in the business of slander. My only wish is to preserve the integrity of the organization. Believe me when I say that I think it is threatened now in a way it has never been before.'

Now Fadden butted in. 'Cameron, you sound as apocalyptic as John himself. If we are to believe what you say, I don't see why we shouldn't believe him also.'

Smyth retorted, 'Because one set of facts is exclusive of the other.'

Fadden was not persuaded. 'Well, I don't see the logic in that.'

Fforde had been brooding over his whiskey, as was his custom. 'If you are questioning my integrity,' he said, 'and through me that of the organization, then you ought to know, Cameron, that the source for all . . .'

Smyth interrupted. 'I am merely saying there has been a

grave deception somewhere. As I'm sure you're aware, not all documentary evidence is what it seems.'

Now there was total confusion. One member looked to the other for confirmation. Smyth and Fforde stared down the table. The soldier decided that his only course of action was to stake all on an outright attack.

'Gentlemen, listen to me and then decide whatever you think best. I shall simply tell you what I believe to be the truth. Within three weeks, it is likely to be announced that Ulster will be handed over to the Republic against the wishes of the majority of her people. We are sworn to oppose such an action with our lives if necessary. It has been our extreme good fortune that we have inherited a potent weapon which can immobilize all those who are essential to the smooth implementation of such a policy. In the crucial weeks, when the most difficult and demanding decisions must be made, those very politicians who are to ensure its success will, to all intents and purposes, be made senile and incompetent. And no one will be able to discover anything, except that they all suffer from the same affliction. This will give us exactly the opportunity we need to mobilize our support and prepare for a Unilateral Declaration of Independence. We will gather our men, arm them, and prepare for battle. We will guard the border and patrol the streets, regardless of the British Army, and we will appeal to all our friends to stand by us. We will thus ensure that the political solution we offer is the only one that is practicable. The advantage will be ours, not theirs, for we will have wrested it from them.'

Fforde paused to sip from his glass, then intoned, 'No surrender!' which sent a shiver along Fadden's spine. 'What did our forefathers fight for, if we are now to hand over our country and theirs without a struggle? Do you think they would have flinched, do you think they would have shielded behind their own cynicism and disbelief, if such an opportunity was presented to them to rid themselves of traitors once and for all? Are we to dishonour our history? Gentlemen, if we do not act now, we will sacrifice the lives of thousands in a rearguard action we can never win. We must strike first. We must ensure that our enemies cannot defeat us.'

Another silence ensued, this time filled with the echo of Fforde's rhetoric. Fadden and Balkwill exchanged glances. Wylie fiddled with his pen uneasily. At length Smyth put one hand on the table, and with the other cupping his chin, spoke slowly and morosely.

'I have only two things to say and then I will leave this meeting, for I have more pressing matters to deal with.' He leant back and continued in the same voice. 'First, if what John says is true about the imminent betrayal of our country, it is indeed a grave moment in our history. Is it then a time to be prattling about cannibals and premature senility? I find it hard to credit. Is it not rather a time when we should be seeking to apply political pressure in the right circles, a time when we should make clear to the people of Ulster that they have a moderate and responsible, though still determined organization in their midst, prepared to represent their legitimate interests? Simply because others may have agreed yet again to gamble with our future, does it mean that we have to delude ourselves in order to try and thwart their interference? John refers to our forebears. Well, let me say that with a steadfast and decent resolution, they triumphed in the early part of this century. I believe that with a similar policy, we shall be successful now.'

Smyth, too, sipped from his glass, though it contained no substance more potent than Fforde's well water, before he continued. 'Secondly, I must reiterate my belief that the organization is being subverted in a most insidious manner. I have worked in politics for many years and I have a nose for these things. It seems to me that we have allowed ourselves to be hoodwinked at the very moment when we should be most vigilant.

'In conclusion, therefore, I would submit that, instead of concentrating our resources on making ridiculous gestures of defiance more fitting in a children's history book than a twentieth century democracy, we behave like moderate and sensible patriots. To this end, I think that the General should do the honourable thing and spare us any more of his delusions. I call upon you, John, formally, to resign.'

Smyth smoothed back his hair and stared at the old soldier, who was again studying his glass like a miniature oracle. The mood had switched from the heady thrall of impending diplomatic and military action that Fforde had conjured with his bombast, to the dull resolution of Smyth's notorious pragmatism. It was this which decided the eventual complexion of alliances.

Fadden said solemnly, 'John, I could never second such a proposal.' He turned to Wylie and asked, 'Terence?' The banker turned his usual nod of assent into a hurried negative.

Wilson added, 'I remain loyal to the commander-in-chief. I am certainly not prepared to accept Cameron's version, unless he provides us with substantial evidence for his claims.'

Fforde, with tears in his eyes, thanked them all, even Balkwill, who still remained determinedly uninvolved. Smyth arose, gathered his papers, and said, 'This is a black day for us all. I only hope that I can change the course of events before it is too late. Then, sir, you shall have your evidence.' Mitchell opened the door for him and he left with a long, determined stride.

Wilson was the first to speak in his absence. 'John, I must admit I find it as hard as anyone else to believe that this could contain such a potent weapon.' He gestured to the wallet on the table. 'But I am prepared to believe it if you say it is so. In the circumstances I would have thought that whatever we can do to try and interfere with the summit is worth a go. If I may echo an absent colleague, what is there to lose?'

Fforde bowed his head. 'Thank you, Sam. I knew I could rely on you. The chief reason I have asked you to attend tonight is that I want you to join Mitch as my right hand man. We must mobilize the men immediately. And that means issuing equipment, weapon training, drill, the lot.'

Wilson, in turn, inclined his head. 'I am glad to be of service. Who knows, even the news that we are gathering our forces may have some effect.'

Fforde said, 'It may, though I doubt it. Anyway, that's Malcolm's department. I myself am prepared to stake my life on the efficacy of this thing here.'

Wylie ventured, 'I must say I'm glad we have more

conventional weapons to back it up.'

Fadden was still pursuing his own ponderous line of thought. 'John, if this is what you claim it is, that's one thing. Getting it into Hillsborough is another.'

Balkwill spoke for the first time since he had given his medical evidence. 'Excuse me for what might seem a foolish question, but isn't it the case that once something of this magnitude is agreed, the disability of the politicians involved wouldn't in itself be enough to undo it?'

Fforde turned to him forbearingly, 'Perhaps not. But that isn't the point. As I have said, in terms of logistical policy what we need is an interim in which to seize the initiative. If our enemies are more concerned with the incapacity of their own people, that initiative will be ours.'

Fadden persisted. 'You have still to answer my question, John.'

'I will,' said Fforde, now undisputed master of proceedings. 'I asked Harry here on two counts – one to explain the virus, the other to give us the benefit of his experience in the civil service. Now then,' he turned again to Balkwill, 'are you not, Harry, in a position to oversee the Environmental Health Inspection which – I have confirmed – is a prerequisite of such meetings?'

Balkwill again assumed his knowledgeable tone. 'Not directly, though I do have some kind of overall authority. But, as you may know, the English have their own body of civil servants in Ulster. In a case such as this, they will already have appointed a Health Inspector from their ranks, along with all other security personnel.'

Fforde frowned. 'I see. What I suggest then is this. We have at least five men in your department.' Balkwill raised his eyebrows. 'Yes, yes,' said Fforde. 'I will make them known to you later. Then you must do your best to ensure that one of them replaces the official inspector, for whatever reason you can come up with.'

Balkwill nodded. 'It might be worth a try, I suppose.'

'If you are blocked, this will leave us a single option. You must arrange forgeries of the required documents and precise information of when and how the inspector should arrive at

Hillsborough. Since this whole thing is my responsibility, I shall be the one to enter the castle with the virus. Sam and Mitch will arrange it that I replace the reál man en route.'

Balkwill was silent. He was again struck by the seriousness of what he had become involved in. He could sense that the others were waiting for him to agree. He said he would do whatever he could.

Wilson then asked him, 'And is it really feasible that what is in there could debilitate all those who attend the conference?'

Balkwill was forced to say, 'Indeed. The germ would be in the form of a solution. The Russians have an establishment at Novosibirsk in Siberia where they work constantly on this kind of thing. The most effective means of administration would be a straightforward application onto the food itself, or perhaps the cutlery. It wouldn't be difficult for someone to do this in the guise of a Health Inspector. Otherwise it would have to be done by a member of the kitchen staff.'

Fforde said, 'That was the Russian angle, you can be sure. This, however, is all that is available at such short notice.'

Wylie interjected, 'I suppose the prospect of the instability this would cause in the respective governments wouldn't trouble the Communists. In fact, it would be to their advantage.'

Fforde was quick to respond. 'Does it trouble you then, Terence?'

But Wylie was not ready to share the fate of the departed politician. 'I am concerned only with the future of my country, John. I must admit the image is, all the same, sufficiently bizarre and unsettling to make me reluctant to consider it possible.'

Fforde was determined to brook no further resistance. 'Any more so than the scurvy betrayal of a whole people? Any more so than talk of delusions and conspiracies on the part of those few who are determined to oppose it?'

The banker was silenced, for all his efforts at diplomacy. Fadden then declared with a broad smile, 'Well, I myself would not find it altogether so bizarre if some of the politicians I knew were diagnosed as prematurely senile.'

Their subsequent laughter was infected with excitement

and relief. The conceit had been implicit throughout; only now did they feel they could afford to recognize it.

Fadden added, 'I take it our action should not be made publicly known?'

Fforde answered, 'If it works, it shall remain a mystery for all time. If by any chance it does not, no one will be any the wiser.' He then returned to the civil servant. 'Harry, I'll expect you to contact me first thing tomorrow morning, though of course you'll hear from me tonight with the information you require. Meanwhile we must make arrangements for the mobilization.' He turned to Wilson. 'Sam, I want you and Mitch to organize the training straight away. We need all the proficient gunmen we have briefed as soon as possible.'

Wilson replied, 'That should be no problem.' Then he inquired, as if casually, 'What about Paddy, should we have him in?'

Fadden took out his silver box, pretending not to hear. Fforde agreed, 'Yes. We need all the men we can get who are familiar with Soviet rifles. So long as he's paid, he'll be no problem.'

At this point Balkwill felt that he could witness no further bellicosity and rose. 'If you don't mind, I think I'd better leave now. Will I be driven to Belfast?'

Fforde too, rose. 'Certainly, old boy. Sam will be taking you. You don't mind, do you, Sam?'

Wilson shook his head amenably. Fforde issued his orders. 'So. If you could return to Cremorgan at 1300 hours with Paddy. I'll have the others contacted tonight.' He turned to Fadden and Wylie. 'I presume, gentlemen, that you will stay over as is your custom?' They nodded. 'Good. It'll give you a chance to acquaint yourself with all the facts.' He picked up Mitchell's report and waved it in the air. 'Here's the report. Perhaps you'd care to glance at it now. The microfilm is at your disposal. It is contained in the small cylinder.'

Mitchell came and took the wallet from the table, disappearing once more into the library. Wilson rose now and left with Balkwill. The General waved an inebriated farewell from his crumbling porch. Then he turned back indoors to gloat over his success with his still somewhat reticent colleagues.

While they were discussing logistics at Cremorgan, Cameron Smyth had climbed into his Rover with a desperate air. His intention was simple: to discover exactly what had been going on at the department of the Secretary of State, even if it meant breaking Emerald rules. Depending on the outcome, he would then know where Fforde stood in relation to the conspiracy. He would have to gather his allies in the organization as quickly as possible.

He drove hurriedly through the Fforde estate onto the main Belfast road. He was unaware of any change in the handling of the car or any other threat to his safety. It was not until he approached the border that he sensed some hazard. He put it down to his general nervousness following the meeting. The next minute, as he came in sight of the first barrier, ten pounds of high explosive detonated under the chassis. The main body of the car was blown through the air into the no man's land between checkpoints. That part of Smyth held by his seat belt remained there; otherwise, he was scattered in the fields of two countries. It was left to the Ulster statisticians to record another political assassination.

Chapter 13

Harry Balkwill was halted by traffic several miles from his Belfast office. He had long since suffered from a peptic ulcer, and recent events had exacerbated the symptoms. He leant his hands heavily on the wheel and held his breath; an open packet of antacid tablets on the dashboard bore witness to his distress.

The news of Smyth's death had filled the headlines in the morning papers. In keeping with Emerald's normal practice, Wilson had driven home by an alternative route the night before. Balkwill had only learnt of the killing as he sat at breakfast. His immediate reaction was one of shock and incredulity. After reflection, his attitude became more practical. He resolved that he must be seen to do his utmost to secure Fforde's initiative at Hillsborough. If he could not change the inspector, he would need to arrange bogus security papers. He would certainly make no complaints about the task he had been given, nor show any interest whatsoever in the details of Smyth's assassination. So it was, he reflected, that military zealots had, throughout time, commandeered the loyalty of their men.

He arrived at his office on the fifth floor of Dundonald House shortly after eight o'clock. He would normally have prepared a mountain of work for his personal assistant when she arrived an hour later. This morning he was not interested in normal duties. He stood and gazed from the window, crisscrossed with anti-explosive tape, at the grey mass of Belfast. Through the haze he could observe mile upon mile of factories, shops and houses, dominated by the cranes and derricks of the shipyard – a city wheezing through the twentieth century like a patient with terminal cancer. Balkwill sighed. His love for the Belfast of his youth was undiminished by the antics of terrorists and soldiers who had turned it into an urban battlefield. He had his own vision of an ideal Ulster. It was this vision which had brought him to the ranks of Emerald: a sentimental re-creation of the province as it used to be, when the Catholic minority had no notion of civil rights, when their privileged superiors enjoyed the wealth provided for them. Whether his vision coincided with that of his associates he could not be sure; but the common allegiance was enough to prompt him, with more personal considerations now, to accept the risks of doing what was required of him.

Half an hour later, when he had penetrated that maze of civil service bureaucracy which opened least of all to its chief officers, he discovered what he had suspected would be the case. The Health Inspection for Hillsborough prior to the summits was a matter supervised from London, and only the most cursory consultation was made with Belfast. Any hope of negotiating the replacement of the English choice was very slim. Nonetheless, he made the effort to contact his counterpart at the Elephant and Castle. His tentative suggestion that Ulstermen should be involved in the administration of their own affairs was met with polite indifference.

This left him with the simpler, but illegal alternative. He sat for some minutes controlling his frustration and then phoned through to one of the officials Fforde had identified as a fellow member in a telephone call the previous night, and told him to report to his office. While he waited, he took the opportunity to contact a number of other colleagues in government departments, to see if he could not glean some information which might further enhance his standing in Emerald. All he could come up with were rumours; though the rumours themselves to some extent substantiated Fforde's claims of English duplicity.

At least the task of forging a Health Inspector's security papers was within Balkwill's capability. All that was needed were the bona fide official's particulars and the precise time of his proposed visit to Hillsborough. With the help of a junior official, the necessary research was undertaken later that morning. By lunch time the relevant information was on his desk. Balkwill had details of the Inspector's age, present address, family situation, even his car registration number. The visit to the castle was scheduled for the very morning of the day on which the summit was due to begin. Balkwill telexed Fforde at Cremorgan with a report on his progress, carefully veiled in abstruse language. Then he sat back in his chair, satisfied that he had achieved as much as he could for the cause of an independent Ulster.

Fforde received the news from Belfast with some satisfaction and retired to his bedroom, to try to catch up on some of the sleep he had lost over recent nights. He had not yet had time, in the midst of his frantic preparations, to reflect fully on the implications of the other piece of serious news he had received that morning. One thing he knew: he could not allow it to interfere with any of his plans.

But when he lay down and closed his eyes, the image of his murdered associate, the disdainful and fastidious politician, stalked through his mind. Who had been responsible for his death, and with what precise motive, he did not yet know. Few details had been released. It could have been the work of any of Smyth's many political enemies. The fact that it had coincided with the struggle for power at Cremorgan was a source of both disquiet and relief. Fforde could not decide how he should react. In this confused state, he fell asleep.

An hour later he was awakened by gunfire from the stable yards, as if Cremorgan was under attack. He hurried from his bed, pistol in hand. Even as he rose, another round was fired. He ran across the gallery. From the windows there, he had a clear view over the outhouses. He was immensely relieved when he saw his own man Mitchell and the Catholic gunman O'Mara standing in a group of volunteers, firing at a row of wine bottles lined along a wooden fence. Wilson was also among them.

Now that he had recovered his composure, he hastened angrily downstairs, out into the yard. 'What in damnation's going on? There is to be no firing whatsoever on these premises. Mitch, I'm surprised at you, I am truly.'

The batman, who himself seemed to be in a state of some agitation, lowered his gun and walked away. Fforde turned to O'Mara. To his surprise he saw that the Catholic's cheek was split by a long blackened scab. Two fingers of his left hand were bound together; and under his shirt a bandage dressing was visible. 'My God, whatever happened to you?'

O'Mara scowled. 'Nothin', nothin' at all.'

Fforde tutted. 'Fighting, I suppose. Bally Irishmen. Never happy if you're not scrapping in some backstreet brawl.'

O'Mara did not react predictably. 'Aye, well, there's no need to go losin' your rag anyhow. Sure, we was just havin' a wee shootin' match here.' He seemed at once familiar, and yet wary, with the General.

Fforde sighed, 'I see.'

Wilson then stepped from the ranks of the other riflemen who were standing sheepishly, uncertain how to behave. 'It was a foolish challenge, John. Paddy here bet anyone he could outshoot them and Mitch just took him up on it. I should have stopped it. It's my fault.'

Fforde said, 'Well, I suppose there's no harm in a bit of healthy rivalry, what.' He could not resist asking, 'And who won?'

Wilson replied, 'Paddy won, sir.'

Fforde looked across at Mitchell who was standing with his back to them. 'Well, it's not on, anyway. We have to be extremely careful. All firing of weapons takes place in the mountains. Is that understood?' He turned to the whole company, some 20 strong. 'You are here only to be briefed on the details of the training you are to supervise next week. If I hear another shot, I shall not be as lenient with the culprit again.'

Fforde turned on his heel and disappeared into the house. He went straight into his sitting room and poured himself a drink. He had fallen uncomfortably into a fitful sleep and had been woken with equal discomposure. Again his thoughts returned to Smyth, as he stood in the cool musty gloom of the room. The gunfire had shaken him. He found himself thinking for the first time that perhaps there had been some substance in the dead man's allegations, after all. There might be a group at work within the organization whose intentions were not constructive, but which had murdered one of its leaders and could be preparing to remove the other. That business about Roy Moore and his Catholic girlfriend worried him now. If it were true that there had been some interference by Republicans, the consequences for the Hillsborough project could be very grave. Fforde resolved to speak to Sam Wilson as soon as the briefing was over. Clearly, Smyth had enlisted his support, and then had had reason to be displeased. Whatever had happened, Fforde was determined to find out.

Wilson was equally determined that his commander-in-chief should remain in ignorance. To this end, he had already spent a valuable morning. He had reached Bettystown soon after Balkwill had contacted his fellow civil servants. O'Mara was not to be found at the cottage, but a short search on the beach revealed him hunched in a sand hollow, watching the sea.

Wilson, too, had reacted predictably to his scarred appearance. 'Christ, Pat, what's been going on?'

O'Mara sat upright, putting his hand on his knife in its sheath. 'Are you tellin' me you don't know?'

The big man sat down beside his former cellmate and offered him a cigarette. 'I don't know, no. But if you tell me who it was, I'll make sure they don't do anything like it again.'

In spite of his reluctance, O'Mara was affected, as he had been in the Maze, by his companion's equanimity. He had harboured many suspicions since Smyth's visit, and these, with the wounds inflicted on him at McKee's Ridge, had taunted him continually. It took Wilson a considerable time to overcome his hostility. But eventually, with his familiar air of candour, he forced O'Mara to believe that he had played no knowing part in the 'coincidence' concerning Moore.

O'Mara lit the cigarette. At length, he said, 'Well, I dunno what's goin' on, but I tell you I'm fucken mad about it.'

Wilson then drew out of him exactly how he had received his injuries. O'Mara related the whole sequence of events, including Smyth's visit. It was clear from the way he spoke that he had not bothered with any means of keeping in touch with the world beyond the dunes at Bettystown.

'So how did you get back here?' Wilson inquired.

'Sure, I footed it over the bogs to Mac's – it's a bar on the road to Belfast – an' I put my knife at his throat, an' the oul' bastard thought I'd come to kill him for somethin'; anyhow I got him to drive me south.'

'No trouble at the border?'

'You know as well as me there's a thousand ways across. Anyhow, he got me to Dundalk, an' they took me into hospital. Only they said I'd be needin' skin grafts an' all, they wouldn't stitch the cuts in case they started beelin', so it looked like I'd be hung up there for ages. There's no way I'm goin' to wait round till some fucker from the north comes in an' works out who I am, so soon as I could I checked out an' came down here.'

Wilson asked, 'And how is it now?'

O'Mara winced as he moved position. 'Pretty bad. I learned some first aid an' all up in Belfast like the rest, but it's not enough. My stomach's still weepin' an' my shoulder's swelled up. Only I can't go to none of the doctors round here, sure, I can't afford to draw attention to meself so long as I'm livin' in one of your places.'

Wilson said suddenly, 'OK, look. I've been ordered to take you up to the estate to brief you on some rifle training. I suggest we stop off somewhere on the road and get you in to see a doctor privately. You've got money, haven't you?'

'Aye. Your man Cameron gave me this cheque an' all. He says I can cash it anywhere so long as I have them check it out by phone.'

Wilson, 'We'll do that first then. I'll go in. Is the number on the back?'

'Aye.'

'Good. I take it you're not immobile?'

'Och no. It hurts like fuck but I'm no cripple.' He stood and flexed his muscles. 'So what's the set-up now then?'

They stared together at the misty horizon where a single fishing boat was slowly crossing. O'Mara listened attentively as he was told of the general mobilization due to take place over the next few days, and the part he was required to take. Wilson concluded, 'I'll tell you the rest on the way. There's money in it. And you'll still be able to keep out of harm's way.'

O'Mara watched the sea breaking laboriously on the strand. A drizzle had begun to fall. Across the dunes, the small cottage appeared vacant and gloomy. 'OK,' he said, 'what do I care who runs the fucken place? You're the only guys that don't want me dead.'

Wilson smiled strangely at this. 'As I said, I'll tell you the rest in the car.'

They drove quickly to Carrickmacross. There, Wilson entered the bank and cashed the cheque with Emerald's special account; the number was already familiar to him. At the next village, he took the wounded gunman to the local surgery, where he had his wounds dressed again, a heavy shot of penicillin, and antibiotic pills to take with him, along with a week's supply of bandages. At the sight of £75 the doctor conveniently overlooked any questions he might otherwise have asked.

Once they had driven some miles in the direction of Cremorgan, Wilson leant back in his seat and said, as if he were relating a piece of gossip, 'By the way, before we go any further, Pat, I ought to tell you that Cameron's dead.'

O'Mara stiffened and exclaimed, 'Holy Christ!'

Wilson explained, 'I didn't tell you before just in case you chickened out. You see, I need you, Pat, and I'll tell you why.'

The gunman lit a cigarette with trembling fingers as they drove on towards Ballybay. 'I reckon they took him out because he was on to something,' Wilson went on. 'If you ask me, everything that's happened has been engineered from inside the organization itself. I don't know where your girl came into it, but I'm sure Moore's the chief architect, along with the General.'

'Christ, I wish you people'd talk straight.'

Wilson spelled out his meaning. 'I think it's a kind of coup. The General's getting rid of anyone who stands in his way. He's a fascist, Pat, and he's getting old. He's going to make one last bid for what he wants before it's too late.'

'Sure an' what he wants is to be King of Ulster like Cuchulain or O'Neill!'

Wilson smiled. He paused carefully. Then he said, 'Now I'm sure they've found out about that visit you had, and that Smyth paid you to do a job. Only you can bet your life they won't let you know until . . .'

O'Mara interrupted. 'Why the fuck are you takin' me up there then? You let me go on thinkin' . . .'

Wilson in his turn cut him short. 'They won't touch you till you're no further use to them. They need you for the rifle training. You see, it's all part of the takeover – getting the men armed and ready to fight, making sure the politicians are out of the way.'

O'Mara said, 'It wouldn't be the first time, sure enough.'

'You're with me so far, then?'

The Catholic nodded. 'Aye. There's people like your man all over, only they don't get where he is now.'

Wilson admitted, 'Maybe. But you haven't heard the crunch yet. He's got good reason for thinking he can pull this off.'

'Has he now?'

'Now listen, Pat. In about two weeks' time there's a political summit to be held at Hillsborough Castle. You know about it?'

O'Mara joked, 'Och, another one? They'll be talkin' till the cows come home.'

'Ah, but this is no ordinary meeting. Even your own people are going to be there, the paramilitaries and all.' O'Mara let out his breath. Wilson went on, 'Straight up. And there's only one reason for that. There's going to be a deal.'

O'Mara looked straight across at his companion, who kept his eyes on the road. 'Are you havin' me on, Sam, or are you?'

'I don't know the details,' said Wilson, 'but the General's out to stop it happening. That's where the whole Moore set-up comes in. Don't ask me how, but they think they've found a way. They're going to make sure the deal can't go through.'

'Jeez, man, I always said you fellas had more money an' guns than you could handle, but I never reckoned you'd come up with somethin' like this.'

'I told you before, you shouldn't let appearances deceive you. They mean to hit everyone who attends the summit, somehow or other.'

Wilson steered along the narrow country road, now only a few miles from the Fforde estate. O'Mara retorted, 'Aye, an' they've got the Martians comin' down to help them.'

Wilson continued to ignore his cynicism. 'Moore's the one with the plans. He's a dangerous man.'

O'Mara recalled the Protestant's conduct at Buncrana. 'I

wouldn't call him superspy meself.'

Wilson replied, 'Men in his line of business are never what they seem.'

A silence ensued while O'Mara reflected again, this time on Moore's more potent manner the night before the murder. Wilson waited with the same patience he had shown in the prison cell. Eventually the Catholic decided to take his account seriously. 'So what's your angle, then? Sure, you're still one of them, aren't you?'

'I'm like you, Pat. The only thing I care about is looking after myself. And the way things are going, my skin's no safer than yours. We've got to take hold of things before they go too far. It's not just the politicians who'll get it in the neck. It's people like you and me. There'll be a bloodbath sooner or later. You can help me, Pat. I mean to stop it happening.'

O'Mara smiled bitterly, 'You sound like a guy that's just been buried.'

Wilson replied, 'They won't bury me.'

There was a further pause while O'Mara pondered. 'But I can't see where I come in, no way at all.'

'Well, I can't tell you that,' said Wilson, 'but I can tell you what you've got to do to get out of it.'

'I get Moore?'

'When the time's right. The Hillsborough conference is on the eleventh. There's not long enough now to find out who's with them and who's not, and we can't afford to make any mistakes.' Wilson spoke as if he was calculating his policy there and then. 'No. The only way's to wait until they all come out into the open. And that means the day itself. In the meantime, there's enough people I know I can trust to put in the right places, so that when the time comes the whole thing can be scuppered.'

O'Mara drew heavily on his cigarette and said, 'That's your crack, Sam, not mine. Moore's all I want.'

'You couldn't get him now, that's what I'm saying. He's taken himself off and he won't be back until it's underway. He's done his bit for now.'

O'Mara inquired, 'OK, so what do I do?'

'You stick around. You're safe so long as they're using you, and the training will go on at least until the conference and probably after. They know you rely on them and you won't go to anyone else, so you wait till Moore gets back and then you take him and the girl. I'll tell you when it's right.' Wilson waited. Then he added, 'The only thing is it would be worth taking the precaution of moving out of the cottage. When this sort of thing's going on, the right hand doesn't know what the left's doing half the time. You wouldn't want to be the victim of a misunderstanding.'

'So where do you think I'm goin' to go? This country's a fucken minefield when you're on the run, man.'

'I'll look after that. There's a safe house in Belfast. I'll take you there.'

O'Mara exclaimed, 'Belfast! Christ, you're away in the head.'

Wilson answered stolidly, 'I'll guarantee your safety.'

His passenger looked at him again with the forlorn gaze of one who seemed to have no choice. Then he asked, 'Who'll pay me for the hit then?'

'I will. Only you'll have to wait till the job's done.'

'In other words you reckon I'll lose me bap again.'

'I can't risk it, Pat. Everything's got to work, and it's got to work in secret.' No more was said, while they passed through Clones. 'Now, when we get to the General's, go on as if I hadn't told you anything. You know Cameron's dead but that's all, OK?'

O'Mara sighed. 'I dunno.' At last he managed to convey his sense of dejection. 'Shite! Serves me right for thinkin' I'd be on a safe bet with a load of fucken Prods.'

Wilson smiled peculiarly again. 'There are no safe bets in Ireland these days, Pat.'

He then drove on quietly, so that O'Mara could be left with his reflections on his precarious position. Shortly afterwards they reached Cremorgan. It was after that, in a blatant assertion of his new role, that O'Mara challenged his sectarian rivals to a shooting contest.

The training brief was short and concise. After a cursory outline of the general reasons for the mobilization, which projected a betrayal by the British Government without giving details, Wilson listed where and when each body of men would encamp, and which gunman was to supervise their duties. He and Mitchell would patrol regularly from one platoon to another, ensuring that all volunteers were both physically and morally primed. The details of their eventual deployment through Ulster would only be revealed once the training was under way. But it was made clear that all officers in Emerald's army would assemble at Cremorgan on the evening of the eleventh to finalize plans for the successful implementation of a Unilateral Declaration of Independence.

It appeared that only three men, including O'Mara, were familiar with Russian weapons. The supply consisted mostly of 762 AK Assault Kalashnikovs, with 30 round magazines and target sites graduated to 800 metres; as Fforde had recognized, these were one of the most efficient of all military rifles, difficult to jam and operated with minimum maintenance. The other members of the company were well acquainted with the less sophisticated weapons they would be using; so no further instruction was necessary. They were then told that they would be given coffee and sandwiches before they were taken home. Over the next fortnight, vans driven by Fforde's estate workers would call on them at specified times, while other provisions would be made to transport the vast bulk of volunteers from towns and villages throughout the province to their military camps in the mountains of Mourne.

It was not in Wilson's brief to add that a vigorous propaganda campaign would coincide with the mobilization. Devised by Fadden, the campaign would draw attention away from any possible designs on the Hillsborough conference itself, but would vilify the English, and rally the people of Ulster to the Loyalist cause. Private notice would also be given to allies on mainland Britain that the men of Ulster were again ready to fight for their independence. By 11 August Emerald's forces would be poised to snatch power.

After the briefing, Wilson entered Cremorgan House and found the General slumped in his chair, a glass of whiskey on the arm, a sheaf of papers in his hand.

'Briefing over, sir,' he said, waking the old man who blinked and stuttered.

'What, what?'

'I said, with your permission, sir, I'll head back to Belfast now. I've done the necessary.'

Fforde struggled to recover his senses. He looked worn and aged. 'Keep dozing off, old chap. Not up to all this, I suppose. Must get in a good night's sleep, what.' He straightened up and resumed a military bearing. 'Good. Anyway, well done, Sam. Knew I could rely on you.' Wilson turned to leave but was not surprised when the General said, as if he had suddenly remembered something, 'Wait a minute. I want a quick word if I may.'

'Certainly. What can I do, sir?'

Fforde sighed dramatically. 'It's a terrible business, isn't it?'

'You mean Cameron? Yes, I suppose it is.'

'Don't know quite how to take it, Sam. I can't say the man wasn't a thorn in my flesh, because he was. Only I wouldn't have wished this on him.'

'He had many enemies, John.'

The old soldier appeared to be seeking some reassurance. 'Newspapers say it was remote control. Don't know about that, though. Right on the border, what. Apparently no one's claimed responsibility as yet.'

Wilson remained impassive. 'You can be sure the Republicans will, sooner or later.'

Fforde agreed, 'Good for prestige. Indeed yes. As we know only too well ourselves.' He lowered his voice. 'Damn stupid of me, I know, but I've been thinking about that nonsense of his, conspiracies and whatnot. Can't help feeling there might have been something in it, all the same.' The General, who was now standing with his hands behind his back, still appeared unusually tired and infirm.

Wilson said merely, 'You really think so, sir?'

Fforde stuttered, 'I mean, what with all the publicity and so on, and then this business with Roy and the girl . . . Do you really think it's part of a plot? I mean, what was Cameron on about?'

Wilson said plainly, 'If you ask me, sir, Cameron had some personal grudge and he was using the organization to work it off.' He stepped close to the old man. 'If there was any conspiracy, then it was more likely to have been one of his own. He was antagonistic towards you too, John, as you're well aware. I wouldn't have put it past him to have been trying to find some less formal means of removing you from your position than he attempted at the meeting.'

Fforde fingered his moustache. 'I see, I see. It's just that it's been such an uncanny coincidence. I feel almost guilty myself, you know, after all that carry-on last night and then . . .'

Wilson smiled warmly and offered some words of encouragement. 'If I were you, sir – I hope you don't mind the impertinence . . .' Fforde waved a hand graciously, 'I wouldn't worry in the least. Cameron is dead, for good or ill, and that means there will be no opposition in our ranks to what is the most vital operation we could ever plan. You must see that whoever was responsible has done the people of Ulster a great favour, no matter that you feel compassion for the victim now. As commander-in-chief you can't afford to hold such feelings for too long. There is a momentous task on hand and you are the man history has destined to accomplish it.'

Fforde's eyes gleamed. He was becoming more mercurial each day. 'By God, you're right! I mean, if a commander spent his time worrying about every little rumour of mutiny, he'd never enter a battle, let alone win it, what. This is no time for faintheartedness. Let the dead bury the dead.'

Wilson agreed. 'Is that all now, sir? I should be making tracks. I've decided to look after Paddy myself for the time being, at one of the houses in Belfast. It's not that I don't trust him, but in the circumstances we'd better be safe than sorry. I'd like him to be where I can keep an eye on him.'

'Sam, you are invaluable,' Fforde declared. Wilson bowed slightly and shook the General's open hand. 'Thank you. You've rather put things in perspective again. It needs a young man to do that sometimes.'

Wilson said, 'Sir, you will outlive me yet.'

'Yes, yes. No surrender, Sam, no surrender!'

Fforde called his batman in and went up to the library to finalize his strategy for the crucial months ahead.

Chapter 14

Wilson found O'Mara deep in thought sitting apart from the other men, who were clustered round Mitchell.

'Come on now,' said Wilson, 'it's time we were away.'

O'Mara immediately rose and, flexing his shoulder, followed him to the car. 'What was the oul' fella sayin'?'

'Trying to find out whose side I'm on. I'll keep him guessing.'

They drove out of the demesne and on to the road that Smyth had taken the night before. Wilson could sense that O'Mara's private thinking had already reached a point where his allegiance to an old cellmate was not uppermost in his mind. He had a sly glance in his eyes, a new air of independence.

'So where's the place in Belfast?' he asked.

Wilson replied, 'Wait till you get there. I'm sure you'll know the area.'

'An' I'm to stay there till the eleventh?'

'Your first stint in the mountains is two days off. Otherwise you'll have to stay out of sight and rely on me for food and anything else you want.'

'Some fucken life.'

'It is a life. Anyway, you've no choice now but to trust me.'

O'Mara might have been expected to resume his forlorn attitude, but he merely nodded slowly. Wilson noted it with satisfaction. He added, 'So you might as well make the best of it. At least it's better than the H Block.'

They turned off the main road and crossed the border at a secluded spot on what was little more than a track, and drove circuitously to Belfast to avoid any road checks. The safe house was set in an inconspicuous terrace off the Donegall Road in the Protestant enclave of Sandy Row.

O'Mara exclaimed, 'Well, fuck me, if it isn't oul' Sandy Row!'

They hurriedly disappeared inside, though there was no one in the street but a small snubnosed boy playing with a wooden rifle. The house was typically furnished. Only the bullet-proof windows and heavy locks on both doors distinguished it from any other in the road.

For the next two days, while the Loyalists of Belfast were being rallied all around him, O'Mara remained ensconced in the house. Wilson brought food and a daily paper, taking in the milk each morning; he made coffee and dressed the Catholic's wounds. There was a television which O'Mara watched constantly, his feet on the glass table stained with the marks of former occupants; chain-smoking and dropping ash in to an empty beer can. Even though he was effectively imprisoned, it pleased him to be back in the city where he had spent his youth. His mind was full of distant memories.

The main drift of his thoughts was not, however, one of childhood recollections. Ever since Wilson had informed him of the ominous struggle for power taking place in Emerald, an idea had grown slowly at the back of his mind. The paradox of his precarious reliance on a hostile organization was not lost on him; nor was the fact that he was now equipped with sufficient information to cause his traditional enemies considerable damage. He realized that he had, against all likelihood, been handed the opportunity to avenge himself in more ways than one.

On the third day, he was driven to a spot in the mountains near Kilkeel, where he was scheduled to give training on the use of Kalashnikov and Armalite rifles. The antibiotics had begun to heal his wounds, and he was full of his customary manic energy. It meant that his preparation was possibly the most effective in the whole corps. As Smyth had remarked, he knew his trade, and he treated it for the most part with commitment. A further roll of cash in his pocket was a just reward.

If this were all he required, O'Mara would have been compliant enough, but he was growing tired of the solitary life of a mercenary. When he gazed from the windows of the safe house towards the Falls about a mile away, a powerful longing grew in him that he had never expected to ever feel again: to be back with his own kind. He was less than half an hour's walk from his family home; the proximity deeply affected him. That life appeared to him better than one spent hiding in the midst of his lifelong adversaries. The position that he found himself in could yet provide passage to a land from which he had too long been exiled.

After Wilson had left him, with the proviso that he would come for him in a further two days' time, and that he himself had business to see to which would prevent his return until then, O'Mara stood on the landing smoking, and watched, through the net curtains, the small boy playing with a group of his friends at those warlike games which were their daily pastime. All the prejudice and antagonism of his childhood came back to him. He might almost have run out and attacked the small gang, riven with the impotent hatred common to many thousands of adolescents in the city. Instead he made the simple, quick decision of a man. He went down to the back door, let himself out in such a way that he would be able to re-enter, climbed painfully over the garden wall and dropped onto a piece of waste ground behind the Donegall Road. He knew exactly where he was. It would take him 20 minutes to reach his destination. On the way he made one brief but vital phone call. Then he pulled his collar round his ears and hurried through the drizzling night.

He was unaware of the inconspicuous figure who shadowed him expertly through the small dark streets of Belfast.

Black's Bar, a Republican club he had last visited with Mary McKee on the night he had been shot, was now a prefabricated hut standing in an area of squalor and desolation. One of Moore's High Security Fences had been built around it, which made the low building look more like a concentration camp than a bar. He approached the wire gate and waited for it to be opened. The doorman did not recognize him, but when he mentioned the name of the person he had come to meet he was let in.

The all-male gathering became silent as soon as he entered. He still wore the beard he had first grown in the H Block and with which he had disguised himself at Buncrana; his red hair was growing long again; the scab on his face had almost healed. Many knew him, and those that did not were soon whispered the information. He crossed the bar, making towards a door marked Private. No one went near him until one of the barmen rushed out suddenly and stood in his way.

'Where the hell do you think you're goin'?'

Before O'Mara could answer, the door opened. Facing him, with the build of a heavyweight boxer and a stack of greasy black hair brushed forward almost to his eyebrows, was the man he had come to see.

He stared him fully in the eyes and said, 'I've come to trade.'

The answer was quick and straight. 'Too right you have, son. An' if we don't want what you've got, you're not goin' out again.'

He was ushered from the bar, and the door closed behind him. Immediately, the hut was full of muttered imprecations, while the story of O'Mara's traitorous exploits was told again and again, with many an invention added to suit the teller's particular bent.

The heavyweight was known as Mallon, a prominent Provisional officer, and member of the Central Army Council. He was sitting at a battered table, flanked by two other men. One of these O'Mara instantly recognized as an elder brother of the prisoner who had shared his protest in the H Block, and who, he knew, had operated from Black's Bar for many years. Dermot O'Hanlon stared back at him with contempt. The other was a squat, unshaven character he knew only vaguely as a hit man who had come to the city shortly before his own arrest. All three had so far negotiated the troubles without any convictions. Mallon himself had been so effectively protected that the police did not even dare to publicize his photograph for fear of litigation, and the security forces were ordered to avoid tangling with him. He was the nominal owner of the bar, a legitimate business, which meant that his cover was always assured.

The room was cramped and poorly lit; the only furniture, the table and three plastic chairs. O'Mara remained standing before his inquisitors.

'Well lads,' Mallon said at last, 'this is Patrick O'Mara, if you don't know him already. He's a fly man, though by the looks of it it's not been doin' him much good lately.' Their visitor stood saying nothing. 'Come on now, we're waitin'.'

O'Mara looked to the elder O'Hanlon for some hint of

encouragement but he found nothing, only the same contempt. Nothing could be achieved by stalling. 'I want a full pardon,' he said, 'an' a weapon. An' good money for a job.'

Mallon leant back, turning a pencil in his fingers. 'Is that all, son? Sure, you're playin' with high stakes. I hope you know what you're doin'.'

The elder O'Hanlon spoke his first words. 'Christ, there's nothin' he can have that'll let him off the fucken hook.'

'OK Dermot,' said Mallon, 'we'll hear him out anyhow.' He looked across at O'Mara again. 'The floor's yours.'

The gunman put his hands in his pockets and made his appeal. He began the story of his last months as if he had quit the H Block with the vague intention of some kind of undercover work, though he admitted he had lost his nerve after he had heard news of the Kelly bombing. But he struggled to make clear that once his cellmate had pressed him to operate for the Protestants, he had agreed only in order to be able eventually to earn a pardon from the IRA.

When he came to the time of his release, he paused to see what effect his statement was having. His listeners were clearly not impressed. In fact their attitude seemed only to have hardened. In the dim light, their steady gaze was more hostile than ever.

During the next few minutes O'Mara could feel the atmosphere change. He first described what he called his infiltration into Emerald, giving details of the Protestant organization that the IRA had long laboured to collect. He pinpointed the military headquarters and described a number of prominent members. He also revealed that it was they who had been responsible for the death of the Russian agent who had been so helpful to the Republican cause in recent years. He stressed that he did not know the precise identity of the assassin.

Again he paused. This time Mallon muttered, 'Go on now.' He had begun taking notes on a grubby pad headed with the name of an Irish brewery, and was plainly anxious now to hear more.

Second in O'Mara's personal armoury was the revelation that he knew about the Republicans' proposed participation at the Hillsborough talks. This caused a vigorous reaction.

'An' how the fuck do you know that?' cried Mallon.

O'Mara replied calmly, 'The Or'ngemen know about it, man.' He added that, not only were Emerald informed about the Republicans' potential involvement, but that they were intending to hit all those who attended the summit. For O'Mara this was the crucial point. Until now he had spoken only of what he knew himself; but when asked how the Protestants could possibly handle such an operation, he was forced to invent. 'They've got at least three different plans. There's plants inside the castle an' the village too. If you ask me, it's the Brits workin' some kind of double cross.'

For some moments there was a sceptical silence, but the significance of his revelation was such that it had to be treated seriously. Mallon said again, 'Go on,' meanwhile continuing to make notes with his pencil.

'The man behind the operation is called Moore, Roy Moore. He's some kind of top agent, MI6 an' all. He's bein' paid to set the whole thing up along with the guy who runs the army side of Emerald. An' that's not all, they're already gettin' rid of anyone that tries to stop them.'

O'Hanlon asked reluctantly, 'How do you mean?'

'It wasn't youse that got your man Smyth. I don't care who claimed it. They did him themselves 'cause he was gettin' in the way.' He paused. 'See, they're mobilizin' all the Or'ngemen in the country.'

This was widely known. Mallon said, 'Come on, that guy Fadden's always shootin' his mouth off. They're just makin' a scare.'

'You're wrong, man,' said O'Mara. He again looked closely at his listeners to gauge their mood. His next move was definitive. 'I know, 'cause I'm trainin' the bastards. An' what's more, I'm trainin' them on your guns.'

The small hit man at that point sprang from his chair and aimed a punch at O'Mara's head. He parried it with his sound arm and looked hurriedly to Mallon for support. The heavyweight made no move. The next punch hit him full in his wounded stomach. As he bent forward, a clenched fist came down on the back of his neck. The hit man stood over him.

With the last strength in his body he managed to straighten up and stand with an unexpected dignity.

'An' that's why,' he said between laboured breaths, 'I'm the only guy that can help you out.'

Mallon rose from his seat, motioning the assailant to retire. He now stood in his place and said, 'Finish what you have to say, O'Mara.'

It took him some moments to regain his composure. He did not complain of his attack but asked to be allowed to sit down. Mallon reached a massive hand over the table and dropped a plastic chair in front of him.

'On the eleventh, in the evenin', all the military command's goin' to be at headquarters. It'll either be for some kind of debriefin' session or they'll be workin' out tactics, I dunno, only they'll all be there. An' the last thing they'll be thinkin' of is a visit from you boys.' He paused as he felt a twinge of pain in his shoulder. Then he went on, 'There's only one time to hit the bastards an' that's it. They'll be hidin' away till then or else they'll be up in the mountains. An' after, it'll be too late.'

Mallon looked for the first time to his companions as if to share his growing conviction.

'I can give you a plan of the house an' all. The rest you'll have to check up with the boys at Castleblaney, that's the nearest ASU.' O'Mara came to his final point. 'Your man Moore, he won't be there so far as I know. But I can find out where to get him, an' that's for why I want a weapon an' a decent fee.'

'That's it?' asked Mallon.

'That's it.' O'Mara sat back, proud of himself. As he had planned privately, he had not said anything about Mary McKee; his intent upon her was as unpolitical as it had ever been. When nothing more was said, he exclaimed, 'Christ, man, I've just saved your fucken skins! They mean business, these fellas.'

Mallon leant back against the table with arms crossed. 'Listen to me, O'Mara. If we find out you've come here talkin' a load of shite, I'll take you out meself. Now I'll tell you what I'm goin' to do. I'm goin' away now to make a few inquiries, an' while I'm gone Dermot here'll look after you.' O'Hanlon was about to protest but Mallon waved him down. 'When I come back you'll either have a deal on your hands or you'd better have your prayers said, OK?'

It was exactly what O'Mara had hoped for. 'OK.'

Mallon grabbed a leather coat from a nail on the wall and signalled to the small man to follow him. As he left he called to O'Hanlon, 'See that he gets a drink, Dermot, he must have a thirst on him after the talkin' he's done.'

O'Mara had a good idea where Mallon would be going. The Brigade Headquarters never stayed in one location for more than a few days but could always be found in the heartland of Catholic Belfast. When he last knew of it, it had been based in a council maisonette near Lenadoon, vacated for the purpose by a family with no known Provisional ties. There the Big Five, as they were known, had installed themselves with an SSB Radio with a loop aerial concealed in the building, and other paraphernalia of an urban guerrilla command unit. Mallon's journey would not take long. Whatever time he spent would be witness to the thoroughness of his inquiries.

In fact it was some three hours later when he returned to the bar. His entry, with the hit man in tow, ended a long silence in the backroom where both man sat smoking moodily. O'Mara looked up expectantly. What he saw in Mallon's eyes made his heart leap.

Mallon said merely, 'I want you back here, Monday, 1700 hours, with your plans of the house an' anythin' else you can come up with. Are you with me?'

O'Mara stood up and cried, 'Holy God! I'm with you, man, I'm with you all the way.'

Then Mallon turned to the subdued O'Hanlon, 'See him off the premises, Dermot.' As O'Mara left he said, 'Wherever it is you're hidin' out, you'd better make sure you stay put, O'Mara. No one's goin' to hear of this till we're sure you're on the level. You're still a marked man.'

O'Mara replied, 'Sure, I've been hidin' long enough. Another couple of days won't make no difference, man.'

O'Mara's return to the safe house in Sandy Row was as well monitored as his departure. He himself was less vigilant now, thrilled with his apparent success. He still looked back at every corner and took a devious route across the waste ground to the rear of the house, but his follower found his task less demanding than it had been earlier.

The gunman spent the next day making drawings of those parts of Cremorgan with which he was familiar, including the outhouses and enclosures at the back of the building. He also put down the location of the camp near Kilkeel, with details of the Protestant battalion and its weaponry.

When Wilson arrived to collect him for his second training session, it was clear that O'Mara would have some difficulty trying to conceal his change of heart. The big man noted his latent excitement. When the Catholic asked, as if merely a matter of academic interest, what defences were customarily used at Cremorgan, Wilson gladly passed on what he considered to be suitable facts. O'Mara by now believed that he had a passable appraisal of Emerald's military headquarters.

The same drill was followed on their return to Belfast as before. Wilson left the gunman, promising to return and collect him for his last stint in a further three days' time. In the evening O'Mara put the final touches to his plans. The next day was spent in his usual state of impatience, hovering between the television and the window; no more distracted by what he saw in one than the other. By Monday 31 July, he could no longer control himself, though this was one rendezvous he would have to make precisely on time.

Belfast, that summer, was dismal and heavy. A whole series of British commercial firms had announced that their factories in the city were closing, which would mean still more unemployment. Almost, it seemed, in reply, there was an increase in the already high number of civilian bombings. The city smouldered, each narrow street a concrete touch-tape to an invisible source of violence and discord. August was always a time when the anniversaries in both communal camps made some trouble inevitable, but now there was an added fervour in their ranks. The publicity given to the mobilization of the Protestant forces had stirred the Catholics of Ballymurphy and Turf Lodge into a frightened rancour which took them out onto the streets, though they were chiefly represented by their children, some no older than the boys O'Mara watched from his window, who swapped wooden rifles for bricks and petrol bombs and some of whom were hideously maimed by the British Army's plastic bullets. This was not, however, the sole trigger for disorder. There was an indefinable tension in the air. Rumours were spreading about the possible outcome of the Hillsborough talks; hinting at everything from a re-imposition of internment to an invasion from the Republic. No one seemed to know anything for certain.

O'Mara's haven was not impervious to such turmoil. His private need was to know exactly how much of it was a direct result of his own actions. He heard on the television news how, in three separate incidents, junior officers belonging to Emerald's volunteer force had disappeared and been found on waste sites several hours later with bullets through the backs of their necks. He saw how the barricades were going up across the Falls Road, the lorries and buses burning at the Monagh Roundabout and the Glen Road, the mobs rioting across West Belfast. He saw also how the ferment was spreading to towns throughout the province. The whole Catholic population was rearing up like a stricken animal, though, as far as O'Mara knew, this could be as much a straightforward reaction to the activities of their adversaries as to any more subtle persuasion.

It was with a nervous uncertainty that he arrived at Black's Bar that Monday afternoon and waited at the gate. The bar itself was packed, as usual, with the unemployed men of the area. He noticed that this time not all the glances directed at him were hostile. He knocked at the inner door and went into the back room.

Mallon was waiting for him with the same two henchmen. O'Hanlon stepped forward and closed the door; then he motioned O'Mara to a chair which had on this occasion been provided for him, before returning to his post behind the table.

'Listen to me now,' said Mallon. 'I'm goin' to spell it out plain.' He glanced down at his notebook. 'One. We've been checkin' up on your Or'nge friends. Maybe you've noticed.

Anyhow, it seems what you said about them all gettin' together stands up.'

O'Mara grinned nervously. Mallon went on.

'Two. As to the place. We've had the Castleblaney boys go down an' take a look. The way it's run no one'd suspect what they're doin'. That's why we never sussed it before. Anyhow we know now. That means it all checks out, O'Mara. So I've been told to tell you, if you have your plans on you, you have your pardon in return.'

O'Mara hurriedly handed over his scruffy papers. 'Here you are, sir. There's a few other wee things there an' all.'

Mallon nodded as he took the papers. Both the hit man and the elder O'Hanlon seemed reluctant to accept O'Mara's return to their ranks. They scowled. Mallon continued.

'I've not done yet. Three. It looks like that eejit Fadden means what he says for once.' Mallon added snidely, 'Only I don't have to tell you that, do I now?' He leant forward and stared O'Mara firmly in the eye. 'Anyhow, I've been ordered to let you know we appreciate your warnin'.'

O'Mara grinned again, looking at the others with sardonic pleasure. Mallon concluded, 'We'll take care of them Or'nge bastards. As far as you're concerned, you keep right where you are with your nose to the ground. When the time comes you get that guy Moore. There's an Armalite waitin' for you. Soon as you do the job the weapon comes back to me, OK?'

O'Mara asked, 'An' I get paid?'

'You're back on the payroll, so you get paid. Only if you screw it there's plenty queuin' up to take your fee.'

O'Mara grinned a third time, now openly challenging his two reticent colleagues. The small hit man stared back, measuring his rival. O'Mara then said, 'Aye, but what about Hillsborough?'

Mallon rolled his pencil in his fingers. 'That's nothin' to do with you. You just carry out orders.' He rose and looked down at the prodigal volunteer with distaste. 'An' if you hear somethin' else, you come straight here.'

O'Mara agreed to do so. There was nothing more to be said. He rose. His manic energy made it impossible for him now to remain in the dim smoke-filled room.

Mallon said, 'Dermot, give him his gun, then get him out of here.' He held up his pencil and pointed. 'O'Mara, you may have saved your neck this time, but you try any more of your tricks an' there'll be no more deals.'

O'Mara knew it was not simply his fee that others in the Provisionals would be queuing for. He turned on his way out of the room and replied, 'Sure, but you needed this an' no mistake.'

Mallon gazed at him, his eyes suddenly weary with the toll of long years of urban warfare. 'Fucken bollocks!' he said as O'Hanlon closed the door behind them.

When Wilson called at the safe house the next evening, it was with the knowledge that his guest had twice visited Black's Bar in the Falls Road, and on the second occasion had returned with a small case of the kind carried by uillean pipes players, plastered with beer mats and folk club stickers from all over the country, whose contents were not difficult to predict. The way in which the gunman now tried to conceal his exhilaration behind an impression of amity and enthusiasm was more transparent even than before. Wilson was happy to play an appropriate part, confiding that he felt unwilling to share his mood since his own dealings had proved so far unsuccessful, and he felt only despair at the way things were moving, both in the organization and in the province itself.

'Still,' he said, as O'Mara listened with unusual attentiveness, 'your part's straightforward enough. I've some good news for you.' The gunman realized what he was about to say. 'Moore and the girl are due back on the tenth. I'll give you details when the time's right. You'll take them both as quietly as possible.'

O'Mara's eyes were black as he said, 'An' quiet it'll be.'

Wilson added, 'I'll personally see to it that you're armed. And as I said, I'll pay you when the job's done.'

O'Mara said nothing more, and Wilson drove on in silence. When they reached their destination, where a large tent and a number of men in Fforde's uniform marked the site of another temporary training camp set up by Reverend Fadden and his colleagues in the mountains between Ballymena and Larne, Wilson stopped the engine and looked across at his companion. 'Pat,' he said solemnly, 'I hope I can trust you to do your bit.'

O'Mara refused to look back. For a moment he was torn between his wayward affection for the big man and his desperate urge for self-reliance which had somehow, once more, become confused with the struggle of his fellow Catholics. He said, 'Sure you can, Sam, I'm your man.'

Wilson smiled. 'I'm glad to hear you say it. These are troubled times. I'd hate to think I'd trusted the wrong man.'

They left the car and crossed to the tent where O'Mara picked up a waiting rifle and addressed the assembled company.

It so happened that while O'Mara was instructing the Protestant volunteers in the use of the Kalashnikov, one of his Provisional colleagues, the elder O'Hanlon, was ambushed by two hooded men in Norglen Parade. Shortly afterwards, the Protestants themselves were said to have killed him in reprisal for attacks on their own number. At that point O'Hanlon was still alive.

The news reached O'Mara when he had returned to Belfast and had put his feet up to watch the early evening bulletin on television, with a beer and a cigarette. He began trembling immediately and spent the rest of the evening and the whole of the night pacing the house in darkness, wondering how much his pardon would be worth if the murder turned out to be more than a coincidence.

Two days later O'Hanlon's body was discovered in a ditch off the Horseshoe Road. It bore all the authentic signs of a sectarian killing. Those two days, though, had been spent, not in the hands of the Ulster Volunteers, but in a special cell at the chief interrogation centre in East Belfast. The bullet had not entered the Catholic's bruised head until he had finally confessed that the IRA were planning simultaneously to boycott the Hillsborough summit, with a demand that the talks – of whose specific nature they had only a slender idea – were postponed and reappointed, and to despatch their most lethal force to Cremorgan on the evening of 11 August to annihilate their Protestant adversaries.

In that same period of time the victims of two other 'reprisals' found their way to the interrogation centre: less prominent Republicans, whose resistance to pain was more easily overcome. Their lists of IRA and INLA members tallied with and added to the information Roy Moore had left in the Irish Alliance Bank in Royal Avenue on the day of his departure to Sligo. This, in turn, was a corroboration of knowledge gathered over many months throughout Ireland by members of the combined Intelligence services of three nations.

In his safe house off the Donegall Road, Patrick O'Mara's renewed confidence had quickly turned to dismay. There was no telling now who would survive the days ahead.

Chapter 15

When he had dropped O'Mara after his last training stint, Wilson drove across the city and parked off Ladas Drive. He then went on foot to that same stark building he had been taken to whilst still nominally a prisoner, and from where he had been receiving orders since his release. It had remained unscathed during the recent unrest; the area was heavily patrolled and strongly fortified. He was checked in by an armed guard who accompanied him down to the office. He knocked on the outer door and entered alone. The thin figure of the Commander of British Intelligence Operations stood in profile talking to his private secretary. He turned and greeted Wilson in his customary forthright manner. The latter smiled. In a curious way, it pleased him to think that while he had been dangerously involved outside, this academic character had been installed here, giving purpose and direction to apparently random events. When he was ushered into the office he was equally gratified to find that nothing had changed: the desk was still tidily arranged, with the small chairs, bearing the faint imprint of other occupants, ranged neatly around it.

'I wanted to see you in person, Sam, before the balloon goes up, so to speak. I've been meeting all those working at top level over the last few days. I had our American friends in yesterday. I have to admit I still find their mercenary demeanour somewhat daunting.'

Wilson replied, 'They certainly seem to have been busy lately.'

The Commander sat behind his desk and motioned his subordinate to do likewise. 'Everyone has been working hard, Sam. No one has disappointed us.'

He paused while the obligatory tea tray was brought in by the secretary. As Wilson took his cup he could not help contrasting the even manner of the Englishman with the fanatical intensity of the leaders of Emerald. He inquired, 'I take it we're on schedule, sir?'

The Commander replied confidently, 'There's a chap under interrogation at this very moment who should let us know once and for all. As it is, we have enough to go on. I personally have no doubts that we're on target.'

Wilson felt a thrill of anticipation. Even his superior betrayed a hint of excitement as he said this, though he concealed it with an air of confidentiality. 'But first things first. Anything you want to ask me yourself?'

Wilson paused before he said, 'Actually there are a couple of points I'd like to raise concerning my work, sir.' The Commander waited for him to go on. Wilson was not afraid to show a sign of humanity. 'First, if all goes according to plan, I should have to oversee the disposal of an innocent man with no political connections whatever. Unless this is absolutely necessary, I would like to perform my own duty before it takes place.'

The Commander nodded sympathetically but replied in a dispassionate voice, 'It's as simple as this. I'm afraid we can't afford to run any risk of loose ends. You must not break cover at any point.'

Wilson drew a breath and said, 'Then I have no choice in the matter.'

The Commander drank from his cup and again resumed an informal manner. 'What else is on your mind?'

'It also concerns disposal, sir, though I understand the necessity in this case. What happens to our absentees on their return?'

The Commander folded his hands and said, 'I should have raised the point myself. I'm afraid we must act clinically here also. I've received certain news concerning the nature of their relationship which puts the issue beyond doubt. As you know, there is a cottage in the mountains. I can think of no better scene for a crime of passion. You must make sure your chap is there on the morning of the twelfth. I will take care of the rest.'

Wilson assented, 'Right sir.'

The Commander now seemed anxious to dismiss the other's personal role. 'But these are minor details. I can't impress upon you enough how important it is now that you understand how closely we are all working as a team in the wider context. Let me give you a few illustrations while you're here.'

Wilson listened as his superior then spoke at length about strategic arrangements which had been made over recent weeks. His own brief was so specifically delimited that he was flattered that it had been thought appropriate to inform him of affairs outside his domain. It was consistent with the subtle manner in which the Commander had liaised operations in Ulster from the early stages of planning and recruitment to the present time. Wilson found himself thinking that if the political mandarins in whose service he worked had treated their negotiations with even a modicum of the Commander's vision, success would be assured.

Eventually the Commander finished his lecture. His listener, who had throughout asked only pertinent questions and restrained his sense of ebullience, gave voice to it now. 'Sir, I just hope the politicians will take full advantage.'

The Commander relaxed his tone. 'Sam, I was asked to undertake a certain task in your country. And, with the help of men like yourself, that is what I have done. In a few days' time we will know whether or not we have succeeded. Howsoever the powers that be make use of our endeavours is not our concern.'

He noted Wilson's momentarily disappointed expression and decided to continue. 'It goes without saying that we all share a common cause, and that that cause is rooted in our fundamental belief in freedom and democracy. We must be grateful that our senior allies in the west have, over the years, proved so eager to uphold these values. Beyond that, we must leave political discussion to those who make it their trade. Our province is action, Sam, and we are trained solely to that end.'

Wilson now seemed satisfied. He said, 'Sir, thank you for all you have done.' He stood up to leave. 'If you'll excuse me now, I'll go and get on with the job.'

The Commander also stood and proffered his hand. Wilson shook it firmly, again recalling the occasion when he had last seen his superior. 'Everything will proceed as planned, Sam,' the Commander concluded. 'The twentieth century must come to this country whether it will or no.'

They said goodbye, and Wilson made his way up from the basement. He was checked again by the guard before he was allowed to leave.

He had been in the secluded office for over half an hour. Emerging into the light of day he was, even more than on his arrival, struck by the aura of calm and insularity within it. As he drove across Belfast, carefully avoiding those routes where he might encounter any hostile mobs, he was no less susceptible to the influence of the city than was O'Mara in his safe house. It had always been rough and provincial, suffering a scale of deprivation rarely experienced in mainland towns. But now its condition was such that it seemed to have reached a point of no return. He recalled the Commander's last address and felt genuinely moved; he told himself that if the price for transforming the battered province into a territory without poverty or civil strife was the sacrifice of its more violent citizens, then it was little enough to pay. If, in the process, there were some unfortunate victims it could not be helped.

In Sligo, on the west coast of the Republic, while events in Ulster were moving so rapidly, the holiday season had passed much as usual, with radiant sunsets, ceilidhs, and good fishing. On the evening of 9 August, two figures could be seen walking along the harbour as the sun fell over the Atlantic. It would have seemed a romantic interlude except that, by their manner, it was plain that they were both more concerned with their own thoughts than with each other's company.

They had left the province in a febrile state that had not diminished. On their arrival in the seaside town, Moore had insisted on taking Mary to the local hospital where he had paid for an extensive private medical examination which revealed that she had sustained no internal damage and that the embryo – which was confirmed to be there within her – had not been harmed in her ordeal. He had now had several days to reflect on the significance of what had happened. Once she had resisted his initial suggestion that she consider an abortion, his attitude had steadily softened. On the long picturesque journey over the mountains by the lakes of Fermanagh, whenever he had glanced at her sleeping fitfully beside him, he had felt a resurgence of his instinct to protect her; and in spite of his reticence, it had grown in him ever since.

During this time, they had shared the same bed in a first floor suite at the Glencar House hotel on the outskirts, posing as man and wife. The evidence of her maltreatment did nothing to diminish the pretence. Mary remained fragile, although, as her wounds healed with the effect of the sea air and long hours of rest, she found she could at least think more clearly. She was relieved at the way Moore treated her, but she was still suspicious, aware of how heavily she relied on him. And while the mere thought of O'Mara made her overlook her fears of dependence, she could not help but regret that she had ever been forced into the situation.

A convenient outlet for her bitterness had appeared in the person of the hotel manager, with whom her companion was often found drinking. She knew that, while he talked with a strong Sligo accent and put on all the indigenous airs to be expected of him, he was in the same camp as Moore, which was why they had come there. Since they spent most of their time within easy reach of the hotel, they were constantly under his scrutiny. He made her realize that she, too, was a renegade in her own country, and she was quick to resent it.

For all this, she and Moore still came to share a kind of tenderness, sustained by the idea of the child they had conceived. At night, in the cover of darkness, lulled by the soothing rhythm of the sea's turn and fall and the pliant warmth of their bodies, they made love slowly and openly, as if in bed at least they could express what was uncomplicated between them. But inevitably, the next day, their sense of claustrophobia returned, trapped among the carefree ranks of tourists from all over Europe.

This sullen mood had reached a pitch now, after ten days in Sligo. When they had changed after strolling by the harbour, and it was time to go down for dinner, Moore went out onto the balcony with a glass of whiskey and said over his shoulder, 'You go down now, I'm not into it tonight.'

She came out to him in a white summer dress with a black crocheted shawl over her shoulders. 'Och come on now, you don't mean it.'

He said moodily, 'I need a break.'

She wondered if she should not leave him alone but she decided to challenge him instead. She snatched his glass and finished his whiskey. 'If you're not goin', nor am I.' To anyone listening from neighbouring balconies, their impression of a married couple could only have been enhanced.

Moore was still taken aback by the vehemence of her reaction as he watched her go back into the bedroom and fumble in his jacket pockets. She held up his car keys and made towards the door. 'What the hell are you doing?' he called as he followed her through into the corridor. 'You never told me you could drive.'

'You never asked.'

He looked into her fiery dark eyes and felt a sudden urge to throw off his sense of responsibility. He wanted to relax; he was tired of treating her as a prisoner whose freedom he was instructed to negotiate. 'So where are we going?' he asked as they descended in the lift.

She said, 'I don't mind. Up into the mountains. Anywhere out of this.'

They left the hotel and walked to his company car parked a few streets away. As soon as they got in, she turned on the engine and pulled off noisily. Moore swore to himself as she drove with the naivety of someone who had not been at the wheel for some time.

When they reached the winding road into the mountains, he could not help being reminded of Buncrana; it strengthened his reckless impulse. He looked at her, frowning as she negotiated the tight corners, and laughed, 'You'll get us both killed if you're not careful.' In response she accelerated round another bend, throwing him against her, then eased down as they hit a steep climb.

Night had fallen over the west coast. Curlews hovered and cried above them. The winds raced from the Atlantic; the sea was a mass of white surf and flickering moonlight. To the other side, the mountains towered in a jagged pile glistening silver with waterfalls. They drove on until they came to a small inn set under a rocky face. Mary pulled in to the car park and turned off the engine.

Moore stepped out and sniffed the air. He looked back in the direction they had come, past Ben Bulben, where the road dropped craggily to the dunes, the fairy tale castle of Classebaun, and the glimmering lights of Sligo.

Mary came to his side and pointed along the coast. 'That's where they got Mountbatten.'

Moore sighed, 'You have such tact.' His thoughts passed briefly to another, more recent assassination, but he quickly resolved to put it out of his mind.

She shrugged her shoulders and went off into the inn, where she ordered salmon sandwiches and pints of Guinness. Moore followed her. Looking round him approvingly at the homely interior, he sat down by the fire burning in a stone hearth, stretched his legs, and seemed ready to fall asleep.

His companion, however, grew more animated with every minute. 'I reckon it's about time we got a few things straight, don't you?' she said as she sat facing him.

He sighed again heavily. He had expected something like this. He did not want to respond. After a moment's consideration while the food and drink were put down beside them, she went on, 'See, I can't afford to get into any more trouble.'

At length he replied, 'I understand that. I wouldn't let it happen.' He avoided her gaze. Ever since her attack he had felt vulnerable if she appeared to accuse him.

She leant forward and forced him to look at her. 'You mean we will live together?'

'I suppose it might have to come to it.' He looked away again into the fire. 'I can't say I've got any reason to think it would work.'

Although he had already told her the details of his marriage, she was determined not to let him spoil her mood. 'Havin' a wee 'un would change all that.'

Moore finished his drink and ordered a second round for them both. 'I suppose you'd have it baptized?' he said with a renewed sense of irritation.

She laughed at him. 'Aye, a good wee Catholic soul fit to go to heaven.'

He kept a straight face. 'Folly and superstition.'

'Maybe. Even so, it's made this country what it is. Sure, you look around an' you'll find it's at the heart of everythin' that's good an' powerful. If you ask me, it always will be.'

Moore grew even more restive. 'You can talk like that while you're here but the moment we go home you keep your ideas to yourself. I happen to belong to a people who don't want your so-called goodness and power. And I'm sorry to disappoint you, but the truth is that as far as our country is concerned, we're never going to have to take it.'

She looked at him over the rim of her beer glass. 'You'd know more about that than me.' As she went on, he leant back in his chair as if he was not listening to her. 'Just 'cause I've got no choice but to try an' look after my own interests doesn't mean I don't care any more. I spent a lot of time workin' for what I believed in. As far as I'm concerned, there's only one country an' we're all part of it. An' it makes me ashamed to think what I've done. So don't you start tellin' me what I'm not allowed to say.'

He responded wrily. 'Spoken like a true martyr.' But he had no answer to her evident sincerity.

'All I'm sayin' is you treat me with respect. If I'm goin' to have your child that's the least I'm askin'.'

He allowed himself another glance at her. She was still sitting on the edge of her chair while he maintained his sullen posture. He felt almost compelled to tell her that even now he was not in a position to guarantee her future: he would not know his orders until they returned to Ulster. Instead he put out his hand to take hers and said merely, 'I'll do what I can.'

She pressed his hand, satisfied she had forced him, too, to be sincere. They finished their meal, washing down the succulent salmon with long cool draughts of stout.

Moore paid the bill and followed her out to the car. He insisted on driving now and took the road towards the coast north of the town. Mary pointed out of the window with an ingenuous enthusiasm. 'Drumcliffe churchyard. Yeats is buried there. "Cast a cold eye on life, on death, horseman pass by."'

He smiled as he concentrated on the winding road. Before long it skirted an old wooded demesne whose flint walls were broken by impressive gateways. Mary indicated an open gate and an empty lodge, saying suddenly, 'Turn down there.'

A few hundred yards along a narrow lane they came to a deserted strand enclosed by the woods. The sea rolled and crashed onto the gleaming sand. Mary got out and hurried off towards the waves. Moore sat in the car with the door open, smoking a cigar, as he watched her take her shoes off and paddle in the shallows. Now that there was nothing more to be said, he began again to share her exuberance; reflecting that it was a long time since he had found himself looking at life simply for the pleasure it could afford him. It had once been his sole occupation.

When she turned round and came back to the car, he was already stripped to the waist. 'Coming?' he asked, continuing to undress until he stood naked before her.

He grinned as she hesitated, the moon lighting his white body. 'Aye, aye, I'll come.' She began unzipping the back of her dress.

He walked off across the sand, leaving her to undress. She soon followed him. At the edge of the surf he turned. She ran ahead of him into the broken waves which surged swiftly past her dark figure, making her gasp with cold. Moore laughed and ran after her, leaping in the fringes. He fell. For moments he disappeared in the swirling shallows. She called out, a note of panic in her voice. Then he surfaced behind her, put an arm round her waist and dragged her down, shrieking with shock and delight. They wrestled in the surf, he bowling her over, she splashing water in his eyes, until the cold grew so intense that she was shivering like a child. He took her hand and led her back across the beach. He covered her in a blanket from the car, while he dried himself with his shirt.

When he looked up she seemed to be waiting, shivering, to be warmed, measuring his body as if they were about to fight. He grew aroused by her watching, so he stepped close to her again, put his hands on her cheeks and drew her lips to his. Still she shivered, but the salty warmth of her kiss confirmed his instinct. He lifted the blanket from her grasp, let it fall and pressed his body against hers. Later, he settled into his rhythm as the boughs above them creaked in the wind. They rocked together on the sand, her legs set apart, cradling him wholly in her, clutching his buttocks arched over her, running her nails over his back as they moved steadily faster, until with a violent shudder he came and her gasping turned to a cry of shock and delight, holding him in her while their bodies slowly grew still.

They lay in silence until the cold grew oppressive, then they put on their clothes and got into the car. They looked at one another, briefly, before they left the beach. Neither seemed unwilling now to confess how close they had become.

The next morning, after they had spent the night sleeping soundly in each other's arms, Moore woke to find her standing in the bathroom doorway drying her hair. She had a warm, jocose air.

'How'd you like to come to Mass?'

He laughed. 'You mean you're going?'

'Sure I am.'

He turned over again. 'Well, say a prayer for me then.'

She grinned. 'So I will. You need savin'. Your soul's as black as they come.'

Within half an hour she was in the dim interior of Sligo Cathedral, along with the holidaymakers and old people who attended the early weekday communion. She did not know why exactly she had come, but it was as much to recover a sense of her own roots beyond the current conflict, as to play with Moore's cynicism. She did in fact kneel to pray, but in spite of the smell of incense, the candles on the altar, and the loveliness of stained glass, it had been too long since she had tried to quieten her own mind for her to become involved now in any kind of dialogue. This did not trouble her. It was the ceremony she wanted to experience, to sit with others in the hushed church, sharing a common inheritance. While she watched them take communion, she thought of the life growing within her and how she would become responsible for its future. It made her think, once more, of her father, whose body would before long be buried in the soil of the divided country she still cherished. When she eventually walked out into the light of day, it was with a new resource of determination.

Meanwhile Moore had been occupied with more mundane affairs. A call had come through for him from Belfast. On being informed by the manager that a business associate was on the line, he had hurried down to his private office. The brief was unequivocal; he was to return to Ulster immediately with the girl and wait at home for further orders. As he passed him in the lobby he nodded to the Sligo man, who seemed to know precisely what had occurred.

By the time Mary returned, he had packed their bags and was sitting in an armchair prepared to leave. He told her that they had to be back in the province that day. She was momentarily shocked; she went onto the balcony and stood gazing out to sea, then came back in and made herself ready, with the same resolve she had felt on leaving the cathedral. They went out to the car and packed the boot. While she waited in the passenger's seat, Moore settled with the manager. Then they left Sligo as hurriedly as they had arrived.

On the journey back, Mary announced that she was not prepared to go into renewed hiding at Moore's home unless he first took her to see her father in the Belfast City Hospital. He at first refused, saying it would be an unnecessary risk. But she was so adamant that he eventually agreed, reasoning that an hour's diversion could not cause too many problems. And besides, he was curious to see the old man who would, if he lived long enough, become the grandfather of his child.

When they reached the border, and had been strictly searched by paratroopers, they drove swiftly along the motorway to Belfast. Their reaction to what they saw on the journey was inevitable. Once they had left the peaceful, falsely reassuring countryside and driven into the city along the Donegall Road – not a stone's throw from O'Mara's lodging – the evidence of unrest was all around them. There were barricades across the side streets. Clusters of armoured vehicles stood ready for an assault, while crowds of rioters gathered at the corners; young children in baggy trousers and heavy boots, descendants of the Tartan gangs, were conspicuous among them. It was plain that sectarian sentiments in the city had reached a new pitch. They both realized that in the present climate it would not have happened accidentally.

When they arrived at the hospital they hastened along the long corridors to a side ward, where six old men were propped up in their beds among the usual miscellany of flowers, fruit and cards. John McKee lay against his pillows, his gaunt face surrounded by straggling grey hair, his shoulders heaving as he drew breath with great difficulty. Mary went quickly to him while Moore remained at the Sister's office to ascertain for himself if there was any hope of recovery, and if not, how long he was expected to live. Then he joined Mary at the bedside.

The old man was looking at his daughter with a weary recognition. According to the staff, his prognosis was uncertain; he could go on another week or six months, depending on the strength of his spirit. So far he had shown an unusual resilience to the effects of cancer in both lungs.

It shocked Moore to see the family resemblance so strangely drawn, as the girl sat holding the old man's hand, answering the accusation in his eyes with her own tears. Her father's sense of time was not accurate; he knew only that he had been deserted by her, not for how long. But such was the generosity of his spirit that his reproachful stare soon turned to a weak smile of gratitude.

Mary introduced her lover nervously. She had it in mind to tell her father of her condition, but the sight of the rosary beads clutched tightly in his hand, and the honest gaze with which he held her eyes, deterred her.

McKee glanced at Moore and nodded. 'So you're the one that's kept me wee girl from me,' he said, speaking laboriously between short shallow breaths.

Moore smiled and replied, 'I'm afraid so. If there's anything I can do for you . . .'

McKee would keep his pride until the moment of his death. 'I can look after meself,' he said without bitterness.

Moore waited to see if Mary would make any attempt to explain her absence, but she said only, 'I'm goin' away soon, da. I want to be sure you're alright.'

McKee drew a sharp breath. 'Och, have you come all the

way to tell me that now?'

She went on, 'I've got meself into a wee bit of trouble. I can't stay on at the farm.'

Now his initial reprehensiveness returned as quickly as it had vanished. 'Sure, you wouldn't be happy till you'd brought a bad name to the place.' They said nothing. Very quickly the pall of a hospital bedside loomed over them in their silence. 'Still, it's yours now, you know that,' McKee said eventually, looking directly ahead of him. 'It's not much, sure, but it's all I have to leave you.'

The effort of this seemed to take the last breath from his body. His head lolled to one side. Mary leant forward and whispered, 'Da, I can't be sure how far I'll have to go.'

He made a final attempt to speak, now looking back at them with another kind of accusation in his deep blue gaze. 'This was God's country once. It's the devil's now.'

Then he closed his eyes and sighed. The two visitors glanced at one another and rose from his bedside. Mary kissed his brow. They turned away and left the ward. A nurse passed them as they reached the door, looking pointedly at the girl, as if to neglect her father for so long and then to come only to hurt him was as much as could be expected of her.

Moore said, 'Come on now, there's nothing more to be done.'

She let him lead her along the maze of corridors towards the light of a gloomy afternoon. At the entrance, Moore saw she was about to break down and said quickly, 'He'll be looked after, don't worry about it.'

She drew in her breath and replied, 'Aye, like the way he always was. Jeez, I'm sick.'

They drove through the same bleak streets into the countryside to Templepatrick. They felt even more oppressed now. The echo of the old man's words seemed to haunt each derelict site, each smouldering barricade, while the rioters and armoured cars performed their vicious dance across the city.

Chapter 16

On the morning of Friday 11 August, Jim Knight was woken by his alarm shortly after eight o'clock. The semi-detached house on the Newtonards estate had been home for himself and his family during his duty in Ulster. The job had involved him in various Health Inspections, from the kitchens of primary schools to the seats of regional government.

He proceeded to the bathroom, where he washed and shaved. There were still a few weeks of the summer holidays to run, which ensured that his children remained asleep next door. His wife followed him downstairs. Tying her dressing gown round her waist, she walked along the short hallway to the kitchen. He appeared at the breakfast table a few minutes later and ate the meal of eggs and bacon that it was her daily habit to cook for him. Then, kissing her cheek, he took his jacket and walked out to his Chevette parked in the road.

His wife waved to him from the porch as he pulled away. When she closed the door, she noticed a silver Cortina parked some yards up the road which drew off shortly after her husband. She waved at a neighbour taking in the milk and thought no more of it, went back to make the bed and to dress herself before the children awoke.

Knight left the sprawl of Newtonards and swung towards Comber. Strangford Lough lay below him. The main Hillsborough road stretched beyond the rolling countryside of small hills and patchwork fields struck by the early morning sun. He glanced at the view with a particular pleasure. This was one of his last scheduled assignments. He would soon be free to return to the land he knew. He could afford to appreciate the finer aspects of the province. He checked in the glove compartment that his papers were intact, including his security pass and directions. In his briefcase were his sample apparatus, notebooks, and other equipment necessary for a thorough inspection. He was an able, conscientious man. He expected promotion on his return to the mainland for his work in Ulster.

As he drove on, glancing from time to time in the mirror, he noticed that a silver Cortina he had spotted earlier seemed to be keeping deliberately behind him. He accelerated over a mile of straight road. The car remained with him. Then he drove slowly for a further mile. Instead of passing, the Cortina settled some fifty yards behind and followed at a sedate pace. Knight turned onto the Hillsborough road. It was then that the car drew level and eased past. A luminous sign appeared in the rear window, POLICE STOP. The driver was waving him down. Beside him he could see another man in an RUC uniform. There was a third passenger in the back of the car.

Many thoughts raced through his mind as Knight slowed down, from fears that he would be prosecuted for speeding, to fancies that some disaster had befallen his family at home. He stopped as the Cortina pulled into the verge. The front seat passenger got out and came back to him, leaning on the window frame, a well-built man with benign features, the stripes of a sergeant on his sleeve. Knight felt immediately reassured.

'Mr Knight?'

'Yes?'

'We've been ordered to direct you to Hillsborough, sir.'

'But I know the way,' Knight said shortly; his sense of relief turned quickly to irritation. 'And if I didn't, I have directions.'

'Perhaps you do, sir. But I'm afraid there have been some changes in security arrangements. In fact I have been ordered to ride with you while my colleagues go on ahead. I'm sorry for any inconvenience, sir.'

'Look, I hardly think this is necessary.'

'I assure you it is, sir. There's a blanket check on all travellers to the castle. Some kind of scare. You won't be admitted unless we travel with you.'

Knight pouted as he looked at the large candid face close to his. 'I suppose I have no choice then. Climb in, Sergeant.'

'A moment, sir.'

The man returned to the Cortina and spoke with the driver, then strode back to Knight's car and settled in the passenger seat. They had not been driving for ten minutes when he said briskly, 'Left turn here, sir. Follow the car. Diversion for security purposes.'

Knight turned left as he was told. Whatever was taking

place, it was clearly cause for more than mere irritation. The new road was narrow, the surface poor. His mouth became dry, his hands began to tremble. The silver car drove on ahead, then came to an abrupt halt.

'Right, sir. If you'd just stop here.'

'I beg your pardon?'

'Just stop.'

Knight pulled to a halt behind the Cortina, parked on the grass verge running over a small ditch. There were no other vehicles in sight. The sun touched the trees and hedgerows with gold.

'Now sir, do as I say and you'll come to no harm.'

The burly man climbed out of the Chevette and told Knight to do likewise. As they stood waiting for the others, the Health Inspector decided to call their bluff.

'Right, Sergeant, I am going to make a formal complaint about this. I want your full name and number.'

The other said nothing, watching the driver of the Cortina climb out and open the back door for his passenger. They approached with an air of determination. The next thing Knight knew, the small driver was standing behind him with a revolver pressed against his spine.

'OK,' said the Sergeant, still in the same even voice, 'turn out your pockets.'

Without another word of protest, Knight again did as he was told. He had no idea who his captors were, or what they wanted from him, but he was resolved that he should come to no harm. The third person, an older man in civilian clothes, ducked into the Chevette and searched the interior until he discovered the security papers in the glove compartment. He also removed the briefcase. These he added to the small pile of possessions on the car roof.

'Right, this way.'

As Knight was hustled towards the Cortina, he saw the civilian climb into his car, put a briefcase of his own on the back seat and a set of papers in the glove compartment. The small man buried his property in the ditch. The Chevette then turned in the narrow road and drove off in the direction they had come.

The Health Inspector allowed himself to be bundled into the back seat of the Cortina; the small man climbed in beside him, keeping the gun pointed at his chest.

'Please, would you tell me who you are and what exactly is going on?' he asked.

Again there was no answer. The Sergeant put the car in gear and drove off down the road. The man with the gun was staring at him intently. Knight, who had managed to keep control of himself until now, began to panic. He considered all kinds of options, from flinging himself out of the door to trying to crash the car in the hope that he would survive. He sat shivering with the gun at his chest.

They drove only four or five miles before turning into a farmyard. No sooner had Knight been pushed from the car than he tried to run. The man with the gun caught him before he could leave the yard and spun him over expertly. The Sergeant then motioned to his colleague, drew his baton, and taking the hapless civil servant by the scruff of the neck, pushed the stick between his legs and, turning it parallel to the ground, pulled hard. In this fashion he ran him into a large derelict barn. There he was tied firmly with binder twine.

The farm seemed deserted. The barn was full of rotting hay, roosting birds and broken machinery. Knight sat, curled in on himself, a strip of gag burning his mouth, the bonds biting into his wrists and ankles.

Fforde drove steadily along the Hillsborough road in the stolen Chevette. In the glove compartment in front of him were his forged security papers, including a driving licence, all in Knight's name, but mounted with his own photographs. On the back seat his briefcase contained everything he needed for the job in hand. He was pleased at the smoothness of the operation so far. He was nonetheless nervous about what was to come.

In half an hour he had reached the small tidy village of Hillsborough with its period houses and hilly streets. He drove straight up to the great gates of the government property. There he pulled up at the sentry boxes manned by British Army personnel.

A soldier with hand radio and clipboard marched over. 'What's the name, sir?' he asked in a thick Scottish accent.

'Knight, Health Inspector.' Fforde proffered his pass.

The soldier took the document, glanced quickly at it and ticked the name on his board. He walked round to the front of the Chevette and checked the registration number which tallied with his records. He briefly searched the car, asked the passenger to step out and frisked him peremptorily, then inspected his briefcase. He inquired what was contained in a small metal canister and was told it was a solution necessary for the taking of bacterial swabs. The soldier asked no more but helped the visitor back into his car, then waved to another sentry who opened the gates electronically. Fforde resisted a strong urge to salute and proceeded into the grounds. The castle stood some 50 yards within the perimeter wall, a sandstone building resembling more a country house than a fortress. Its construction was probably contemporary with Cremorgan, though there the similarity ended. Hillsborough gleamed with new paintwork and elaborate restoration.

Fforde noticed both soldiers and RUC men with guns and radios patrolling the grounds. He was directed to the rear of the building into an area marked CAR PARK – VISITORS ONLY. He locked the car and with a steady gait walked to a small door designed for tradesmen, carrying his briefcase in one hand, his papers in the other.

'Stop there please!' A voice called sternly from behind. The muscles in his groin tightened; he turned quickly to see a tall guard approaching him. 'Move your car, please sir, it's too close to the house.'

Fforde smiled effusively, returned to the car, parked it where he was told, and retraced his steps, watched all the while by the armed policeman.

'Better there?' he inquired politely.

'Thank you sir.' The RUC man continued on his patrol.

Fforde was now at the rear entrance to the building which towered over him. He loosened his collar and looked up; a close circuit camera gazed down from the eaves. He rang the bell. After some moments he heard footsteps, the door opened, and another armed policeman faced him. He, too, checked the forged papers before allowing him entry, then motioned to a subordinate and said, 'Tell the chef to look lively. The Health Inspector has arrived.'

They walked along a short corridor and entered the kitchen, where the ceilings reverberated with the roar of extractors. The chef, a dour-looking, middle-aged character, dressed in his traditional garments, came to greet him.

'Knight,' said Fforde, 'pleased to meet you.'

'Hogg's the name. Same routine as usual, I suppose?'

Fforde hesitated, but quickly recovered. 'Well, we all tend to do things somewhat differently, old chap, but I'm sure it'll be along the same lines.'

The chef made a gesture of indifference then said, 'Well, anything you want, just ask me.'

Fforde took some papers from his briefcase, laid them on a nearby table, and made a cursory examination. The ritual was, for the most part, self-explanatory: sample-taking, regular inquiries. He saw that the sombre chef was watching him from a distance as he supervised his staff. Fforde said to him loudly, 'If you could just take me round the dry stores, cold room, food preparation areas and so on.'

'Certainly.' The chef conducted him on a tour of his kitchen with evident pride. Fforde took notes and, putting on a pair of transparent gloves, managed to make a passable imitation of taking samples from the stores.

'How many staff have you?' he asked then with an official air. He noted the answer and added, 'No difficulty catering for these numbers at the conference?'

Hogg smiled superciliously. 'You've seen the facilities yourself.'

Fforde said, 'Indeed. And I must say I'm favourably impressed. May I ask what you intend serving for luncheon?'

Hogg replied with the same affectation, 'I take it you mean the set menu. Egg Mayonnaise. Soupe Maigre. Sole Lyonnaise. Roast Fowl à l'Allemande. Boeuf en Daube à la Provençale. Pears Bonne Femme. Rice à l'Imperatrice.'

'Excellent. You make me wish I could be there myself. And what about this evening's dinner?'

'Beef salad. Conger soup. Fricandeau, Salmon au Citron.

Roast Saddle of Leveret. Apples à la Normande. Apple Tart. Assorted Cheesecakes.'

Fforde nodded appreciatively. 'Now I'd like to take a look at the ovens if I may, Mr Hogg.'

The chef willingly obliged. The General peered through the glass at the shoulders of beef and bacon cut into cubes cooking in a moist red wine marinade. He put his fingers to his lips and ostentatiously blew a silent kiss. The chef accepted it as his due.

'Well, that just leaves the instruments you will be using, Mr Hogg. Carving knives, ladles, spoons, forks, plates, you know what I mean.' Fforde was led to a long table covered with cooking utensils where he said nonchalantly, 'Just take a few swabs, what. Satisfy my superiors.'

'What are you looking for exactly?'

'Oh, bacteria, that sort of thing. Can't be too careful, old chap.'

The chef scowled and watched over Fforde's shoulder as he opened the briefcase and took out his small canister and a packet of swabs and test tubes. He lifted a knife from the table and broke the seal on the canister, then with shaking fingers tried to loosen the cap. All the while his breath was short. Beads of perspiration stood out on his forehead. The chef grew impatient and said, 'Look, if this is the last thing, perhaps you'd excuse me. I am very busy.'

'Of course, old chap, by all means.'

Hogg returned to his ovens. Fforde heaved a sigh of relief. He at last managed to remove the cap on the canister. He dipped the swabs one by one and delicately laced the carving knives, the ladles, the cutlery. When he had finished, he closed the canister, corked the swabs in their tubes, placed the whole apparatus in a plastic bag which he sealed with care and packed it in the briefcase.

When he had removed his gloves and was washing his arms and hands in a nearby sink, the chef returned. 'So that's it then?'

'Indeed,' said Fforde in a faltering voice. 'All present and correct.'

'I take my work very seriously, Mr Knight. I look upon the

hygiene of my kitchen as a matter of personal honour.'

Fforde replied, 'I'm sure you do, Mr Hogg, I'm sure you do.'

At 10.30 the General politely took his leave and walked unhurriedly to the car park, climbed into the Chevette and drove down to the gates. The guards waved him through. Within an hour he had parked the car in one of the large anonymous car parks near the Dublin Road, a short distance from the centre of Belfast. He then walked to the Central Station and caught the Express Bus for the Republic. He sat gazing out of the window barely able to contain himself. When he reached Clones, he strode proudly down a long street once named after his ancestors, but changed in 1922 to commemorate an obscure Republican killed in the uprisings. In his mind a Unilateral Declaration of Independence for Ulster was soon to become a reality. There would be many streets in years to come bearing the historic name of Fforde.

The kitchens at Hillsborough had become a scene of anger and confusion. While Fforde was on his way to Belfast, the chef was informed that there would be no visitors for whom he should prepare his extravagant fare. The venue for the conference had had to be changed for security purposes. On the various kitchen utensils Fforde had swabbed, a thin film of sodium hydrochloride evaporated, while the chef and his minions protested to one another about the total lack of civility and consideration on the part of Her Majesty's Government.

At the deserted farm there was no such disturbance. Fforde's orders had been explicit: his two right-hand men were to wait until midday, then dispose of the Health Inspector in such a way that he would not be found for many weeks to come. Then they were to drive back to Cremorgan for the meeting due to begin at six o'clock.

By mid-morning there had been no hitch in the plan. Knight had fallen into a kind of trance, numb with shock. His two captors paid no attention to him. Wilson had removed his sergeant's jacket and was sitting on a milkchurn smoking a cigarette. The silent Mitchell had left the barn to take guard at the concealed entrance to the yard. The minutes passed laboriously. The only sound came from the birds in the rafters. The thoughts of one man were unknown to the other. Though Knight's apprehension and Mitchell's singleminded intent would have come as no surprise, Wilson's private cogitations were a different matter.

The sun rose brilliantly in the sky, clearing the last remaining clouds from the day before, though in the barn only a few dusty shafts filtered through the cracks in the roof. There, the sparrows and starlings continued their territorial disputes. The smell of hay mixed with decayed compost and the odd scuffling of a rat made it an oppressive prison. Knight was sweating profusely. His nose was blocked and his limbs were numb. He could not come to terms with the fact that on a routine morning, filled with thoughts of his return home, he should end up in this purgatory. He could only listen to the panic within him, thinking brokenly of his family, all he had planned, all he had failed to do. He still had no idea what was happening, or why it had involved him, but he was certain of one thing: the bitter feuds of Ulster had caught another victim.

Wilson glanced at him as he had many times, then at his watch. He rose from his perch and, checking the gag and bonds, left the barn. Mitchell returned in his place and gazed coldly at the trussed prisoner. Knight quailed. In spite of all that had happened, he was still strangely consoled by the big man's presence. His companion had the ruthless bearing of a murderer. He had said nothing throughout the morning; there was no telling what he would do.

It was a few minutes before twelve when Wilson returned to the dim recess of the barn. Mitchell looked up quickly. He, too, now consulted his watch. Both men nodded. They approached the prisoner and stood over him as he peered up in fear.

Wilson took his legs and turned him round so that he faced a broad stack of hay. Then he stood back, lifted his jacket and put it on. Mitchell glanced at him again, took out his gun, a Walther 9 millimetre, removed the magazine, checked it, replaced it, and flipped the action back. A bullet jumped into the breech. He released the safety catch and pressed the muzzle against Knight's neck.

The captive turned his head against the pull of the gag and looked up at his executioner. The nape of his neck was smooth and white in one of the shafts of light, his eyes were a glimmering green. Mitchell hesitated, as if considering the mute appeal for mercy. Then he pressed the trigger. In the same moment a bullet from another revolver entered the back of Mitchell's head and exploded in the centre of his brain. He slumped forward over his victim, covering his face with the detritus of his own skull.

Wilson stepped forward to make sure that both were dead. The gun was still in Mitchell's grasp as his nerves conducted their last bizarre dance. Beneath him lay Knight's body still gagged and bound. The big man did not trouble to cover them with hay, as had been the General's plan for the single corpse, but turned on his heel and hurried out to the car.

He then drove straight to Belfast. He stopped at an address in the city long enough to make a call to the safe house in Sandy Row. He informed the Catholic gunman still installed there that a gun would be delivered to him that evening and he should proceed to Ballymacford the next morning to account for his victims. He agreed to meet at the house in two days' time.

Wilson would not be at that meeting. Changing his clothes, he threw a few belongings in a holdall and drove to Aldergrove. A seat on the next shuttle to Heathrow was immediately arranged for him. By four in the afternoon he was in London, where he would stay until it was deemed safe for him to return to Ireland.

He did not know that shortly after he had left the scene, the innocent man who had apparently been murdered recovered consciousness for a matter of seconds – long enough to feel the weight of a dead man over him, and smell the odour of his broken skull, to hear the birds still squabbling in the eaves where the sunshafts fell mistily – and then disappeared into darkness for good.

Chapter 17

Aldergrove was originally a military airfield and it still shared its facilities with the adjoining RAF base. On the morning of 11 August, while the normal flow of civilian traffic continued uninterrupted, a small number of official aircraft arrived, whose passengers then proceeded by helicopter, not to Hillsborough, but to British Government Headquarters at Stormont, for a summit conference which was to determine the future of Ulster.

The agenda indicated that the talks were to span three days, though a general agreement was to be signed that evening. At a specified late hour, journalists stationed in the province would be called to a press conference at Stormont where they would be furnished with broad details of the resolution and its consequences for the people of Ireland. It was also planned by those allies who had masterminded the whole operation that another kind of announcement would be made shortly afterwards. Together the two pieces of news would serve to ensure the acceptance of a new, momentous policy throughout the island.

While the last helicopter landed on Stormont's immaculately groomed lawns, a 38 hundredweight Ford Transit van pulled away from Gough Army Barracks and headed along the main road towards the border with County Monaghan. When it reached the checkpoint barriers, it received automatic clearance from both British soldiers and Gardai, and travelled on into the Republic.

The van arrived at the Cremorgan estate late in the afternoon. Its passengers were not furniture removal men as the motif on the side panels suggested, and any search of the visible contents would confirm. Nor, indeed, were they American tourists in search of their Irish roots. The two CIA mercenaries who had been on active service in the country for the best part of four months, and who were engaged on their last, vital mission, were as cool-minded and secretive as they drove among Fforde's dwindling forests as they had been when they first arrived. In the unlikely event of failure, regular forces could accomplish their present task conventionally in weeks to come. But the essence of the combined operation in Ireland had, throughout its course, been an emphasis on secrecy and the power of deception. This attitude was about to be taken to its logical conclusion.

The vehicle which they manoeuvred into place on a small track just below the summit of a wooded knoll, known as Sentry Hill, three miles north of Cremorgan House, had been specially prepared by the British Army Advanced Vehicle Unit in Essex: a twin rearwheeled transit, with a detachable van section, fitted with hydraulic rams activated by the power take-off from the engine. When lowered, the pick-up section could be detached and driven away, leaving the van like a large box standing on its jacks.

The mercenaries' final brief with the Commander in his Belfast office had been straightforward, the last rehearsal of an action for which they had prepared themselves throughout their time in Ulster. In the van lay a concealed section 18 inches deep, protruding over the cab. Within this, a Whistler missile had been secreted: a top US infantry weapon designed for the European war zone, three foot long with a maximum speed of 700 miles per hour and a range of five miles. The compartment also contained an SLR rifle with image intensifier, a laser launching gun, and two NBC protective suits. The men had been ordered to drive the pick-up away from the van on the concealed vantage point overlooking Cremorgan and to remove the front panel of the missile compartment. One was then to retire with the laser gun some 30 yards from the van and conceal himself in a suitable hiding place. The other was to make his way, with the rifle, undetected through the woods of the demesne down to the banks of the River Finn which flowed into Fforde's lake. In these positions they were to wait until dusk, when it was confidently predicted that the Provisional IRA's most efficient fighting units, despatched with their most prestigious weapons, would make an attack on Cremorgan to annihilate the crack forces of their adversaries.

1700 hours, 11 August. General Fforde, in full battledress complete with medals, had been waiting in his dining hall for two hours. All the members of Emerald's committees had arrived, and been duly informed of the General's successful exploits at Hillsborough that morning. There were reports of considerable activity at Government Headquarters, but these were dismissed as the Secretary of State's personal preparations for the summit. The mood of the gathering was such that only their own actions appeared of any real significance. The higher ranks of the military force began to arrive on schedule. Fforde himself moved from group to group, clapping his men heartily on the shoulder and plying them with port and whiskey. He was in his best form, and they responded to him eagerly. Though inwardly troubled by the absence of his two right-hand men, he was determined not to allow this to affect his behaviour. He was confident they would arrive sooner or later with a suitable explanation. This was the hour when he must assume the mantle of a leader; there could be no room for personal weakness.

The agenda for the meeting consisted of a speech by the General, which would include detailed descriptions of both political and military strategy for the next weeks, and a statement by the Reverend Fadden on the essential role of propaganda in the campaign, designed to rouse the spirits of the company with fiery rhetoric. There would then be a series of toasts proposed by committee members. Finally there would be a separation into small groups to discuss specific tactics and their employment. After the meeting the men would return to the north along several minor routes.

At 1815 hours, Fforde decided he could wait no longer to inaugurate the proceedings. He stood at the centre of three oak tables and called for attention. Emerald's final meeting was underway.

In the small town of Castleblaney, 20 miles from the estate, another gathering had been taking place throughout the day, but in a manner designed to attract the least attention from the local citizens. At dusk, a radio signal came through from the Provisional IRA's Belfast Headquarters that the time had come to move out. The information they had received concerning Cremorgan and its visitors had been checked and rechecked since the disappearance of Dermot O'Hanlon and others, but no inconsistencies had been discovered. The message to Castleblaney was simultaneously picked up at Gough Barracks and relayed to the American hidden on Sentry Hill, who in turn signalled to his companion stationed by the river below. Some 80 men, all of whom were seconded from different Republican battalions, made their way from safe houses in the town to rendezvous points in the surrounding countryside. They travelled in cars and vans to isolated spots on the road skirting the north east flank of Cremorgan. There they disembarked and scurried into the wooded demesne. They had been well armed by the Castleblaney quartermaster with Kalashnikov and Armalite rifles and a small number of Russian grenades. None would have carried a personal weapon except on a specific job, and there was not a single convicted man among them. In clothes ranging from creased Sunday suits to denim jackets and jeans, they spread out through the woods with the stealth and determination of the most disciplined guerrillas.

On Sentry Hill their movements were observed for half an hour or more. It was clear that their intention was to approach Cremorgan House across the river so that any follow-up operation could be prevented. At 2130 hours an advance party of five men, led by a heavyweight with a shock of black hair protruding from a beret, arrived at the river. Three of them rowed across in an inflatable rubber dinghy. They then hastily constructed two bridges, using a simple rope system. The three who had already crossed then proceeded through the woods to within a hundred yards of Cremorgan House, where they counted the small number of guards posted around the building. Meanwhile, small groups of men converged on the makeshift bridges and crossed the river, their rifles strapped to their backs. The remaining two men from the original party were left to guard the bridgehead.

Within a short time the IRA units were moving towards the house, where the assembled company was listening to General Fforde's closing remarks. The mercenaries signalled to one another to prepare for action.

Some 70 miles away across the border, the home of the director of Moore Security stood silent and secluded. Its owner was absent on private business. The sole occupant, surrounded by a recently fortified alarm system, including a circle of floodlights, was a young Catholic woman, seven weeks pregnant.

Since their return from Sligo the day before, Moore had worked hard making final arrangements for the proposed contracts from the British forces. The work would have to be quickly and efficiently done if, as seemed likely by the signs of civil unrest, the reported political resolution being negotiated was soon to be put into practice. He had ordered new machinery, and agreed to the employment of a further 15 workers at his factory. It did not escape his attention that other firms in the city were involved in hasty contraction. Throughout his endeavours, he was troubled by a sense of risk and uncertainty; he could not overlook the fact that his affair with Mary McKee had gone palpably beyond the bounds of his brief, and that he had in the course of events betrayed traces of irresolution. Though his employers had shown no evidence of dissatisfaction, he had already been treated equivocally, which left him in some doubt as to his future status.

It was this which explained his absence now. At six o'clock he had boarded a charter plane and flown to the Isle of Man for a prearranged rendezvous with a bank director he had known for many years. He carried with him £10,000 in twenty-pound notes, with which he instructed the banker to open a private account under a fictitious name, to which access could be obtained through the use either of his own signature or Mary McKee's. He stipulated that no communication should be attempted with him as depositor in any circumstances. As soon as this was arranged, he flew back to Ulster; knowing that no matter what course his personal fortunes should take, he had insured the immediate future of his child in the only way he was able.

It had become a hot dewy August night. In the garden around his home the air was heavy, the elm trees still and soundless. Halfway across the lawn stood a clump of laurel. At the edge of this Patrick O'Mara crouched, face darkened, a pair of binoculars in one hand, an Armalite rifle in the other. Unable to contain his usual impatience, he had arrived from Belfast an hour before and hiked over the fields to the south side of Moore's property; he hoped that he could carry out the task for which he had been promised payment on two counts, and which, more than any other murder he had committed in his terrorist career, he wanted to put behind him.

The lights illumined an area 30 yards square around the modern building. The gunman spotted conventional alarms fitted to the doors and windows. What other systems Moore had devised for his own safety, he could not begin to guess. He spent some minutes wondering whether or not he could afford to risk detection in pursuit of his quarry. Then he came to a decision. Crooking his rifle across his forearms, he crawled some 20 or 30 feet over the lawn to the next place of cover, a willow tree only a few paces from the gravel drive. He lay under the dangling fronds, motionless, he had triggered no alarms as yet, nor was there any sign of close circuit cameras scanning the grounds. There were many lights on in the house. The gunman was so close now that he had no need of binoculars. He took up a comfortable position with the gun and waited. Sooner or later someone would cross the window and figure in his sights.

It happened once, then again, and then a third time over the space of half an hour, as Mary McKee passed in front of the lounge bay windows. O'Mara strived to control his feelings, telling himself he had been hired on strict conditions to carry out an assassination, and could not afford to be distracted. If he bungled the job, his own life would once more be at risk. To some extent he succeeded in ordering his thoughts. Though it would have been easy to shoot her there and then, it would put his main contract in jeopardy; he had known all along he would have to take Moore first. Yet for all his efforts, by the third time she passed through his sights, he was consumed with the same strange mingling of passions as he had been before, crouched on the ridge over McKee's Farm. Whether Moore himself was there or not – and it seemed likely he was not – the prospect of waiting under the willow as Mary McKee walked back and forth in front of him was too much.

O'Mara slithered back across the grass. He reached the laurel. There he lifted his head and cursed. Then he made his way across the grounds towards the hills, and the village of Ballymacford.

There was no hesitation or retreat at Cremorgan as O'Mara's Republican colleagues, led by the massive figure of Mallon, settled into their positions in the woods around the ancient mansion. In the absence of any floodlights or alarms, five sentries patrolled the porches and stableyards. Inside, the dining hall was a scene of noise and light. Nearly a hundred men had assembled there, predominantly military personnel; the focus of their attention was a clerical figure proposing the last toast, who had earlier loudly proclaimed the holy virtues of patriotism and the Presbyterian church. Seated beside him was the small effete figure of a banker sagely nodding, as the rowdy ranks of noncommissioned officers reacted euphorically. In the hallway outside rifles were stacked. The sentries continued to patrol the perimeter of the house, watched closely from the fringes of the woods. At the sound of a single ululating cry from Mallon they were simultaneously gunned down by small calibre 0.223 bullets from identical rifles to the one O'Mara carried as he stumbled over the fields. The bullets travelled at such speed that the sentries were knocked back several feet as they fell.

There was enough time for the mood in the house to change dramatically to one of panic, as the soldiers ran from the dining hall to gather their arms, and the civilians tried to take cover under the tables.

After the first exchanges, when the IRA units prepared to storm the building, blowing the main doors apart with a volley of grenades, the senior American hidden on Sentry Hill aimed his launching gun at the house. Using his laser sights, he pressed the trigger for three seconds. A laser beam was now locked on target, and a sequential operation began which launched the missile and brought it onto the co-ordinates established by the gun. The Whistler was fitted with a cluster warhead, containing VR 65, the latest development in non-persistent nerve gas, fatal up to 300 yards from its target area, but with a potency of only a few minutes. It exploded within moments of its launch.

The second part of the mercenaries' operation involved the removal of the IRA men left by the river. With the aid of the night sights on his SLR rifle, the other American accomplished this without difficulty. His attack was ruthless and effective. Once he had destroyed the rope bridges, so as to ensure that any Provisionals who had remained with the cars and might try to advance on Cremorgan would find their way blocked and be forced to retreat, he returned to his companion. They exchanged a thumbs-up signal, and then climbed into the pick-up. One of them primed a timed device which would fire a small charge in the napalm lining in the van's structure, burning up the stationary vehicle and destroying all evidence of its military capacity. They had five minutes to make good their escape.

The scene they left behind them was one of surreal desolation. Among the border trees and on the gravel, the IRA's elite force had been completely destroyed, some authentically gunned down by Emerald's swifter marksmen, others inexplicably eliminated in the midst of action. The advance party had reached the main porch. At their head the figure of Mallon lay splayed over the threshold.

Apart from the shattered entrance and countless broken windows, the house itself stood intact, though a fire was quickly spreading from the hall. In its path lay some ten or fifteen men who had been caught in the act of retrieving their rifles when the Whistler had exploded. In the dining hall, surrounded by the bodies of those who had taken up firing positions at the windows, the tables were still standing and the civilian guests still gathered beneath and around them. The Reverend Fadden lay sprawled under his chair, as gross and unappealing in death as he had been in life; his silver box was open beside him and its contents spilled out over the floor. The Head of Finance had fallen not far away in a kneeling position, as he had tried to shield himself under the table, his head and arms over his thighs like a praying Moslem. The effects of the gas had been lethal immediately.

Some yards from the two inner committee members lay General Fforde, face down. The decanters he had earlier lined up along the tables had all been smashed. Like a fallen drunkard, he was soaked in whiskey, which would soon catch fire and immolate Emerald's military commander, clutching his pistol, his wizened face set in a mask of defiance. There were no survivors.

By the time the Americans, once more dressed in blue overalls, had reached the border and driven on towards Belfast, the flames had spread throughout the old house, cremating its occupants without ceremony. The last family portraits in Fforde's gallery perished. The library, with all its sophisticated equipment stowed among ancient books, was also burnt. Outside, the Provisionals lay oblivious.

As the mercenaries submitted themselves for their last debriefing, even now retaining the dispassionate anonymity of their breed, the inhabitants of Clones and the nearby town of Ballybay, who had already gathered in the streets, watched the advance of Eire soldiers sent in to cordon off the area around Cremorgan. The subsequent examination of the battlefield carried out by military experts led to certain unavoidable conclusions. The IRA had achieved their purpose: the higher ranks of Emerald's forces were destroyed. All that was left of the Protestant paramilitary group was a collection of volunteers dispersed throughout the province. Without leadership or organization, these people would quickly return to respectability and make no effective opposition to the plans even now being announced at Stormont. Similarly, the Republicans had lost the greater part of their strategic fighting units. The bulk of the armoury of both groups now lay in the hands of official forces. Moreover, while the cordon around the estate was consolidated, a series of raids in towns and villages from Derry to Crossmaglen, at addresses where incriminating material was to be found, resulted in the detention of all those known to have been involved in paramilitary activity over the previous five years. In the process, the Supreme Head of the Provisionals was shot dead at his sister's home in Dungannon.

The principal forces of sectarian violence in Ulster had thus been removed in a single calculated act of modern warfare. They had appeared to destroy each other. It would be a long time before a true version of events could be compiled. Those with any subversive motives would long since have been driven from the island, in the name of peace and democratic government.

Chapter 18

Morning broke mistily over the north of Ireland. The late summer dawn was already chilled with the first touches of autumn. Roy Moore woke to the sound of sparrows squabbling on the roof. He opened his eyes wearily; he had no idea how close he had come the night before to never waking again. He had arrived home only an hour after the man who had come to kill him had faded into the darkness, and exhausted from work, he had sat down to listen to his music, then followed his lover to bed. They had both slept deeply through the night when others were frantically discussing the news from Stormont.

Now he turned over to embrace her, only to find the bed empty. Tying his silk dressing gown, he went down to the kitchen. There he found her standing with her back against the sink drinking a cup of coffee. His transistor radio stood on the table. A news programme was in progress.

He said from the doorway, 'I didn't know you'd got up.'

She appeared to ignore him. He asked, 'What's the matter?' She nodded to the radio. He heard only the tail-end of the report: 'We will bring you more of this historic news before the end of the programme.'

He raised his eyebrows and was about to ask her exactly what had happened when the next item was announced. He stood listening, open-mouthed.

'. . . But this was not the only announcement made at Stormont late last night. The Secretary of State also reported that a military action had taken place in the Republic at Cremorgan House, County Monaghan, in which it appears the Provisional IRA made a full-scale attack on the previously undisclosed headquarters of Emerald, the Protestant paramilitary group responsible for a great deal of recent sectarian activity, including the mobilization of men in the province. Such fierce fighting was said to have followed that the majority of both forces were killed. Numbers of dead are estimated at over 150 though this has been impossible to confirm since the area has been cordoned off by soldiers of the Irish Armed Forces and no one is permitted to enter.

'The Irish premier travelled immediately from Stormont, where he was attending the talks, and visited the scene. He declared that he had seldom before witnessed such unmitigated horror. However, he also stated that in the present circumstances such an event could prove a peculiar kind of blessing to the prospective unification of the island. This sentiment was echoed by the Secretary of State's prepared speech, which implied that the confrontation between the two illegal organizations had been brought about by apprehension about the Stormont agreement, through leaks made by members of the civil service who were now being held under interrogation. He added that the reaction of those not interested in the rule of law was tragically predictable. It would serve as a timely warning to the people of Ireland that such episodes in their history should now come to an end. The violence of this action was on a scale that could have meant only one future for the province of Ulster, had the unification of the island been delayed any longer: a more formal state of civil war in which countless innocent lives would have been lost.

'It was for this reason, the Minister said, that all known members of the Provisional IRA and other paramilitary groups had been arrested in a series of raids after the battle at Cremorgan had ended yesterday evening. Ireland could not repeat the turmoil of the 1920s, when a desperate band of renegades held the country to ransom in pursuit of ideals that were both undemocratic and unlawful. The declared Provisional aim of achieving a Marxist Republic was not concomitant with the aspirations of a free Irish people. Nor was the mobilization of an illegal army, the fomenting of sectarian hatred, or the appropriation of a country for the anachronistic aims of a minority.

'The people of Ireland, especially those living in the north, should recognize that what has been resolved is in the best interests of all Irish citizens, and that any alternative would lead only to the kind of carnage witnessed in County Monaghan last evening.

'As a result of the army raids, we now know that a number of men were shot while resisting arrest. Among these . . .'

Moore could listen no longer. 'Look, what the hell's happened?'

The girl put down her cup and said quietly, 'They're talkin' about a United Ireland. The Brits are goin' home. The Yanks are comin' in.'

Moore drew in his breath. 'What do you mean?'

'They're settin' up missile bases.'

'What bases, where?'

'Sure, if you listen they'll tell you.'

He could see she could not make up her mind how to react to what she had heard. He shook his head. 'I don't believe it.'

She said, 'Aye, well, where does that leave us?'

He ignored her. 'I'm going down to Templepatrick to fetch the papers. I want to know exactly what's been agreed.'

'Och, look, stay an' listen to the radio. There's no point . . .'

'He was already halfway out of the door. 'I'll be back soon.'

Still in his dressing gown and slippers, he drove into the village, leapt from the Jaguar, and bought one British and one Irish newspaper in the local newsagent's. The occupants were so preoccupied by the news that they scarcely noticed his appearance. He returned to the car and hurriedly scanned the papers. The headlines were explicit but it was not drama, only details, that he wanted. He turned to the inside pages of the British paper, with a frown of concentration.

> Only the barest outline of the agreement was given and this was deliberately withheld until late at night, though it was enough to make the intention clear. The British Government has agreed to withdraw its troops from the six counties and to relinquish all governmental authority. The border is to be removed and the seat at Stormont abandoned. In its place the Dáil is to assume responsibility for all domestic and foreign affairs, while Westminster will continue to be involved in certain economic areas. There will be an interim period when co-operation between the two governments will be essential to the maintenance of law and order and to a degree of political consistency. Details have yet to be finalized as to how exactly this

interim will be terminated. However, it is thought that the British will require at least six months to a year before they hand over to their Irish counterparts and the latter assume independent authority in Ulster.

But these are the logistics involved in such an agreement. The central tenet remains uncomplicated: the island is to be united. Great Britain is to withdraw its interests.

What, then, is the vital factor which has brought about a state of affairs which successive British Governments have vowed would never occur? It seems that the whole arrangement has been overseen by the Americans. The existence of a destabilized Ireland has long been a source of concern to the Western Alliance; the only solution apparent to the US has been the eventual reunification of the island under a sympathetic administration in Dublin, committed to NATO.

The bargain has been struck in order to ensure this commitment. In exchange for the annexation of Ulster and a guarantee of long term funds to bolster its extremely volatile economy, the Eire Taoiseach has agreed to the siting of two nuclear missile bases on the island; one in the north at Ballykelly, to include the whole Magilligan Peninsula; the other taking in the peninsula at Black Head, south of Galway Bay, equipped with an airfield and a radar base on Slieve Elva. Intercontinental ballistic missiles will be established in deep silos in the rocky areas around both bases, which, in accordance with international law, will become sovereign US territory. The Americans will therefore not only gain an important new nuclear leverage but also fill the radar gap which has existed between their bases in Greenland and West Germany, and which has led to an unsatisfactory dependence on Great Britain.

Moore looked up in exasperation. He could not have known how subtly Fforde had been deceived. The bait had been specifically prepared to lure the General into action, in such a way that even if he had decided to alert the citizens of Black Head to the fact that their local environment was about to be endangered by the siting of a conventional British naval base, he would have been disbelieved. And all the while, American nuclear missiles would be primed secretly in their silos in the hills nearby. Moore had never, for all his anxious curiosity, managed to extract details of the British stratagem for the future of Ulster; a stratagem that, he had been led to believe, was compatible with the aspirations of the Protestant majority. Now that he could see the real plan, he was stunned by its sophistication.

He turned to the Irish paper. The reports here were less formal and spoke elatedly of the prospect of a close alliance with a great nation, a vast proportion of whose citizens were originally from Ireland. The stress was so strongly on the withdrawal of an unwanted presence and its popular substitution, that it read almost as an account of a liberation. It was not explained that the chief contact with the new allies would be official; nor that the chief presence on the island would be one of concealed nuclear weapons aimed at countries beyond the Iron Curtain, countries which would in turn deploy similar devices aimed in the opposite direction. The enthusiasm was absolute and there was no apparent awareness of a further escalation in the threat to the future of humanity.

> This is a truly historic hour. Once and for all our nation will be free of her bitter and divided past, free to point a bloody finger at the perpetrators of her captivity, no longer fearful of reprisals, invasions, states of martial law, free to govern her own legitimate interests in the sight of the world.

Moore sat motionless in his car, which was parked in the main street of Templepatrick, and gazed into the distance. Any of the local inhabitants could have been forgiven for thinking he had lost his sanity. A whole series of connections was taking place in his mind. Eventually, he turned to the papers again for reports on the battle at Cremorgan. He read them voraciously, and then once more sat and stared blankly. He had been so concerned with his personal involvement in the secret work of those he considered allies that the only disappointment or betrayal he had thought possible was his own. Only now did he begin to realize what had been at stake. He shared responsibility for the deaths, not only of those bombed at Kelly's Motor Inn, but of a small army of his fellow countrymen, in the name of a cause he had mistaken, and whose long term effects he could not even start to calculate.

He threw down the papers and drove home. When he came into the kitchen, Mary McKee was no longer there. He sat down at the table and looked round him. He felt at once numbed, angry, tired. He put his head in his hands and closed his eyes.

She came in, dressed, a few minutes later and asked aggressively, 'So what happens now?'

He made no answer, keeping his face in his hands. When she repeated her question, he lowered his fingers and said, 'I don't know yet.'

She herself was still evidently confused. 'Och, well, maybe you'd like to tell me when you do.'

Moore watched the door close, fiercely stroking his moustache. After some moments a sudden blackness came into his eyes, he lifted his arm and swept everything from the table. Then he hurried out of the back door into the garden, where he wandered moodily – as had once been his habit – for over an hour, watched by Mary from an upstairs window.

The sound of the telephone recalled him from his bleak thoughts. He ran back into the house. Mary McKee waited expectantly at the top of the stairs as he lifted the receiver.

O'Mara had spend the night curled up in the heather midway between Templepatrick and Ballymacford. Shortly after dawn, he rose to beat some life back into his cold limbs. Once the feeling had returned to his legs, he slung his rifle over his shoulder and went on quickly towards the village in the hills. He avoided the roads and made his way through the mist as it swirled over the fields.

He emerged on the main Belfast road, 100 yards from Mac's Bar. His knee had plagued him for the last mile, but now that he was in sight of his destination he hurried on, arriving at the squat building shortly after its owner had risen from his bed.

There was no question of his being admitted once he was recognized, so he limped round to the back of the building, climbed onto a pile of crates and hoisted himself onto a low roof running on a level with Mac's private quarters. He thrust the butt of his gun through the kitchen window, then pointed the barrel at the only occupant. Mac was sitting at his table, listening to the radio, drinking his third cup of tea, when the glass shattered.

'Holy Christ!' He leapt to his feet and peered at the gun. 'Sure, you'll not kill me now.'

O'Mara said briskly, 'One more wee favour an' that's it, Mac. Now let me in.'

The landlord opened the window timidly for O'Mara to climb into the kitchen. 'But Pat,' he said, 'You've heard what's happened, surely. Listen now, it's on the news, they're . . .'

O'Mara stepped forward and switched off the radio without bothering to listen. 'Right this minute I don't care if they're goin' to rape the Queen. Shut your matherin' an' listen to me now, you oul' shite.'

Mac would not argue with a gun aimed at his face. 'What have I to do?'

'First you make me some breakfast an' then you take the van up through the village to the wee girl's cottage.'

Mac was blatantly relieved. 'Sure, is that all? Och well, you sit yourself down, Pat, an' I'll make you the best fry you ever saw, an' a nice pot o' tea for a young fella that needs a good feed.'

'Don't give me any of your oul' lip. Just you get on with it.'

O'Mara sat down, while the fat man nervously cooked for him, with the gun still aimed at his head. Mac made one attempt to talk while the gunman was eating, but a single wave of the barrel quickly silenced him. O'Mara made short work of his meal. Drinking his tea in three gulps, he stood up again and said, 'That's powerful, Mac, you always was a good cook. Now you go an' get the car an' meet me downstairs.'

Without protest, Mac locked up his bar and brought the small van, in which he had taken O'Mara to Dundalk some three weeks before, round to the rear of the premises. There the gunman climbed into the back, pressing his rifle against the driver's neck.

'Now drive on up to McKee's Ridge. An' drop me a wee way down the hill.'

Mac nodded against the rifle and pulled away. Within a few minutes, he had stopped in the lane some yards from the cottage gate. 'There you are, Pat, an' you're right welcome. Sure, any time you want to call in just you come, son. No need to go breakin' the windows, no need at all.'

O'Mara climbed out and bent down by the driver's window. 'Now you head straight back an' say nothin' to no one, you get me, man? 'Cause if you do you won't be worryin' about your windows.'

'Aye, Pat, I will surely. Anythin' you say. Take care now, I'll be seein' you.'

O'Mara watched Mac disappear down the lane and then made his way surreptitiously towards the cottage. Once he had made sure that no one was there he climbed in through the pantry window and unlocked the front door.

Moore immediately lost his temper again when he heard the familiar voice on the line. The English manner he had once found so engaging was anathema to him now. 'And what the hell do you call this?' he cried.

'Now don't be bitter, Roy,' he was told calmly. 'It's in everyone's interests in the long run.'

'I disagree. In my opinion it's treachery.'

He was quickly rebuked for his attitude. 'Our intention has always been consistent. It was up to you to interpret it in your own way. That has been the case with everyone involved, so don't think you are any exception.'

He swallowed hard. There was a long silence before he asked, 'Where does it leave me then?'

The answer was as he had expected. 'In rather a difficult position, I'm afraid, unless you continue to co-operate with us. If you do, I can assure you we will honour our obligations and ensure your business interests in the new community. Unlike some of your fellow sympathizers, we would make certain any former political allegiances were not taken into consideration.'

Moore drew a deep breath. He had not wasted his hour's reflection. 'I see no alternative,' he said. 'Though I want you to know that if I did, I wouldn't hesitate to take it. I'm furious at what has happened.'

The caller seemed uninterested in his subjective response. 'I thought as much. In that case, I'll be brief and to the point. Your current private relationship should stand you in good stead for the future, as far as all legitimate parties are concerned. But for the time being it would be foolish to take unnecessary risks. The next few days will prove a delicate period. What is more, you must personally submit yourself to a process of debriefing, so to speak. I therefore suggest you separate until things have been cleared up.'

Moore said impulsively, 'Perhaps we could deal plainly for once. I'm tired of all this.'

The response was equally blunt. 'Certainly. Nothing would please me more.' There was a brief pause. 'You should return the person concerned to her own home immediately and then drive on to Belfast. You will be met at McGlade's Bar at eleven hundred hours by one of our representatives.'

Moore realized that there was no purpose in any further prevarication. 'Right. Then I imagine I will see you shortly. Goodbye.'

He replaced the receiver and looked up at Mary McKee, who returned his gaze inquisitively. 'So,' he said, 'I have to take you home again. It's only for a day or two. I'll come for you as soon as I can.'

She looked away, knowing that now more than ever she should force herself to tell him the chief cause of her fear for her own safety; but the fact that she had kept it from him all this time, and the hope that the information had not been exaggerated that all known terrorists had been taken into custody, made her decide to keep silent. She said only, 'Just so long as you do. I'm trustin' you now,' and disappeared into the bedroom.

While she collected her belongings, Moore picked up the Jaguar keys from the hall table and waited in the car. Eventually, she joined him, throwing her bags into the boot with an air of resignation.

As she settled into the passenger's seat, she asked, 'Are you sure it's goin' to be alright?'

He started the engine without replying. Then, as they left the driveway to take the road to Ballymacford, he said quietly, 'I'm not sure of anything any more.'

She glanced at him briefly and put her hand on his as he steered up into the hills.

Such was their uncertainty that when they arrived at McKee's Ridge, Moore parked behind the hedge and told her to stay in the car.

'I'll go in first,' he said, 'just to make sure.'

Mary was resolved to stick by her decision. 'Aye, if you say so. You know best.'

Moore banged the car door behind him. All around, the fields were empty and tranquil in the morning sun. A mist lay on the hills above, and would slowly glide down into the valley as the day wore on. Its first cool fringes were easing round the cottage. There was no sign of life, no smoke pouring from the chimney. The long single-storey building had the deserted appearance of other homes abandoned in the uplands of Antrim.

Moore went slowly to the door. He found that it was not locked. He pushed it open and stepped inside, instinctively apprehensive. Facing him in a chair set a few feet from the doorway was the lean figure of Patrick O'Mara, his face bent over his rifle, his eyes at the sight fixed on Moore's forehead.

'How's about ye, Or'ngeman. Glad you could make it.'

Moore could not move. There was no chance of escaping. His stomach turned. 'Christ,' he muttered, 'now what?'

'Sure, you don't need me to tell you.' O'Mara stood up, still with the gun fixed on Moore's face. 'So where's the wee slag?'

Moore resorted to the obvious ploy. 'Look, how much do you want? You can have whatever you ask.'

'I'm gettin' all I want for you, man, I don't need your bread.' The gunman watched as the victim's eyes turned inward, in a manner reminiscent of his own reaction on the evening that Cameron Smyth had visited the cottage at Bettystown. Even in his recent anxiety, Moore had not consciously believed that he would meet this kind of fate. He asked, 'So you've been hired to kill us both?'

O'Mara grinned, 'Och, they're all after your skin, man. Now tell me where she is.' Moore made no answer but went to lean on the doorpost. O'Mara made a quick decision. 'OK then. Put your hands on your head an' march.' He did as he was told and turned. 'That's right, an' don't stop till I tell you.'

They walked down the path from the cottage through the small gate. When the gunman saw the Jaguar, he prodded Moore towards it. But there was no sign of Mary McKee. Kicking at the flared wing, he said, 'So she can wait. She'll not get away from me now.' He made Moore walk back up the hill between the high hedges. Once they had turned a corner he ordered, 'Kneel down there.'

Moore looked round for a possible means of escape, but none appeared to him. He knelt in the middle of the lane, his hands on his head.

'Now this is what you might call a wee trial,' said O'Mara. 'An' I'm your judge an' jury, right?'

Moore swallowed his fear, listening to the sullen voice behind him, unable to turn. 'So what's the crime?'

O'Mara laughed bitterly. 'You think I'm goin' to tell you? Och no, this is Northern Ireland, man.' He intoned solemnly, 'Whereas it appears to me, on the recommendation of the Chief Constable of the Royal Ulster Constabulary, that for securing the preservation of the peace and the maintenance of order . . . Sure, I can't remember the rest.'

Moore said angrily, 'That's all past now.'

His captor ignored this. 'So all I have to do is decide who I'm goin' to kill you for.' The gunman was clearly enjoying himself, savouring the humiliation of a man he hated. 'Have a wee guess now. No, have three guesses an' then I'll tell you who's payin' me for your scalp.'

Moore sighed with a desperate understanding. He hung his head and, staring at the ground beneath him, muttered a single name.

'Right in one. Good oul' Sam,' O'Mara cried. 'I didn't think you'd have it. Sure, an' I bet you was thinkin' he's as bold a fella as ever you met. Was that it, Moore, were you thinkin' he's your best buddy, eh? Sure, I bet you were.'

Moore did not reply. He could see the whole image of his

future disappear like a mirage, leaving him to stare at his own shadow on the road.

O'Mara went on, 'Now, the way I see it, the Boys won't be payin' me the same, an' you might say there's somethin' I like about the idea of you bein' done by your own people.'

Still, Moore remained silent. He had never before realized how it felt to be a real victim. Now it seemed to have come to him too late to serve any purpose.

O'Mara grew impatient. 'Have you nothin' to say in your defence, Mister Moore, sir?'

Instead of speaking, he did the only thing he could think of; he sprang from his knees towards the hedge at the side of the lane, trying to grab at the small branches hanging over the verge and pull himself into the field beyond. O'Mara's reactions were swift. Moore fell back into the dirt, writhing in pain.

'Don't think I'll let you off the hook, man. You're goin' to dangle till you die.'

The gunman had fired deliberately at Moore's legs. The bullet had passed through his left thigh just above the knee. He cried out as he lay on the lane, clutching his wound.

'Sure, I reckon that one's for the Boys. I think I'll leave the best for oul' Sam. That'd be justice, wouldn't it now?'

White with pain and fear, Moore could not see his assailant clearly, but he could hear what he said as if it was the taunt of a less mortal tormentor. He asked breathlessly, 'Have you no compassion?'

O'Mara spat in the dust. 'Fuck you, Or'nge bastard.'

He was so involved in his trial that he did not notice a small figure moving up the lane behind him.

After Moore had left the car, Mary McKee sat trying to contain her sense of anxiety, but it was not long before it forced her to get out and peer through the hedge towards the cottage. When Moore turned in the doorway, she saw the gunman's silhouette. Clutching the briar, she felt she would faint. But she realized immediately that there was no time to be weak. She quickly scurried through a gap into the field and made for the shelter of the conifers. Once there, she hastened across the ridge. While O'Mara was marching Moore from the cottage she reached the derelict hut at the edge of the quarry and pulled up a loose floorboard beneath a pile of old blankets. This was where she had long ago secreted the revolver O'Mara had once given her. By the time she had crossed the ridge again, she was weak and breathless. Her determination alone gave her strength. But now she was only yards away from the gunman, with the loaded weapon in her hand.

O'Mara was set to extract the most pleasure possible from his role as torturer. He was, he felt, in no danger of any interference, for even if local people should come upon them, they would never challenge a Provisional in the process of carrying out an official execution. He stood holding the rifle, a thin figure in khaki combat jacket and frayed jeans, his face still blackened, his eyes gleaming with hatred. Moore lay some ten feet away. His next shot would not be the last; he would aim at the lower back, in order to cripple his victim further. He took aim as Moore began scraping in the dirt, still trying to inch himself towards the hedge.

O'Mara squinted along the sights and touched the trigger. 'OK, Moore, if I can't buck the bitch, sure, you won't neither.'

But he never fired his next shot. Mary had crept to within a few feet of him. The sound of her laboured breathing distracted him from his prey. But he turned too late. She held the Webley in both hands, shaking as she took up the 14 pounds of trigger pull. O'Mara's head with its shock of red hair was half-inclined toward her when the gun leapt in her hands. The big lead bullet hit him just over the occipital bone. As with the rival he had challenged to a shooting match, his skull cracked open like an eggshell. He died instantly.

The girl immediately ran forward, not daring to look at him, to the other man whose hands were tangled in the hawthorn. She bent over him, dry-eyed and white-lipped from what she had done.

Moore was in a state of serious shock. He whispered, 'I've been here before. I've seen all this, Mary. I can't do it, not now.'

She looked at the blood soaking his trousers; she had seen the same kind of wound before. She said, 'Stay still for a minute, I'll be back. Stay still.'

She hurried down to the cottage and climbed into the Jaguar. She could not manage to turn in the narrow road so she reversed round the corner. She ignored Moore's cries of pain as she helped him into the passenger's seat. She lifted her dress and tucked the revolver into her underwear, against her pregnant stomach. Then she climbed into the driver's seat and sped off over the hills towards a point where she knew the lane turned down onto the Belfast road, three miles north of the village.

'I'll get you to hospital, it'll be alright, sure it will,' she said as she lurched round a series of sharp bends.

Moore seemed only to panic at this. 'No, it's not safe. Nowhere's safe here. Get over the border. Get over the border.'

'But the border doesn't matter now. It's all changed.'

He gritted his teeth and shook his head. 'The border will always matter. Do as I ask.'

They had reached the main road by the time two cars drew up on the ridge. A number of armed policemen got out and surrounded the cottage. Instead of turning left towards the city, Mary McKee drove straight across on to another minor road, heading out of Ulster for the west coast, the rugged mountains and the sea.

Dominic McCartan belongs to one of the oldest families in Ireland. Coming from a medical background, he travelled extensively as a freelance writer after graduating from university. With his wife and son, he now lives and works in England, but retains close ties with his homeland.